THE
EMERALD
OF THE
NIGHT

Book 1 of *The Gems of Worthington* Series

SELA COLÓN

Self-Published 2020
by Sela Colón

Ebook ISBN: 978-1-7362947-0-3

Print ISBN: 978-1-7362947-1-0

Cover art and book formatting by David Prendergast @ www.ebookscoversdesign.com

Follow me on Instagram @ sela_colon
selacolon.com

About the Author

Sela Colón was born in Puerto Rico and moved to the state of Georgia at a young age, where she was raised along with her three siblings. Her youth was filled with Spanglish, salsa music, rice and beans, sibling pranks, simultaneous conversations, and an importance on the value of family. She studied English Literature with a speciality in British Literature at Georgia College & State University before moving to New York City to pursue her master's degree in teaching.

She began writing her debut novel as a one-act play for an assignment in college representing a given time period. Having always been fascinated with the Victorian era and British history, it was a no-brainer. After graduating college, the story remained a one-act play with notes scrawled in the margins full of ideas for a full-length play and placed on a shelf while she finished her master's degree and then began her teaching career. It wasn't until a case of stress-cleaning two years ago she found the play wedged between a set of books on the top shelf of her bookcase. Shortly after finding it again, Sela found herself a writing coach and began converting the play into her debut novel.

When she's not wearing her author hat, she wears the hat of an elementary special education teacher. She can also be seen reading, watching movies, scrapbooking, talking on the phone with her sister, and walking around Old Town Alexandria with her husband.

DEDICATION

For Mami and Papi, who always
encouraged my storytelling and love of books.
Thank you for always listening!

PROLOGUE

She didn't want to trust him and let him know just how much she loved him. He knew too much about her past already from what she'd told him. She could try to avoid him like she'd done years before, but now he knew her mind and would go after her. Or would he? Did she want him to chase her if she were to accept another man? She'd thought if she could keep him at bay, she would be free of him. Now, as she looked into Cameron's eyes, she sat transfixed, unable to even contemplate departure.

"You look confused. I thought you would be happy to hear about my new plans to remain in London for another fortnight or so." Cameron touched Briana's arm and winced as she jerked it away.

"I... I am happy you want to stay here with your family and..."

"With you!" Cameron interrupted. He seized her hand and gripped it tightly, rendering her incapable of pulling away. She looked up into his deep brown eyes, the ones that had begun to haunt her dreams with their depth and mystery. How could she continue lying to this man?

"Cameron, you don't really know me. You don't have any idea where I've been these last ten years or what I've had to do to keep my family together. You don't even know what I'm truly capable of. I'm not the woman you think I am." Briana looked down to hide the tears she felt stinging her eyes. She couldn't cry again in front of this man. She couldn't cry about her past and about the horrible deeds her father did to her and her mother. She was stronger now, right?

"I think I see who you are better than you do." As if to better make his point, Cameron grabbed Briana from behind the neck and kissed her passionately. His tongue urged her lips apart to allow its entry. The distance between their bodies no longer existed. Briana's train of thought vanished into the fuzziness of delight. Her vision began to blur and, despite her attempts to remain logical, she knew she was his.

They pressed closer in a heat of passion, with a need to become one with each other. Later, they would think about the dictates of society. Later, she would put up her guard once more. Later, he would begin to analyze again. But for now, they were lost in one another's arms.

CHAPTER 1

December 1841

Briana was thirteen years old when she fell in love for the first time. She'd spent almost every day of her childhood near him until he was sent away to Eton. She waited patiently for every holiday to catch a glimpse of him or for the rare opportunity of conversation. Cameron had always been Emily's elusive big brother who, being eight years their senior, never served as a playmate to his siblings. Despite this, he always had a smile ready for Briana. When someone was hurt, would care for them as best he could – all the while scolding them for their unrestrained idiocy. At the age of one and twenty, he was absolutely splendid in his god-like figure. He was tall and lean, with broad shoulders and a dimpled smile. He had a deep voice that carried easily across a room and dark hair that he wore a bit long like his father.

It was because of him that Briana began requesting more green gowns in her wardrobe a year earlier when, after his mother had reminded him to greet her, Cameron had said hello and inquired after her health, noting that she hadn't seemed to grow much since he last saw her. Before leaving their conversation, he'd displayed just how much of a gentleman he was when he told her the green dress she wore was pretty and complemented her brown curly hair, making one think of a tree in nature. It was at that moment that Briana decided green would forever be her favorite color.

Now, at the age of fifteen, Briana found she often stood out in a crowd and it was not because of her beautiful green dresses. No matter how much she wished she could be as beautiful as her tall, graceful, blonde, blue-eyed friend, Briana was quite the opposite. She stood a foot shorter than most children her age when one didn't take her unruly mass of brown curly hair into account. She had pretty amber brown eyes which did not match her unflattering dark brown hair, the color of which refused to lighten no matter how many times she washed her locks with lemon juice. She was scrawny and recently found a dusting of freckles across the bridge of her nose, which did nothing but draw attention to her big lips and toothy smile. Making matters worse, Briana never could keep from bumping into things around her or dropping things, no matter if she used both hands or not.

Briana tried her best to ignore her looks by focusing on enjoying other aspects of herself. She reminded herself daily that she was smart, creative, adventurous, and loyal. These were the attributes Cameron told her really mattered in a young woman when he found her crying at Jake's teasing months earlier. She'd spent a year reliving all their short conversations about each others' health, family, schooling, caring for the land around the country estate, and her rivalry with Jake. In all those conversations, no matter how short and to the point they were, Cameron was never rude. In many ways, she felt years older after speaking with him. Although Cameron would sometimes speak condescendingly, he always made sure to educate and answer her questions and she in turn would always leave him smiling and laughing. She loved thinking she was the only one who could bring this side out in him and that he was the only one who understood her insecurities and helped her find strength within them.

Having come to the Hereford's country estate in Surrey as the family's guests, she would have the opportunity to tell him how much she admired him for all the support he'd given her over the years. Walking the halls of Dalton Place, rather than searching for Emily as she normally would, Briana sought out Cameron before losing her nerve. Turning the corner leading towards the library, the study, and the solarium, Briana found herself face-to-face with Cameron, who was making his way to the entryway of the estate.

"Oh! Excuse me, I didn't see you there." Cameron said as he stopped before crashing into Briana's small form.

"No, it was my fault for walking too fast while being lost in thought and not looking ahead." Briana shook her head and smiled sheepishly. Honestly, she was already making an idiot of herself.

"Well, no harm done. If you'll excuse me, I have to check on the land and the progress being made in the west corner of the estate. If you are looking for Emily, I believe she is not yet home from visiting the vicar with mother. As for Jake, I've stopped asking of his whearabouts," Cameron said dismissively. He didn't understand how his brother was always out of the house when home from school. With so much to be done here, how could someone find the time to traipse about finding new ladies and gentlemen to pass the time with?

"Yes, I knew Emily wasn't back yet. But I thought..."

"Well, you're welcome to use the library while you wait if you'd like. I do believe we have the latest poems by Robert Browning and Lord Tennyson," Cameron said with a quick bow in dismissal before continuing on his way.

Seeing the opportunity to be alone with him escaping before her eyes, Briana followed after him. Reaching his side, she asked, "Do... do you mind if I join you for a spell until Emily arrives? I promise I won't get in the way of your work."

"It can be quite tedious and complicated..."

"Didn't you tell me I was smart before? I am sure I could understand with your explanations. Please? I know I will be bored waiting for Emily and I am sure Jake is probably avoiding me after the prank I pulled on him recently," Briana pleaded, batting her eyelashes as she'd seen Emily do with Cameron before.

"I will never understand you both and the pleasure you derive from such childish pranks." Cameron sighed while shaking his head in exasperation.

"Hmph. It's about outsmarting one's opponent. Can I accompany you, please?"

Touching his fingertips to his lips in thought, Cameron did not respond immediately. When he gave her a half smile, exposing one of his adorable dimples, Briana knew he would allow it. "Very well, I think you may enjoy to see the estate in a different manner. Come along."

Briana followed after his large strides trying to keep pace with him as best possible – a daunting task when she had to take three steps for his one. Walking around the estate, Cameron held a notebook in his hands where he took note of crops, animals, workers, equipment, stable conditions, soil conditions, and time spent on various tasks. He told her that his father had his own notebook with similar notes and that they often would sit together at the end of the day and compare notes on what they'd seen.

With a grin at Briana's pursed lips and furrowed brow, Cameron teased, "With an expression like that, I can only assume you're puzzled why we would do such a thing."

"Doesn't it seem redundant since it is the same information? Well, unless you are surveying everything at different times of the day." Briana replied.

"Interesting. What makes you say that?" Cameron said, his eyes holding a sparkle that was not there before.

Biting her lip out of nervous habit, Briana shrugged her shoulders. When he tilted his head and smiled encouragingly, Briana found her voice saying, "Well, if one were to go in the morning time and record notes and stock of everything and then the other does the same in the afternoon, you would be able to see the amount of growth or depletion."

"Well said, Brie. Yes, that is precisely what we discuss, but comparing our other notes daily also helps us determine the productivity and effectiveness of our workers, as well as the strategies we are using. The notes I keep help me know the quality and quantity of everything in order to assess for areas of improvement that I can work upon and bring possible solutions to my father. If I am to inherit this title, it is my duty to do so to the best of my ability and know this land as well as our finances like the back of my hand in order to continue my father's legacy. Don't you think it would be remiss of me to shirk any responsibility for the mere reason that my father is still capable of carrying everything out on his own? If a man is to wait until the passing of his father before behaving reliably, then he is merely a child in gentleman's clothing," Cameron stated.

Glancing over at her blank face, he slowly closed his eyes in frustration with himself. He was lecturing this poor girl again. It seemed that he often did so when in her company without noticing. She made it so easy for him to voice the thoughts and concerns he didn't often share. It was probably because she stayed in his presence longer than his siblings did and asked questions out of politeness and curiosity.

"I think it is wonderful that you have such a sense of pride in your family title and desire to help your father. I did not think about comparing notes in order to make changes for effectiveness. I merely thought of it as a daily record. I see you are just as wise as your father." Briana smiled up at him with her toothy smile, forgetting to control it as she'd practiced daily in order to make it appear smaller.

Cameron couldn't help but smile back. It was nice to have someone, other than his father, to talk to about his ideas and feel as if he were truly being heard. Pointing in the direction of the stone wall marking the estate boundaries, Cameron asked, "Would you like to sit and listen to the idea I plan to propose to my father tonight in order to make the soil richer and more efficient?"

Nodding her head, Briana allowed him to escort her to the stone wall. Adjusting the ties of her bonnet, which was threatening to fall off at the mere suggestion of wind, Briana sucked in a breath when she noticed just how close he sat to her. Briana breathed in his scent, reveling in being so close to him. It was a heady combination of leather and parchment, with a hint of lemon that made her think of what sunshine would smell like. His shoulder pressed against hers as he began pointing to his notes and the various figures of soil layers he'd drawn in his notebook. Briana looked at his face as he spoke but didn't hear a single word.

Stopping to look at her, Cameron waved a hand in front of her face. "Brie, did you hear anything I just said?"

Giving herself a mental shake to reorient her focus, Briana looked away and said, "Of course. Umm... you were explaining your notes and the different numbers and how this is all very important for the estate soil." Briana bluffed.

"Well, that's definitely a basic summary of what I said. Look, I'll explain the procedure of using potash in our soil one more time and how it is different from what my father has tried in the past. Listen closely now," Cameron said as he moved a bit closer and returned his attention once again to his notebook.

Briana really tried to pay attention to his words, and when he asked if she understood the procedure a second time, she was able to properly respond recounting the procedure in her own words. Seeing him smile and nod at her with the pride of having taught her something, Briana knew this was the moment she'd been waiting for. They'd never been so close before and if she didn't tell him how she felt now, she was scared she would forever remain silent.

"I knew you would make sense of it! You are always quick to understand things and possess such curiosity that makes answering your questions quite enjoyable," Cameron said with a friendly pat on her hand.

Taking his hand in hers, Briana said the words she'd been carrying in her heart for the past two years. "I find you enjoyable. In fact, I think you are the most handsome man I have ever laid eyes on. I have found myself drawn in by your love and respect for your family, especially your father. I care for you in ways different than I do with any other man of my acquaintance, Jake included. I feel safe and secure with you and, well, I do believe I am quite in love with you."

Cameron looked down at his hand clasped tightly in hers and pulled it away. He had not expected a love confession out of Briana. She was like a little sister to him and he knew she always looked up to him. Telling himself she must be confused, Cameron placed a hand on her shoulder and said, "Aww little one, I care for you as I do for Emily. I think you are mistaking companionship as love, since you and I have developed a companionship of sorts during our conversations. Love involves much more than you have experience to know." Seeing her shake her head and open her mouth to speak, Cameron continued hoping to be done with this uncomfortable discussion. "You are to make your debut to the *ton* this year, and I hope you don't mistakenly fall in love with every handsome man who offers you friendship and attention." With a soft pat on her shoulder, Cameron dropped his hand and stood up before asking, "Shall we head to check on the horses?"

Briana felt the tears stinging her eyes. He did not return her feelings and she had made a fool of herself. Standing up as well, Briana said in a broken voice, "You're wrong and the fact that you think that of me shows how little you understand me." With a last look at Cameron, Briana turned on her heel and raced back towards the house. Their relationship would never be the same, even if he insisted upon it. She would tell her parents that she missed London after being in the countryside too long and that they should return sooner than planned. Little did she know that conversation would be the last one she'd have with Cameron for the next ten years.

CHAPTER 2

March 1851

London was abuzz with the beginnings of a new social season. As the flowers were now in bloom, the London *ton* was already beginning to gossip about who the prime debutante would be. It was among this society that Briana found herself thrust into once again. She and her mother, Violet Valmont, Countess of Darby, had left London when she was fifteen years old after her father abandoned them and left them without money to fend for themselves. Those days were behind her now. She would find a rich husband in London during the season, preferably a man she loved, and would thus no longer have to lie to society about her family's social and financial status.

Briana looked out her second-story window and pushed the problems of her past out of her mind. Today marked the beginning of her adult life, the life for which she had prepared herself over the last ten years. Today, she would become the woman she was destined to be, one with love, money, and security she could also extend to her mother. Though she was filled with a renewed vigor and purpose, Briana continued to lounge on her window seat and stare off into the scenery on the other side of the window, which provided her with a glimpse into the world she would come to know more of very soon.

Briana was pulled from her reverie when she heard a knock

on her bedroom door. Pushing herself into a more elegant seating position and smoothing the few curls that had fallen out of her chignon, Briana called for her visitor to enter the bedroom. Her mother entered wearing an expression one could only call anxious.

"Briana, you really must get up and ready yourself for tonight. We have been called upon to attend a ball at the house of Her Grace, the Dowager Duchess of Hereford. Now, I know you remember how close we were with the family, and since we have kept up our correspondence with Her Grace and her daughter over the years, we must carry on like we still have the same status we did then."

"Yes mother, I know. I promise to put on a great act tonight, just like I have done these past ten years. You do not have to worry. I'll put on my best dress and carry myself with such charm that I am sure I will have at least one caller by the end of the night. Please, do not trouble yourself over our situation anymore." Briana closed her hand over that of her mother's and smiled. "I'll take care of everything."

As her mother kissed her cheek and left her to get ready for the night, Briana continued to daydream. Briana would have loved to see the world in order to further her understanding of how others live. Instead, all she'd seen was a small house with few portraits, vases, settees, gowns in the current style made out of curtains by her or her mother, and a mother who had grown so much older than her years because of her preoccupation with keeping up appearances. Briana wished her life was normal, and above all else, easy.

Cameron sat at his large mahogany desk in his bachelor lodgings and finished his bookkeeping of the Hereford estates. He loved his mother, but after inheriting the title and living alone for the last nine years in Dalton Place, the country estate, Cameron couldn't bring himself to stay at the London house with his mother and siblings as he did when younger.

Although he took his position as the Duke of Hereford very seriously, he always felt it was lonely. Cameron was always seen as the reasonable one when paired with his father and his younger brother since he was always concerned with completing all the responsibilities the Dukedom required. His father was a good man who was hardworking but always carefree and joyous until the day of his death nine years ago. His younger brother inherited all of the joy and carefree personality, despite being a Lieutenant in Her Majesty's Royal Navy, while Cameron inherited the hardworking personality. His mother always joked about her son's serious disposition and independence, saying that he came out of the womb with a ledger in hand and the same calculated and disinterested look on his face as his grandfather. He was very different than other children his age since he was always more interested in how his father balanced their books, managed their estate, followed societal rules, and how to properly discuss politics and literature before he even attended Eton. Unlike his father though, Cameron took his work to such extremes that many of his friends and family deemed him a workaholic.

As Cameron laid aside his bookkeeping, he chanced to look outside the windows of his study, which gave him a view of the busy London scene on Brook Street. Cameron loved the energy he found in London because it made him feel less alone, especially since he spent most of the year in Surrey at the country estate. He always managed to make some excuse to come back to London a few times throughout the year. In London, he could always look out into the street to see many people walking by on their way to the shops, to a ball, or just to take a stroll in the park. He had always been one to look at life as a checklist to be completed. In many ways, he knew it was time to complete the next item on his checklist: marriage. As a titled gentleman, he needed a wife. But it was also time for a new mistress.

He had been with the deliciously exotic Serrafina for almost a year now, and even though the courtesan still knew how to make his manhood throb with desire, Cameron never kept a mistress for longer that. It was now time for this partnership to come to an end. Even though he knew she would never wish to marry him – she had been married once before – he knew the longer they remained together and the closer they became, his bachelor ways and the demands that would be placed on her would be less acceptable to her. With a wry smile on his face, Cameron thought, "Well, it wouldn't hurt to maintain her acquaintance for when I'm in town though." He was pulled from his thoughts at the closing sound of the door.

"Hey, what's wrong with you today? I knocked on the door four times before giving up and coming in. You seem distracted, which is odd for a man who is always nose deep in his work," Cameron's younger brother, Jake, said as he strolled into the study unannounced. Jake casually dropped onto the armchair Cameron kept in there for guests. He gave his brother a lopsided grin which seemed to display everything about Jake's personality and his nonchalant attitude toward life. Jake had been home for a little more than a week and had taken it upon himself to serve as Cameron's daily dose of diversion.

"As a matter of fact, I just finished my work and was enjoying a second to take in the day outside," Cameron replied in a short manner. The last things he wanted his younger brother to know were how much he wanted his life to change and how much he wished he could be more like Jake with his laid-back attitude.

"Ah, well, Mother wanted me to remind you about her ball tonight. She expects you to arrive promptly, dance, and participate in the festivities rather than your usual making an appearance before retreating to your study. I know her parties will be the death of us, especially since she keeps trying to marry us off." Jake shook his head in resignation and then ran a hand through his thick light brown hair in order to get the rakish look he had been trying to emulate for some time now.

Cameron smiled at his younger brother knowingly and said, "Yes, well, I think Mother and the rest of the *ton* will be happy when I fulfill my role and responsibilities by taking a wife. You know, I am at the age now where I must look toward settling down and taking a wife to help manage the house and provide me children to carry on the family name. I have the title now, the estates to manage, finances to balance, and the last thing to complete is to find a wife. Yes, a wife is necessary." He smiled to himself after saying this and then laughed as he saw the shocked expression of his brother who looked completely horrified.

"I'm sorry, are you saying you are actually thinking of marriage? To one of the ninnies that will be present tonight? Cam, you have to relax every once in a while. Not everything in life happens on a schedule. In all my travels, one thing I can say for certain is that there are many wonderful women out in the world living life. You know what I mean when I say 'wonderful', right?"

"Yeah, I know what you mean, you numskull. I said I am in need of a wife to provide me children and carry on the title. It is simply a necessary part of life that must happen. Father knew he needed a wife and children to carry on the title and grow his legacy."

"That is true, but Father was still able to enjoy life. He was able to balance everything he needed to do as the Duke of Hereford and yet still found time for joy and pleasure. He welcomed opportunities for life to happen as it may and to share the delights others brought into it on a daily basis. Do you really think Father ever thought his title was all there was to life?" Jake asked.

"Well, that was Father. He had his manner of doing things and I have mine," Cameron replied bluntly.

"What, you don't think you could handle something that isn't planned to perfection?" Jake challenged.

Cameron bristled at his brother's challenge and said, "You know, Jakie, I am sure I can handle anything, just like Father could. I can most definitely relax and enjoy the life London has to offer. I'll start tonight after fulfilling my role at the ball. I'm sure I can slip away with a 'wonderful' woman then."

Although he knew having a fling would not ease his thoughts of the responsibility of finding a wife or living up to his father's memory, he knew it would give him temporary distraction from the checklist of duties he kept in his head. Maybe he could take up a new mistress and shower her with gifts and attention, therefore making him livelier like his father and less lonely. He stood up from his chair behind his desk, giving one last look through his window to the busy street that had now calmed down as the day began to progress into early afternoon. With a smile, he clapped his brother on the back and the two walked out of the study to ready themselves for the dance that night.

Knowing she still had four hours until the masquerade ball that night, Briana decided the only way she was to see the world around her was to take matters into her own hands. So, under the guise of looking for new hair ribbons, she set out with her companion Lucy. As Briana strolled down the streets of London, she witnessed many different scenes and people. There were people buying goods at the open-air market, women dressed in ornate day dresses, children playing on street corners to the constant dismay of their mothers, and men lovingly accompanying women on their shopping errands. Briana wished for that attention, that feeling of being the only one in a room who people see.

"Miss Briana, we've passed the ribbon shop. Should we turn around?" Lucy asked, breaking Briana's reverie.

"No, it's fine. We'll stop by on our way back home. I just want to continue to walk a bit. It feels so refreshing outdoors." Briana took in a deep breath and smiled up at the direction of the sun. She knew she shouldn't remove her bonnet for fear of getting freckles and ruining her complexion, but instinct dominated over reason. As soon as she untied the ribbons, a gust of wind blew the bonnet out of her hand. Before she had time to think of decorum, Briana took off running after it.

Finding the bonnet proved fruitless but revealed the perfect place from which to view the city. Briana sat down on the grass at the top of the hill and waited for Lucy to catch up to her. Fanning out her skirt around her and trying to settle her hair back in place, Briana smiled to herself, realizing she'd just found heaven. She'd found her place to escape from the world she'd known and become an observer of the world she was determined to make hers. Briana removed a small notebook she kept in her handbag and began taking notes about the inspiration she found all around her. She smiled as she realized she had a nice little scene brewing. She knew that her sketches and short stories would never be published, but they were hers alone, a secret that was not a burden but a pleasure she felt many would not understand.

Lucy came upon her, breathing heavily. "Miss Briana, what were you thinking running off in such a manner? And removing your bonnet? What am I going to tell your mother…" She was unable to finish because a man was seen approaching them.

"Excuse me, I found this blowing along the side of the road, and when I spoke with people in town, they directed me this way saying a wild woman was running after the bonnet she'd removed. Does this belong to you?" The man asked from a distance with a cordial smile and eyes that seemed to be studying her.

Briana stood, suddenly shocked at the sudden appearance of the man who held a familiar countenance but one she could not place. Dismissing this thought as unlikely, since she left London at the age of fifteen, Briana pasted a smile on her face and answered, "Yes, thank you." Feeling the need to explain herself to this man, Briana said, "It is beautiful today and I wanted some sunshine to fall upon my face. Some may think that reckless, but I think a woman should be able to do so without being judged by society." Briana finished with her head held high, completely countering the emotions of embarrassment she held inside. She really did know better and would hate to ruin the reputation she and her mother had worked so hard to construct despite lying to the world of their social status.

The man laughed deeply before passing the bonnet over to

Lucy who in turn returned the lost item to her mistress. Keeping his distance, the man stated in a haughty manner, "Well, it certainly was a bit reckless due to the windy days we have been having for the past week. There are rules that we must follow when among society. You are not so young that you would be oblivious to the fact that the *ton* is always judging." Quirking an eyebrow and looking the woman up and down, Cameron assessed that though she was a pretty thing with a warm countenance, she was far younger than he. "You can't be more than three and twenty, if I had to guess." The man's tone held a hint of cynicism to everything he said, and yet it was glossed with an almost silky-smooth coating.

Briana did not know what to make of the man except that he made her nervous. Based on his ornate clothing, she could tell he was definitely a man of worth. Despite his distance, she could tell he was a handsome man with a muscular build, brown wavy hair, dark eyes, and dimples that made him irresistible. There was something in his mannerisms and his dimples that reminded her of her first love, the one she'd left behind as a young child of fifteen. She knew she should be nice and gain his affections for his money alone to save her mother and herself, but she could not bring herself to do so. Also, why wasn't he moving closer to her when speaking? Was he expecting her to close the distance?

Out of a combination of stubbornness and nerves, Briana remained rooted in her spot. Bringing a smile to her lips, she replied, "Yes, I am *five* and twenty and do not believe that my age should keep me from contributing my opinions to a conversation as many others would do. It is ridiculous to think I am merely to smile idly and give short, agreeable answers when I am invested in a conversation. At the look of shocked disapproval on your face, I see that we are simply prolonging an awkward situation, so I will thank you again for returning my bonnet to me and bid you good day." For having some similarities with her first love, the young boy she'd left behind had a warmth to him that was not found in this man's rude and opinionated manner.

Briana smiled tightly for fear her nerves would get the best of her and she would begin to ramble profusely about the rights of women or her bonnet or the sun. Oh goodness, she was already rambling in her head. Briana turned away quickly and motioned to the appalled Lucy. Briana fought every urge to turn around and look at the man until she heard him turn and walk away. As she turned, she was shocked at the sudden blush that came to her cheeks. Telling herself the blush was simply from her irritation at the man's rude manner, Briana turned and continued with Lucy to the ribbon store knowing she could not return home empty-handed if she wanted to avoid answering many pointed questions from her mother.

Briana returned home with a new emerald ribbon which she knew would match perfectly with her best ball gown. She rushed upstairs to her room before her mother could scold her for taking so long to buy a simple ribbon. She opened the door to her bedroom to find the gown carefully laid out on her bed and soon began to feel the pressures of the night's festivities. Looking around at her sparsely decorated room, Briana heaved a sigh and rang the bell for someone to fill the bath.

As she was moving to the bath, her mother knocked on the door and asked to enter. Briana opened the door to her freshly bathed mother, who smelled of the beautiful flower with which she shared a name. The wonderful scent of sweet violets washed over Briana and brought a smile to her lips. Her mother's violet-scented water was something that had never disappeared despite their declining fortune.

"Is everything alright, Mother? You don't look anxious but have an expression I cannot place." Briana studied her mother, who looked so serious, an expression she rarely saw even though it is very close to the anxious expression Briana had come to expect upon her mother's face every day.

Her mother suddenly broke out into a grin. "While you were out at the ribbon shop, I stepped out as well to see

Madame Dubois who agreed to sell me this wonderful mask for the ball tonight. Isn't it gorgeous?" She frowned as she saw Briana's questioning look. "It does not matter how much I had to pay. We were able to afford it because she gave me a wonderful deal. Besides, you meeting a rich man tonight will cover our expenses soon anyway," her mother responded casually and handed the emerald green and gold accented mask. Briana was amazed by the beautiful colors as well as the subtle touches on the tips of the mask that held a small peacock feather on each side that would sit nicely against her dark brown eyebrows. Briana stood gazing at the mask, thinking that tonight was the night she would put on the performance of her life. With a motivating nod, Briana lightly placed the mask on the bed alongside the gown and smiled as she walked into the washroom.

CHAPTER 3

Briana descended the stairs with the elegance that would make the best debutantes jealous. Her curly hair shimmered in the light of the room and her amber brown eyes looked all the more mysterious when paired with the emerald and peacock feathered mask. The emerald gown she wore swept the floor as she walked, mesmerizing all in her wake. Inside, Briana was terrified she would not find any suitors to call on her with offers of marriage. But, on the outside, Briana wore the smile of seductive confidence.

The Valmonts did not have to travel far to arrive at the house of the Dowager Duchess of Hereford since they had decided to take up residence in their old family home nearby and could be considered to be neighbors. Walking into the house, the Valmonts were in wonderment of the decorations that met them. The house was spectacular with dim lighting, setting the mood for a night of mystery. Briana smiled politely to passing guests as she made her way to the hostess and her family. Upon seeing Her Grace receiving guests as they entered the ballroom, the pressures of Briana's purpose began to mount. She held the confident smile she had mastered over the years and stepped forward to greet the woman she had not seen since she was fifteen years old. She and her mother removed their masks momentarily to pay their respects to the hostess, as well as to her daughter and son that stood at her side.

"Lady Darby!" Elizabeth Worthington, Dowager Duchess of Hereford smiled with delight as she looked upon the two women. "Oh! Violet, Briana, how are the two of you? It's been such a long time since we all spoke last," Elizabeth said as she hugged both women, instantly recognizing them despite the years they had spent apart. "I am sad to hear from your letter that your husband will not be joining us tonight, but I am happy he is healthy and spending time with his nephew on holiday." Briana's mother simply smiled and thanked her friend for her thoughts, knowing the importance of using the Dowager Duchess to spread the story of her husband's whereabouts.

Emily too recognized her best friend and following her mother, threw propriety out the proverbial window and enveloped Briana in the hug she had been waiting many years to bestow upon her. "Oh Brie! I cannot believe we've finally been reunited. You are so beautiful and elegant! All the letters we shared, and yet you forgot to mention in your last letter that you would be returning to London!" Emily playfully chastised. Her gaiety was infectious and Briana found herself grinning the same way she had when they ran through meadows and always returned to the house dirty as children. Remembering herself and the restrained manners she should display, Emily stepped back and remained simply squeezing Briana's hand.

"So, the runt of a girl finally grew into her hair, huh?" This was said by the man that Briana instantly recognized as Lieutenant Jake Worthington. When they were younger, Jake would often tease Briana about her short stature and wild hair that was two times larger than her face. Although he was two years her senior, he would often join her and Emily for adventures outside since his older brother was always working alongside their father with no desire to stop for fun. After receiving a letter from Emily about his enlistment in the Royal Navy, Briana was happy to see he still maintained his sense of humor and *joie de vivre*. Brie smiled up at him and couldn't help but laugh as she took in his costume. Where Emily was elegant in a costume of "Starry Night" wearing a dark sapphire tulle gown, dressed with gold stars, a necklace of star-set pearls, white gloves, and a simple blue and gold mask, Jake decided to truly show his personality and have fun with his attire. Jake wore a costume of "King of Hearts" attired in a black dress coat, matching fitted black pants, a white vest dressed with red hearts, a white dress shirt studded with red hearts, a red cape, a faux-gold crown, a simple black mask, and white gloves. To complete his look, he wore his most devilish smile that would surely capture the hearts of many.

"If you are referring to the mass of curls I now wear permanently affixed to the top of my head, then yes, I have. I'll have you know that this hair needs no ornamentation like most other women would wear," Brie replied with a smile before conceding, "Well, that's probably because its fullness already attracts enough attention on its own."

She gave Jake her gloved hand, and as he raised it to his lips for a quick kiss, he smiled mischievously at her and said, "Well, would you like to place a wager for old time's sake?" Never one to back down from a challenge given by Jake, she nodded her head. "I will wager a friendly kiss on the cheek that at least a dozen men will ask to dance and compliment that mane of yours tonight. Do we have a deal?" Briana let out a throaty laugh and was reminded of how Jake would always wager a "friendly kiss on the cheek" no matter what the bet was. That friendly kiss always turned into him pulling some prank on her. But this time, as adults in a very crowded ballroom, she would be ready for any prank his "friendly kiss" could result in.

"Very well, but if I win and nobody pays any attention to my hair, as I think, you must serve as Emily's servant tomorrow and help her respond to any letters from admirers." Jake rolled his eyes upward but smiled and nodded nonetheless.

"If you two have finished, I'd like to take Brie around and introduce her to those she has not seen in some time. Plus, Jake, don't you have some hearts to collect tonight?" Emily threw him a mischievous grin and then grabbed Briana's hand and led her away into the mass of people gathered in the ballroom. It was the grandest room in the Hereford estate with its high ceilings, gold trimmings on the walls, plush floor to ceiling velvet curtains, and the golden chandeliers which hung down almost tempting someone to reach their arms up and try to grab the tiny crystals that adorned it. She loved this room. She loved the memories of spinning around the room with Emily as young girls trying to make their skirts billow out all around them. Now, in the full swing of a ball, this room was more magical than she could ever have imagined. The band was playing a lovely waltz and the couples on the dance floor whirling around the room in their costumes added to the splendor of the night. Briana could not wait to be able to dance; it didn't matter with whom at this point. She simply wanted to feel strong arms around her guiding her through such a magical dance that would transport her to a world where the music and her dance companion were the only things in existence. Briana blinked herself back into the present just as Emily lightly jabbed her elbow into her side.

"Briana, are you feeling alright?" Emily asked with concern in her voice.

"This is all so beautiful and magical. I'm just taking it all in so I remember every detail exactly. Could you ever imagine anything like this when we were girls spinning around in this room? I wish I brought my notepad so I could sketch this scene, although I'm sure it will be ingrained in my memory." Emily chuckled at Briana's innocence, remembering that this was truly the first ball she'd attended.

"It's even more magical once you begin dancing. Come, let us fill up your dance card and introduce you to some nice people," Emily said as she guided Briana to a circle of men and women talking in the middle of the room. "Lady Turner, Lady Phillips, Lord Edwards, Lord Blackstone, let me introduce you to my dear friend Lady Briana Valmont. Briana and her mother have recently returned to London after moving away to care for family. Her father is the Lord William Valmont, Earl of

Darby." Briana smiled brightly despite feeling guilty for having lied to her best friend about the reason for their departure from London years ago.

"Lady Valmont, what a pleasure to make your acquaintance. I trust that now you are back in London your family's health has been restored? My poor late wife could not find herself restored after our last journey to Bath sadly, but one day we will reunite in good health," Lord Blackstone said as he bowed over her hand. He was a man well into his seventies and not an overly tall man but that of average height. He wore a pleasant smile but a look of sadness lay hidden in his seafoam colored eyes.

Briana smiled at him and nodded regally. "My uncle passed away, unfortunately, but we were able to care for my aunt and nephew so they are now in good health. In fact, my father is now on holiday with my cousin as a reward for his doing so well in school," Briana replied, remembering the story she and her mother had agreed to earlier in the day should anyone inquire about their ten-year absence. Smiling, Briana continued, "I thank you for your concern and am very sorry to hear about your late wife. Your love for her is very touching." She reached out and patted his hand in a manner of comfort.

"Lady Valmont, have you been able to explore London since you have returned?" Lord Edwards asked, thus moving the conversation back to lighter conversation. "I wonder if it is much changed since you saw it last." He wore a genial smile on his face, his crystal blue eyes crinkled. Briana could sense he was a man who was genuinely content in his life and whose smile was as honest as he. He looked to be in his thirties, maybe closer to five and thirty. He wore his blonde honeysuckle hair trimmed neatly and combed to the side with long sideburns to complement his lovely visage. Briana liked him instantly.

"I haven't had much time since we only just arrived in London a few days ago. I fear most of my time has been spent helping my mother get the house back in order after years of absence. I do hope to find time soon. Emily has already promised me an outing." Briana smiled.

"Well, if you ladies are in need of a companion, I am at your service." Lord Edwards bowed elegantly. "Lady Valmont, are you engaged for the next dance? If not, may I have the honor?" Briana found that she did not have to feign happiness at being asked and happily gave him her dance card.

"I'll claim the next if you are not opposed to dance with someone as old as I," said Lord Blackstone. "I have a nephew around here somewhere that I can make your acquaintance with as well. He is about your age I believe, and though he can be a bit dull at times, he has a good heart." Briana simply smiled and gave over her dance card once again. The two gentlemen then fell to discussing the best horse for different kinds of races with two new gentleman who had come to join in their conversation. One was a tall and rather gangly looking fellow with a comical mustache that curled up at the ends and a monocle affixed to his right eye. The other gentleman was quite his opposite, except in height, since he was rather muscular and dashing to look at with his soft smile.

"I say, Edwards, you've never claimed to know everything about horses. But, after losing enough bets to you back in our Oxford days, I know better than to question you." This was said by the dashing gentleman who was wearing a black dress coat, matching fitted black pants, a white vest, a white dress shirt studded with black buttons, a red cape, a simple black mask, and white gloves. He had a smooth baritone voice that commanded attention but with the ability to put his friends at ease. Seeing Lord Edwards grin, it was obvious these two men had known each other for some time. "Be careful not to let my mother hear you talking about races. She'll be heartbroken if she believes there is gambling happening at this ball."

"Aw, you know I would never intentionally break your mother's heart. Lovely lady that she is. But, you know I am right about those horses..." Lord Edwards replied with his easy smile.

"But horses will not only neigh gaily when they are winning, you know. We must remember that a happy horse is a winning horse." This was said by the gangly gentleman as he adjusted his monocle. With a nervous chuckle at the blank eyes looking back at him, he continued, "Well, if a horse was sad, one would surely think he would not be a good contender to place bets on. Also, the poor horse would rather not wish to leave his stall and the comfort of his hay. I mean, if you weren't happy, would you want to race or indulge in eating and lazing about. I for one think the key is talking to a horse to see if said horse is happy." Dropping his hand from where it had been curling his mustache ends as he thought, the gentleman smiled unsurely.

Briana couldn't help but smile at the comical suggestion of a grown man conversing with a horse. Before she could wonder if the gentleman would once again receive blank stares from his companions, the gentleman with the red cape said genially, "Lord Burfel, it does not surprise me that while us heathens would think of simply winning bets, you would be concerned with the feelings of the horses. Always the soft-hearted one." Lord Burfel seemed quite pleased with the praise as he smiled and stood a bit straighter.

"Well, putting the feelings of horses aside, I would say that if you were to find a purebred Arabian stallion, the endurance it possesses would prove best for harness racing," Lord Blackstone said, steering the conversation back to its original purpose.

Deciding that these gentlemen would be discussing horses and gambling for a while, Briana turned her attention to Emily and the two ladies, Lady Turner and Lady Phillips, who were now seated at the chairs along the wall and were discussing their favorite costumes of the night.

"Well, of course, both of the Worthington brothers look dashing tonight and will surely leave many women in a daze. Those women looking to make a match will definitely have their sights on one if not both of them," said Lady Turner, who looked to be no more than fifty. She did not wear a costume, but instead wore a beautiful violet tulle and lace gown and carried with her a matching mask she could place over her face at any given second. Before Briana could comment, Lord Edwards was by her side to collect his dance. They made their way to the dance floor just in time to set themselves for the quadrille that had begun to play.

Emily curtsied as Lord Edwards bowed to her. He took her hand gently in his as they moved forward in the beginning passes of the quadrille. The three other couples that joined their circle smiled genially at them and continued their private conversations. "So, tell me Lady Valmont, have you had the chance to visit the shops in town yet?" Lord Edwards began.

"Why yes, I was able to visit a few in order to get some new bonnets and the like. It was very nice to see all the people out and about," Briana replied.

"Ah, yes, women can never have enough bonnets it seems. Although, I must say, it is such a tragedy to have to cover lovely curls such as yours," Lord Edwards said smoothly. Seeing the slight blush that came to Briana's cheeks made him proud. Continuing the conversation, he asked, "Have you been to the book shop? Monsieur Le Rous has the most extensive collection of classic literature despite his emphasis on French literature and comically ruddy complexion. My favorites, of course, are the Greek and Roman philosophers. Where would one be without the knowledge and philosophies of life they bestowed upon us through their works? It's fascinating really. Would you like me to escort you tomorrow, perhaps?" Lord Edwards inquired as he smiled down at her. It wasn't a very interesting topic for her, but he was being so kind that to turn him down seemed wrong in some way.

"Why Lord Edwards, we just met tonight. Shouldn't we at least see each other a few more times before we plan an outing?" Briana replied, smiling and looking up at him flirtatiously. As he chuckled awkwardly and nodded his head slowly, she said, "Maybe someday, Lord Edwards. That sounds nice," Briana replied, hoping she wasn't breaking any societal rules with this noncommittal reply of hers.

"Yes, well, you do seem to have a point. It wouldn't be very proper to rush an acquaintance with such an elegant woman, would it? Well, what do you enjoy doing when not attending to your daily duties? Do you like to ride horses? My mother always said the true measure of a lady was how elegantly she can ride a horse. My mother was the most elegant of women," he sighed sadly.

"She sounds wonderful. Are you very close?" Briana asked in curiosity. The man who had been so cheerful seemed a bit sad when he spoke of his mother.

"We were. I had no siblings growing up and was a sickly child, so she spent a lot of time with me. She was always making me laugh and smile by telling me jokes or describing my future. She was always so clear in her belief that I would be a strong, healthy man with an elegant, docile, and respectable wife by my side." He looked away for a brief second and then returned his sad blue eyes to Briana. "If she were still alive today, she would be very proud to see me dancing with a woman such as yourself now." Briana squeezed his hand subtly in comfort. Although this man didn't strike a passion in her, his kindness and love toward his mother was endearing.

"Ahem. Sorry about all that," Lord Edwards said, clearing his throat and removing her hand from his and placing it back on his arm. "As touched as I am by your concern, you really should be careful with how you comfort others, Lady Valmont. Although what you just did was kind, the look in your eyes along with the gesture was highly improper and I wouldn't like to ruin your good reputation." Briana simply nodded, dumbfounded. "Let's talk of happier things before you think me the biggest dullard in all of London." Briana couldn't help but giggle at the face he made and, like that, they continued to talk about his time in Oxford studying the classics and her love of reading poetry. As the quadrille began to draw to a close, Briana looked for Emily, who smiled at her from across the room where her partner had delivered her earlier.

Emily was gathered in a group of women who were discussing the latest fashion. As she watched her friend dancing happily, she looked around for Jake to shoot him a knowing glance that Jake would surely be the winner of tonight's bet. Although she found their bet to be highly improper, she couldn't stand to be the one to ruin their fun after reuniting for the first time in over a decade. She spotted Jake talking to a few women who were all but swooning at his every glance. Emily rolled her eyes and then, making eye contact again with Briana, went in search of a glass of lemonade.

CHAPTER 4

Cameron stood at a distance staring across the room at the mystery woman in the emerald gown. He had taken to calling her his "emerald of the night" since she was radiantly set apart from any other woman in the room. Despite the dancing couples that separated them and continued to circle in front of his eyes, Cameron never once lost her, as if he was staring through each couple. The longer he stared, the hotter the room became, the tighter his breeches felt, and his cravat became more constricting around his neck. It was ridiculous that he was lusting after a woman his mother would have picked out as a possible marriage match. He saw himself as a bachelor, and though he was lonely and had entertained thoughts of marriage earlier in the day, he knew that kind of woman would only marry him for his title and money, whereas a mistress would want him for the very carnal thoughts he was entertaining in his head about one lovely woman in emerald. He had to dance with her and hold her close for a little bit before he forgot about her completely. In a few long strides, Cameron found himself standing in front of the most beautiful lady in the room. Even though she wore a mask that covered half of her face, Cameron still noticed how captivating her amber brown eyes were.

"Excuse me, are you engaged for the next waltz?" Briana looked up to see two dark eyes staring down at her, hypnotizing her. Unable to speak, she simply shook her head no and handed the man her dance card. "I'm looking forward to the next dance. Until then." The man bowed gracefully and once again caught Briana off guard by flashing her the most beautiful smile she had ever seen a man wear. He turned to leave, glanced back at her once more, and then was lost in the crowd of masks. Briana remained and spoke with Lady Phillips until the dance was over, and then began to make her way through the throng of people and masks in order to find Emily.

Briana found her speaking with a man who seemed to be of the same age as Emily's father and as much of a bore as his conversation of the weather. Emily glanced pleadingly at her friend and was relieved to find Briana ready to come to her aid. Briana paid her respects to Sir Robert Buckingham and begged for Emily's assistance with a stray thread on her gown. As the two ladies excused themselves and made as if they were heading toward the ladies room, Emily and Briana took a detour to the far side of the ballroom where the windows gave a spectacular view of the gardens and breathed simultaneous sighs of relief.

"Oh Em, you look beautiful tonight! I do hope you're enjoying the ball as much as I am. I feel that I have already met so many people that I would normally recognize. But tonight, everyone has an air of mystery and it seems like everyone is revealing so much more of themselves," Briana said, in awe of all the dancing couples and the scandalous bits of conversation she could hear.

"Oh yes, everyone is definitely covered in mystery, but it seems some are revealing a bit too much of themselves tonight," Emily said with clear disdain as she motioned toward the window behind them. Briana glanced at the designated area and, stifling her giggles, simply shook her head in awe of the reckless abandon some women dared to have when thinking they were out of sight.

Before Briana could voice her opinion on the subject, a

31

waltz began to play and her heart began to beat faster as she anticipated her next partner taking her hand again. She thought of his smile and his lips that tempted her to feel their smoothness upon her own. She knew she could never act on this thought, or the rush of nervous anticipation she was feeling knotting in her stomach, unless this man had a large sum of money to his name. But despite her duty to her mother, she sincerely hoped to fall in love with the man she would marry and have his love in return. In a daze, she thought about the other qualities the man must possess, among them generosity with himself and others, an amiable nature and disposition, an astute intelligence, a love of life, and the belief that a woman could indeed be seen as a man's equal.

Cameron walked toward the woman in emerald with the peacock mask and could not help but grin when he saw the dazed expression in her eyes. She was so beautiful and so mysterious, especially since she looked like she was miles away from the place where she stood. He slowed his stride a hair so he could further examine her beauty. She had such an exquisite smile on her face, one that suggested to the outside world that she had a pleasing secret. Cameron's gaze continue to pass over her, ever so slowly moving further south to take notice of her elegant neck, which unlike many other necks in the room was left unadorned by gaudy necklaces. The woman in question was not the typical slender, small-chested, woman with a demure attitude that the *ton* claimed as beautiful. Instead, this goddess in emerald was curvier, but not to the point of being considered portly. She had the sort of body that could drive a man wild with passion and desire simply with a mere glance in her direction. The air about her was a subtle confidence meshed with a seductive appeal which enabled her to stand apart from all the other women Cameron had ever come into contact with.

Taking a deep breath, which Cameron hoped would settle not only his excitement but also the surge of blood that was heading south quickly, Cameron reached Briana and simply put out his hand in front of her, not even sparing a glance for

Emily. Smiling to himself as he noticed her quick little nibble on her bottom lip as their eyes met, he took her hand and with ease led her onto the ballroom dance floor where all the other couples were preparing for the waltz. Having recognized this gentleman and seeing his captivated visage so evidently displayed, Emily realized the two had not yet recognized each other. With eyes trained on them, she sipped her glass of lemonade with a knowing smirk on her face. The night was about to get a lot more interesting.

As Briana and Cameron began dancing, they were transported to a place where only they existed. Looking into each other's eyes and smiling at each other with such ease, the two suddenly laughed slightly as they realized they had yet to make conversation as society dictates. Cameron broke the silence by stating calmly as he smiled down at her, "I saw you pass by earlier and couldn't take my eyes off of you. I hope it wasn't too forward of me to come and ask you to dance."

Briana could not believe that such a gorgeous man, with such exquisite dimples to frame his seductive smile, was dancing with her and giving her all the attention in the world. She had already had to calm her excitement as she walked into the ballroom and saw all the fabulous dresses and suits, the sparkling diamonds which adorned most women, and the beautiful linens and decorations found throughout the ballroom. She looked up at the man smiling down at her and answered truthfully, "I have to admit, I was a little taken aback, but it doesn't seem to bother me now."

Cameron could not help but chuckle in surprise to her answer. "You seem to be pretty straightforward, not demure at all like most women. It's refreshing." Again, he found himself smiling at this unknown woman. When was the last time he smiled so much in the company of anybody, let alone a woman who was not his mistress?

"I'm glad you agree, because I must again be frank. I don't

have much skill when it comes to dancing the waltz...I'm afraid I never had the desire or talent to practice." Appalled, Briana looked down and thought to quickly add, "Of course, I'm not terrible, but you won't find me to be the best dancing partner either." Briana hoped this statement would serve to cover up her mistake of telling this man, who was worth a lot of money (as witnessed by his attire), that she was clumsy, which she had heard her mother say was her worse trait. Hoping to regain her cool, seductive, and charming appearance, Briana chanced another glance at the gorgeous man whose strong arm around her waist was causing her legs to go weak against her will. Caught off guard by his grin and his assessing eyes, Briana stumbled and stepped on his foot. "Oh, sorry!" Briana nibbled on her bottom lip, mortified that she was losing her composure.

Cameron could not help but smile at this woman who was at one moment completely confident and calm, yet the next minute could turn into a bundle of nerves. He was beginning to realize that she had a tendency of chewing on her bottom lip when she was nervous. Grinning to himself, he said, "Well, you have nothing to worry about, because after dancing with me, you will be the best dancer the *ton* has ever seen."

Here was her chance to get back in the game and adopt the seductive and confident demeanor she knew would make this man continue to think of her after tonight. Looking him in the eyes, Briana grinned slightly at him and said, "You seem to be very confident. What happens if you are wrong?" She sucked in a breath and held it, hoping that her game would work to keep him wanting more. Cameron brought his index finger to his chin while sending her a lopsided grin that made it harder for her to keep her mind on playing the role of calm seductress. A lock of Cameron's hair fell across his forehead and Briana fought with all her might not to reach out and touch the silky brown lock.

Cameron had stopped stroking his chin and chuckled as he said, "If I am wrong, you will never have to dance with me again."

"Are you assuming I was going to dance with you otherwise?"

Briana was surprised at the breathiness found in her voice. She hoped that Cameron did not see through her façade even though she felt herself melting further into his arms at the strength of his gaze.

Cameron released another chuckle before replying, "Of course! I'm very irresistible." Briana couldn't help but giggle at the man's audacity. She was enjoying his company and could tell by his dimpled smile that he was enjoying hers. "So how do you know our host?"

Regaining her composure, she replied, "I've known them for years, since I was a young girl. Are you close with the family?"

Cameron could not help but smile. "Very." He wasn't exactly lying to this woman, and the idea of continuing the mystery was very enticing.

"You must be friends with Emily's brothers."

"Oh, you could say that." Cameron tightened his grip on her back and grinned as her eyes met his. "Your dancing seems to be improving. It looks like I am justified in my confidence." He gave her such a smug look that Briana could not resist what she did next.

Purposefully stepping on his foot, she smiled coquettishly and said, "Sorry... I would hold off on the praise. If I don't get better, you are going to look very badly."

He chuckled as he replied, "As will you." Briana couldn't help but laugh in earnest at his wittiness. She was falling for this man and she barely knew him. She knew in the back of her mind that she should probably stop dancing with him soon in order to leave him desiring after her. She wanted him to want her deeply enough to offer marriage, and she knew one way to get that was to make him jealous by watching her dance and flirt with other men. She looked up at his grin and his adorable dimples, and her thoughts of being with anyone else were dismissed immediately.

"I think you owe me more information about yourself since I am saving your image," Cameron said, breaking into her reverie. He could tell she was debating whether or not to leave his company as soon as socially acceptable, but he couldn't let this woman go. He had to keep her talking, interested, and above all, he had to keep her in his arms.

Briana returned his smug impression. She smiled charmingly and said, "Is that right? Well, I suppose I can humor you a little. What do you want to know?"

Without hesitation, Cameron replied, "Anything. What is your biggest ambition?"

Briana bit at her bottom lip in thought. "I don't know. Nobody has really asked me that before. I guess it would be... to be a writer or an artist. Men can do it, why can't women?"

"You continue to surprise me. I think you could really be a threat to those men."

Feeling confident, and completely wrapped up in their own world, Briana displayed an act of blatant flirtation by playfully hitting Cameron on the arm and giggling. "Are you saying that because I'm clumsy or because I am a woman?"

"Both. You know, you're really not as clumsy as you think you are. And even if you are, it would only make you more beautiful." He lifted her chin with his finger. "I feel so comfortable with you, even though I'm only just getting to know you. You give me this sense like I have known and spoken to you many times before."

Briana smiled and could feel herself blush. "I'm comfortable with you too, even if you are overly confident at times." When Cameron's response was a raised eyebrow, Briana returned the quirked eyebrow and said, "Oh, don't look at me like you have no idea what I'm talking about." Looking into each other's eyes, they both found themselves laughing until Briana began to lose her balance and Cameron helped her regain it.

"Would it be too forward of me to tell you that I would really like to kiss you right now?"

Briana stopped dancing and looked around the ballroom filled with couples, matrons, and bachelors all beginning to glance in their direction and whisper. "I'm sorry? I... Well... It's just that... it's just we've danced three dances in a row and I think the *ton* is starting to talk and stare."

Unconcerned, Cameron continued to look at Briana. This

woman who could display such confidence one minute was obviously not indifferent to the opinions of the *ton* like he thought himself to be. "So let them stare. I don't think I'm willing to see you dancing with anyone else. Anyway, it is almost time to take off our masks. I think we are both ready to see each other's identities."

Feeling nervous, Briana said the first thing that came to mind in order for her to get away for a second and catch her breath. "Well then, let's keep the mystery for a little bit longer. I see a friend who requires my attention," she said, motioning to Emily who was standing next to the refreshment table smirking in their direction as she waited for Briana to meet her.

"Promise to come back for the removal of the masks?" Cameron couldn't keep the excitement and pleading from his voice. He was sure that tonight he would meet the woman of his dreams. Maybe she would become his new mistress… or maybe something more? No, he had already decided today not to get married yet, but God she'd be great to call his. To go to bed with her every night knowing that no other man would be able to get the pleasure he received from being with her was almost enough to make him reconsider putting off marriage.

Smiling her calm and seductive smile, she nodded her head and whispered, "Of course." As she turned away from him, she could feel the warmth of his smile on her back. This man had made quite the impression on her. She knew this was the man she wanted. He was wealthy and could cover all her family's debt and she could definitely grow to love this man. She knew it!

As she approached Emily by the refreshment table, she couldn't keep the excitement and happiness out of her manner. "Oh, Em! I think I've found a man I can really connect with. I've been dancing with him all night and have discussed so many different subjects. Even though I kept stepping on his feet, he made me feel so comfortable."

Smiling softly, Emily could only think to reply, "That's great." She hated that what she had to tell Briana would crush all her hopes. Emily knew Briana would hate to find out that the masked man was Emily's older brother, Cameron, the same boy who broke her young heart. Briana had never forgiven him. "Brie, I should tell you something..."

"So, after that waltz I definitely win tonight's bet. Let me see your dance card. I'm sure I can add those numbers to the four men I have already seen speaking with you and then about you all night. Surely, the number will prove in my favor," Jake said laughingly as he came to join Emily and Briana.

"Yes, Jake, I do think I have to declare you the winner of tonight's wager. I do believe I had a dozen men ask me for a dance and complimented me on my lovely curls and costume. I believe if your four men did the same, that puts me at sixteen. I believe I owe you a kiss then." Before she could rise up on her toes to plant the kiss on Jake's cheek, he stopped her.

"Not now, I'll collect later. I hear my brother is begging my presence to save him from any matchmaking attempts my mother has planned. Find me when the bell chimes tonight to remove masks, okay? My costume is pretty unique, so it shouldn't be a problem for you." And with a quick bow, he was off to play the dutiful and pleasant brother before Briana could let him know she had other plans for when the bell chimes.

Cameron glared at his brother as he watched him talking a little comfortably with his little gem. When Jake came over to him, Cameron was ready to toss the glass of champagne he'd been enjoying in Jake's face. Instead, Cameron cleared his throat and stated, "If you are set on collecting the hearts of women just for fun, I don't think that little gem is one to add to your collection."

"Oh no? Why, has the lady caught your eye tonight as well?" Jake teased.

"I'm simply stating that she seems to have more substance than the other women in this room," Cameron bristled.

"She does seem to be exactly the woman you were hoping to meet. You know, the 'wonderful' type that could make life worth living?" Jake grinned secretively at his brother as he lightly elbowed him in the side.

"Jake, you know Mother and my title are going to need me to find a wife soon. I am in no way enjoying the prospect of marriage, but it is my duty to do so," Cameron replied smoothly.

"Well brother, you have to remember to enjoy life and its treasures. You said you were able to relax and enjoy life as well as fulfill your responsibilities just like Father could, right? Don't tell me you can't?" Jake challenged his brother. "Relax and enjoy the women around you!" Jake continued and clapped his brother on the back. "Here, take my crown and tap into your innermost King who can collect the hearts of women easily and use at his disposal." Jake placed the crown on Cameron's head with a wicked grin. "Now, I'm off to meet and collect more beautiful women. Enjoy brother!" Jake called out the last message over his shoulder as he made his way to a tall and slender brunette dressed as a fairy with wings and all.

Cameron adjusted the crown that now sat uncomfortably on his head. He could never be as carefree as his brother to attract many young women. Suddenly feeling a bit panicked and overwhelmed, he made his way to the restroom where he did not plan on running into any women of importance or convenience.

Just as Cameron had turned the corner to enter the passageway that led to the restrooms, his arm was grabbed by a pair of small and tender female hands. "I found you! Since you win, here is your reward." As Briana raised up to kiss "Jake" on the cheek, Cameron turned his face just in time to see his Emerald Lady bring her lips to his. His Emerald was kissing him. Did she read minds and men's desires? This kiss was not the type of kiss he was accustomed to with Serrafina or any of his other mistresses. This kiss had so many layers of innocence, shock, and a burning promise of passion he just had to explore. He couldn't help himself. He grabbed her by the waist and brought her closer against him and deepened the kiss further, urging her lips apart and sliding in his tongue to taste every corner of her.

Briana couldn't believe this kiss was happening. This was Jake, right? No, this wasn't the fun, brotherly kiss on the cheek she'd agreed to. He was kissing her! And she was enjoying it! His lips were so soft and revealed to her the same shock she was currently experiencing, but also had a sense of command and control that she was lacking. He deepened the kiss, exploring every part of her mouth with his tongue. As he pulled her closer, she gripped his arms and a moan escaped from her. She'd never been kissed like this before. She'd never been kissed at all. She felt like she was no longer in her body. She was so unbelievably relaxed and yet wound up so tightly at the same time. How was that even possible? And this was Jake! She had to stop this. This was her first kiss, after all, and Jake had just turned it into part of their bet.

She pulled herself apart from his hold gasping for air. "Jake! How could you? That was too far and well you know it!" Briana said loudly through clenched teeth at him. She could feel her body burning both from the passionate kiss and also from the anger she was now feeling toward Jake.

"Jake? Seems you've got the wrong brother, little gem. You just throw yourself at any man nearby without confirming his identify?" Cameron was infuriated and hurt that his mystery woman was more interested in his brother than in him, just like everyone else. They had shared such a special moment during their dancing and he knew she felt it too, but alas his brother's charm once again won out in claiming yet another woman's heart. "You, ma'am, will garner a reputation as a loose woman if you're not careful," Cameron said while crossing his arms across his broad chest.

"How dare you!" Briana said seething as she reached for her mask. The gong was heard at that exact time. Cameron too reached for his mask and the two removed them from their faces simultaneously. Briana gasped and Cameron cursed under his breath.

"You?! I couldn't have been dancing with you all night. Do you always take advantage of women like this? Pretend to be such a gentleman who really cares about what one has to say..."

"Excuse me? You seemed to be enjoying yourself. Why don't you just admit it to yourself?" He was taken aback as Briana scoffed at him. "Why is it so hard for you to believe that I was being completely genuine?"

"Ha! I know who you are. Rude, arrogant, and you probably have a reputation as a rake! Dancing with you was a mistake – a lapse of judgment. It was the allure of a masquerade ball. I can't believe I thought myself falling for a man like you! Good evening." She turned swiftly on her heel and stormed off. Cameron did the same in the opposite direction toward Emily who was standing by the refreshment table. After looking around to see if anyone is watching, he grabbed a glass of champagne off the table and quickly downed the drink before placing the empty glass back on the table.

"Are you okay? I saw you watching her from across the room before you even asked her to dance and tried to get your attention. When that didn't work, I figured you would find out sooner or later and decided to join Mother and Lord Burfel for a chat on the intricacies of book collecting. Then, the next time I see you two together, you are arguing. I guess the reunion wasn't as happy as I hoped," Emily said with a shrug of her shoulders.

"Reunion? How did you know that I met her earlier today? I didn't think there was anyone else there but the two of us and her maid." Cameron said confused.

"Don't you recognize her?" Cameron simply stared ahead. Emily shook her head softly as she replied, "Cameron, that's Briana. You know, Brie from our childhood?" It broke Emily's heart to know that yet again Cameron was selfishly wrapped up in his own thoughts that he was unable to recognize her dear friend. Cameron couldn't believe this was the same girl who had all but been another sibling in his house growing up and now he had actually lusted after her. Before saying another word, he stalked off, leaving Emily with nothing else to do but go find Briana and help mend her broken heart if need be.

She found her out on the balcony getting some fresh air. "So, you've been reunited with Cameron, I see," Emily said with a hesitant laugh.

"Now it makes sense! I thought he looked slightly familiar when I saw him earlier today, but he was at such a distance I couldn't tell. And then with the costume and masks tonight, I really didn't know. His blunt and confident manner has definitely not changed, but his hair is longer and wavier. His eyes seem to be darker now than they were before as well. He seems much older than his age. Ugh, I should have known it was him by his attitude alone. He called my actions stupid and spoke to me as if I were a child when I met him earlier today!" Looking back at the man who'd returned to his recently vacated spot and was now watching her, Briana felt the need to leave the ball and avoid any gossip. "Emily, get me out of here please. I think I feel faint." Emily nodded and holding her friends elbow, the two women entered the ballroom and made their way to the exit.

Cameron, who reentered in time to see the two women speaking quickly on the balcony before leaving, stood rooted to the spot where the floor fell out from underneath him moments ago. He could not believe it was her. This woman who obviously held him with such disdain and who he believed was reckless and naïve. As he stepped forward to leave his spot, he realized that he was stepping on something. Bending down, he retrieved her mask. "She must have dropped it from the shock," he thought to himself. Staring at the mask in his hands, he found himself remembering their time together. She enjoyed being with him, he knew that. "She may swear she never wants to see me again, but dancing with her tells me otherwise. Why does she hate me? Because of my arrogance? My reputation? Did I not care for her as my own sister growing up?"

Turning the mask in his hands, Cameron couldn't help but remember the feel of the woman who was so adamantly against his person. She not only set his loins on fire, but she also intrigued him mentally as she met his wits easily. "Well, Lady Briana Valmont, it would seem I no longer think of you as a sister. You've changed and there is something that mesmerizes me about you. So outspoken and strong, and yet so fragile too." Cameron spoke to the mask as if the woman in question were standing before him. He shrugged his shoulders and turned the mask over in his hands once again as he contemplated how to change their current situation.

She hadn't seemed to recognize him as well, but would she react differently once she found out? Cameron could barely remember the last words he said to her before she left London, but he had a feeling it was no more than a terse farewell. Putting the mask into his pocket, Cameron thought to himself that spending more time with her would help to change her mind about him. He'd make sure tonight would not be the only night he'd spend with this emerald of the night. He'd make sure of that. Although he had hoped to see her again that night, she never reentered the ballroom.

CHAPTER 5

Briana sat upright on her four post bed with her knees hugged tightly to her chest. She had convinced herself that she could find a man who was as rich as he was good-hearted and who would fall madly in love with her. As she thought back to the waltz from earlier that night, she had deluded herself to a status of grandeur by believing that she in turn could be lucky enough to fall madly in love with such a man. She wished finding someone to solve her financial problems would be as simple as meeting a man and having an instant spark. Of course, that only happened in the silly notions of horribly written romance novels, but she wished nonetheless.

Pulling up the sleeve that had fallen off her shoulder, she slid from the bed and walked to the window to push it open. She needed fresh air from outside to blow away the stresses of the night. Tomorrow, her search and act would start anew as she would hopefully meet with many callers in the morning who would come to express their admiration. She hoped desperately that one of them would prove to be handsome, debonair, rich, and possess an agreeable disposition. She knew love was too much to hope for, but getting along with your husband was definitely rational. She would definitely have to wow them tomorrow with her appearance, disposition, and mystery. How she longed to be done with the façade.

Briana released a sigh and walked to her wardrobe where she examined the few remaining dresses she had left. None of her dresses for morning callers were fashionable this season, and as much as she hoped the men would not notice, she knew they would know her family's financial troubles in an instant. She picked up a gown with a color of lavender that was lucky enough to still be pseudo-fashionable. She would spend the rest of the night changing the neckline and sleeves to match those of society women she had seen this morning on her stroll. Pulling out the sewing needles, thread, and scissors, Briana settled into bed for a long night of reinvention.

The light of morning came in as softly as the landing of a butterfly on a dewy tulip. The warmth of the sun's rays caressed Briana's face and she released a satisfied yawn, but did not open her eyes. Not yet. This was her favorite time of day: the peaceful quietness of morning wrapped in the warmth of her bed sheets before life and its demands took hold of a person's mind and body. She knew she couldn't stay in bed forever, even though she would be delighted to do so.

"Alright, you're going to get up now!" Briana said aloud to herself as she continued to lie in her comfy bed. "Okay, seriously. Open your eyes Briana and get up!" It was the same thing every morning. Although she loved the morning time, she was of the opinion that actually getting out of bed and being productive ruined the majesty and peace. Briana stretched out her long arms, bending her wrist down and up. She had stayed up late the night before sewing and altering her dress, making her wrists and fingers feel cramped. She sat up, let out a deep sigh, and proceeded to get out of bed, hopeful that the morning would see a decent turnout of callers for her to choose a suitor from. She had given the performance of her life at the ball, and she'd be damned if she didn't see the fruits of her labor.

Briana made her way to the wash basin and began her grooming routine before slipping into her now-fashionable lavender morning dress. She was determined that it was going to be a wonderful day! She began to rub a splash of rosewater between her wrists and along her neck as she decided which hairstyle would best suit the dress and yet be simple enough that she could do it on her own. Styling her own hair was always her least favorite part of her morning. If she could leave her curls loose and wild over her shoulders and still be fashionable, she'd do so in a heartbeat.

Making her way downstairs into the kitchen, Briana made herself a simple breakfast of eggs, sausage, and biscuits. She made sure to leave enough for her mother who was sure to be awake and dressed but lying on the chaise lounge reliving moments of a happier time in her youth, before she had fallen in love with Briana's father and lost everything. Briana never minded making breakfast for two, but she hated the nervous energy that hung in the air whenever her mother was present.

Briana carried the tray of food to the dining room table and called across the hall for her mother to join. As her mother prepared her own plate and sat down, Briana was running through the conversation that would commence any second. It was the same one they had every morning.

"Do you think anyone suspected us at the ball? Darla Fendleton was saying that your dress was so bold, she wondered what modiste we visited. She then said that I must be a very confident and lax mother since she would never let her daughter Eleanora out of the house in something so provocative."

"No mother, I don't think anyone suspected. As for Mrs. Fendleton, you know you can't listen to anything she says. Poor Eleanora is going on eighteen and she is still being dressed in the fashions of a thirteen year old girl. I believe I played my part well last night and captivated the attention of many gentlemen and befriended many of their sisters and mothers."

"Hmm, yes dear. You were magnificent! I do hope it wasn't too much though." Her mother wrung her hands together, a nervous habit she never before displayed until after her father had left them destitute and confused. Her mother always began the morning meal by reliving every detail of the previous day's or night's public appearances and questioning how everyone perceived them. It was truly the most exhausting meal of the day for Briana, no matter how well she'd slept the night before.

"Well, I for one *am* hoping it was too much. Maybe then the sitting room will be filled with eligible suitors for me to consider. I promise you, I will get us out of this situation and restore us back to our rightful place in society." Briana stood and gave her mother a hug and a kiss on her cheek. She made this promise every morning, but this morning she believed it for the first time. Briana turned her attention back to her meal and quietly listened to her mother's nervous ramblings of the acquaintances she met at the party last night. In all honesty, she was more interested in the melodious songs of the birds chirping outside the windows.

"Briana! Darling, are you feeling alright? You seem very distant." Briana turned her gaze back to her mother to see a rather confused face that involved squinted eyes and an upturned lip. Briana always laughed when she saw this face because it never quite matched the woman wearing it. Although her mother was seen as nervous most mornings, wringing her hands or drawing her brows together, most of the time her mother was the picture of wistful beauty with a hopeful smile and a dreamy look in her eyes.

"I'm fine, Mother. Just a bit tired. A little more coffee and I'll be fine." Her mother let out a huff. "Now, don't scold me about the coffee again. It's only a little cup and it gives me more energy than tea does. If today is going to be a success, I am going to need all my energy. We should probably finish soon so I can take everything back to the kitchen and let Wallace know to come answer the door for guests." Briana stood up and began cleaning her area. They did not keep many servants in the house since most of them left when they were no longer receiving wages, but Wallace Allen and his wife Cathy chose to stay since they had been with the family since

Briana's birth. Wallace served as the butler and handyman of the house while Cathy served primarily as housekeeper but also played the role of cook. They also had Lucy who served as Briana's chaperone and lady's maid on occasion. Briana left the room and found both Wallace and Cathy in the kitchen eating the remaining biscuits. Although Briana often wished they would join her and her mother for meals, it would not help their situation if someone came by unannounced and found the Valmonts dining with their servants.

"Good morning!" Briana said with a bright smile as she sat down on the vacant stool. She grabbed a nearby apple and began to eat it as Cathy leaned over the table and smiled broadly.

"How was the ball last night? Did you accomplish what you set out to? Was there a gentleman who caught your eye? Or better yet, did you catch the eye of any suitable gentlemen?" Just as Cathy stopped to take a breath, her husband rolled his eyes upward and grinned at Briana. Cathy and Wallace were such opposites, but their love for one another was obvious. Cathy was the open, friendly, and curious extrovert who could befriend a door nail if she set her mind to it. Wallace on the other hand was the cautious, quietly loyal, and pensive introvert who said very little, but when he did, he would make big statements.

Briana laughed. "Well, I definitely caught the eye of many men. All of whom are wonderful candidates that will be able to care for all of us without blinking an eye."

"That sounds wonderful dear, but did your heart skip a beat? Were you truly smiling while meeting any of them? Did you catch yourself swept away and truly enjoying yourself with any of them?" Cathy asked.

Briana smiled in response. "Cathy, it's not important for me to lose myself or to have my heart skip a beat. As much as that would make this process more enjoyable, it's not the point..." Briana trailed off as she remembered her waltz with the mystery gentleman. "But, since you asked, there was one man who made me forget about my purpose in attending the ball. He had a way of making me feel more myself than I had before

Father left. He held me close as we danced and had me talking openly about my thoughts and dreams. Unfortunately, he turned out to be Cameron Worthington, the Duke of Hereford. That man is as arrogant, overly serious, oblivious, and as structured as an old man watching the clock waiting to die. You know, when we were kids, I thought he was the most beautiful and responsible boy ever to walk the earth. He had this way of taking charge and getting results that made me feel happy and safe with him, but every time he smiled at me or walked with Emily and I, he would simply talk about his work and role in the family. No matter how many times I said I wanted to know more about him, or tried to create various scenes to get him to fall in love with me, he never noticed. He was always so concerned with fulfilling the role of Duke that I don't think he ever learned how to be just himself and not the Duke of Hereford," Briana finished as she rolled her eyes. "I don't ever want to think of that man who never gave me the time of day before now. Wallace, if I did my job right last night, we should have many suitors coming to the house to get to know me better. Can you please show them all into the front sitting room?" After waiting for his response, she headed off to her room to check her appearance and prepare. Although Briana said she never wanted to think about him, she knew it was impossible for her to do so. Even with ten years of distance, she always made sure to ask about him in her letters to Emily over the years. Latching on to any information Emily passed along only filled Briana with daydreams of him and a bittersweet pain in her heart.

Cameron sat in his office trying to focus on the account book that lay open in front of him. He had woken up early this morning and, although it was only eleven in the morning, he had already walked the length of the streets outside, spoken with fellow members of the House of Lords, and balanced his accounts. He always enjoyed balancing the books of his estates, even as a young man. Numbers made sense to him. There is no mystery or second-guessing when it comes to numbers. Not like a woman who wears mystery like another layer of clothing. His eyes wandered to the emerald eye mask that sat on the small table across the room by the bookshelf. He had moved it over there earlier in the day in the hopes that he wouldn't be distracted by it anymore. Well, so much for that idea. Cameron stood up and walked across the room to examine the mask for the umpteenth time in hopes that he could garner some clarity for winning over the owner. Just as he was about to put it back, a small rip on the side of the mask caught his eye.

Who was he kidding? He hadn't stopped thinking about Briana since last night, no matter how sloshed he was by the time he fell into bed. His mystery woman, the woman with the lost bonnet, and the young girl who grew up with his brother and sister, were all the same woman. He'd kissed her thinking she was simply this wonderful, mysterious, confident, and sexy woman, and now he had no idea what to make of her. He picked up the mask and stroked the rip on the side softly. The rip was in a piece of green velvet that was soft and smooth, just like the owner's lips. Cameron replayed the kiss in his mind and let out a sigh. Well, even though that kiss was definitely one of the best he'd had, the kiss was meant for his brother. He had been such a cad to her the night before and knowing it was the gentlemanly thing to do, he knew he would have to go and pay his respects to her and apologize for his behavior. She was his sister's best friend, and since his mother was close with Briana's mother, he knew they were going to be seeing a lot more of each other. It would not do for last night's behavior to ruin such friendships. Good thing he was planning on leaving town soon to look after the Hereford country estate. He was restless and needed to put his mind and physical effort into something else besides spending time with the same acquaintances. Putting the mask down gently on his desk, Cameron left his study to ready himself for his apology.

Briana was amazed at how many callers she had this morning. They had come in waves since eleven that morning, with the front sitting room hosting three to four gentleman visitors at a time. Of course, societal rules deemed that they not stay for longer than thirty minutes and most obliged for fear of being snubbed later on by others of the *ton* for breaking such important rules and bringing scandal to a woman's home.

It was now a little past midday and she had received the cards of eight gentlemen, none of which had really caught her eye. Just as she and her mother were picking up their needlework again to keep their hands busy, Wallace came into the room with the cards of two more gentlemen: Lord Michael Edwards and Mr. Dorian Gutterson. Briana smiled at seeing Lord Edwards' name card. He was such a pleasant gentleman and she had enjoyed speaking and dancing with him last night. He was by far her first choice as candidate. Now that she realized her mystery man was Cameron, he was no longer a contender. She could never consider marrying the man who was so cruel to her in childhood, no matter how rich he is. Although, shouldn't he at least stop by to apologize for his behavior or to welcome the Valmont family back to London as head of the Hereford family? Didn't he at least consider the family relationships to be important enough to salvage? She let out a sigh of both frustration and something else. Rejection? Dejection?

Shaking her head to mentally bring herself back to the cards in her hands, she smiled again at Lord Edwards' card and blinked at the other. She didn't recognize the name on the other card, but thought to herself that maybe she'd met this man last night at the ball and could not remember his name since she was overwhelmed with all the introductions. Briana nodded to Wallace and readied herself for their arrival.

Just as Briana and her mother finished fixing their skirts around them, Wallace opened the door to the room and introduced Lord Edwards followed by Mr. Gutterson. The gentlemen both executed a bow as the ladies curtsied and returned to their seats. "Lord Edwards, thank you for coming and paying us a visit this morning. I believe you were introduced to my mother last night by Her Grace," Briana said, gesturing to her mother seated next to her.

"Yes, Lady Darby, it is very nice to see you again. I am glad to find you both well this morning," Lord Edwards replied, smiling kindly to Briana's mother who returned the smile with a nod before turning her attention to the other gentleman in the room.

"And Mr. Gutterson, I don't believe I remember being introduced to you last night. Is my memory leaving me?" asked Briana.

Mr. Gutterson offered a smile that didn't seem to reach his eyes. He was not a short man, per se, but was not as tall as Lord Edwards, Cameron, or Jake for that matter. Being older than these men, he had a dusting of grey hairs at his temples and a slight hunch forward of his shoulders. He had dark eyes, almost as black as oil and carried a walking stick that he treated with the utmost care. Under the guise of dusting something off his lapel, Mr. Gutterson took a minute to enjoy the view of Briana's body up close. His eyes moved slowly down her body and then up again to rest on her lips as his tongue came out and licked both sides of his mouth before he met her eyes and replied, "Surely, you were introduced to so many people last night that you wouldn't remember me. I was dressed as a member of the Calvary, but I dare say there were many of us in similar costumes. Lady Rushton introduced us early on in the masquerade ball along with three other gentlemen. But, please, take this visit as a reintroduction." He once again bowed before her and stood straight as Briana smiled kindly and her mother slowly nodded her head twice in acknowledgement.

Sensing a lull in conversation, Lord Edwards asked if the ladies enjoyed the masquerade ball from the night before. Both ladies shared that they loved seeing all the costumes and thoroughly enjoyed the music and food. "It was very nice to get in touch again with Her Grace and her family again. We missed them so much while we were away. Just like my mother is very close with Her Grace, her daughter is my best friend. So you can imagine how happy we were to be reunited in such a nice way yesterday," Briana responded.

"Yes, I don't think I saw you stop smiling for a second the entire ball. It was a nice to see everyone welcome you both so warmly. Wouldn't you agree, Mr. Gutterson, that it seems the Valmonts were sorely missed by many during their absence?" Lord Edwards replied, looking to the other gentleman.

"Well, of course. And with such an elegant woman as Lady Valmont is, I am sure many men were very happy to see her return. Many were captivated by you last night, as was I." Mr. Gutterson licked his lips again as he directed his gaze to Briana. "I daresay, my dear, the emerald gown you wore last night was a very unique style. Very much keeping with the fashionable dresses of other women, but almost reminiscent of a style from the past as well. Where did you find such a gown?" Mr. Gutterson said with a quick squint of his eye.

"Uh, at a modiste in the town we were living right outside of Bedford. The modiste was a very unique and knowledgeable woman on women's fashion," Briana responded smoothly, although his questioning was making her uncomfortable. Why was he asking about her dress? She'd worked so hard trying to modify it to match the current fashion. Did she fail since there were parts of the dress she couldn't alter due to its construction? No, maybe Mr. Gutterson simply had sharper eyes than most when it came to women's fashion.

Lord Edwards cleared his throat and, thankfully, once again diverted the attention of the ladies by discussing the music from last night's ball. While they spoke, Mr. Gutterson walked the room. He grazed his fingers over the small letter writing table in the corner of the room and then made his way to finger a pair of ruby lusters that sat on top of the fireplace mantle. He waited until Briana made eye contact with him. "Do you enjoy decorating, Lady Valmont? These ruby lusters are very beautifully placed and tie the colors of the room together well.

Are they a family heirloom? You seem to have put a lot of thought into the details, but not as much to the furniture in the room given some of the silk fabric choices," Mr. Gutterson replied with a haughty tone and a hint of a sneer before replacing it with a smile. "You are still very young and unmarried, so it is understandable that you wouldn't know everything there is to home decor and the like. It is a good thing you have your mother to guide you."

"Well, I do enjoy helping my mother with the decorating of the house very much, Mr. Gutterson, and usually turn my attention to the details in every room. As you say, I am still young and can only improve with time," Briana said smoothly, reminding herself to not grind her teeth while speaking. "As per the ruby lusters, they have been in my family for years and are quite irreplaceable to us," Briana answered, wondering how this man had a way with words that made every compliment seem like an insult. How much longer did he plan on staying? She wished he would leave so she could enjoy the last few minutes of the visit with Lord Edwards, who kept sending her encouraging smiles and conversing about topics that were both socially appropriate and kind.

"My mother always said that a true measure of a woman was how she decorated and cared for her home. I do believe that Mother would have agreed with me when I say that you, Lady Valmont, have served your own mother dutifully and have helped her create a beautiful home. I also feel duty-bound to remind my companion that a true measure of a gentleman is how he treats a lady," Lord Edwards said with a pointed look at Mr. Gutterson, who only scoffed and stared out the window as a response to his scolding.

"Well, thank you Lord Edwards for your kind words. My daughter truly is the best I could ever ask for," Lady Darby responded. "I must say that you are welcome to call on us any time." She glanced at Mr. Gutterson before adding, "Mr. Gutterson, I thank you for paying us a visit today." Her eyes were full of anger mixed with worry as she looked at Briana.

"Yes, well, we do not want to overstay our welcome and

will take our leave. Come Gutterson, let's leave these women to their morning." Lord Edwards fixed a pointed look at Mr. Gutterson as he said the words and gestured towards the door. He smiled at Briana with a glint in his eye as he executed an elegant bow. "It was a pleasure speaking with you this morning, Lady Valmont. I hope to have the opportunity to do it again very soon." Mr. Gutterson in turn executed a swift bow before saying, "I too hope for another opportunity to get to know the elegant and mysterious Lady Briana Valmont." He licked both corners of his mouth and smiled at her before leaving the room following Lord Edwards.

"What an insufferable man!" Briana said after she heard the click of the front door close. Briana looked over at her mother ready to discuss how vile Mr. Gutterson had been, but stopped as soon as she saw her mother's face, which had turned a disturbing shade of white. Her eyes were large pools of tears that hovered on the edge of releasing themselves in streams down her face. "Oh, Mother. It's alright. Why are you so upset?" Briana asked as she sat down next to her mother and patted her hand.

"That man... Do you think he knows about us? He was so interested in you and our house. He looked at the ruby lusters with such a greedy and conspiratorial look that I was reminded of the look your father had in his eye many times before." Briana's mother began pacing around the room. She was growing more frantic in gesture and speech as she continued to think of the man. "Do you think they know each other, your father and Mr. Gutterson? I have a feeling I may have seen him and your father together before. We can't let him get close to us, Briana!" Briana, who only wished to disregard Mr. Gutterson's visit completely, was now replaying the visit in her mind a little differently.

"Mother, please! Calm yourself so that we may collect our thoughts together," Briana said as she followed her mother around the room. "Now, we have worked very hard to protect ourselves and will continue to do so. Father left London so long ago that it does not seem possible for them to know each other, or wouldn't Mr. Gutterson have left town as well? Maybe you are simply confusing him with another one of father's acquaintances," Briana reassured her mother, who had stopped her pacing in front of the mantle.

"Not necessarily. What if your father left him as well as us? That is to say, what if your father took something from him and now he wants it back?" Briana stared at her mother, who was waving her hands erratically as she spoke.

"That is assuming, Mother, that Mr. Gutterson's interest in our house and me has anything to do with father in the first place. You heard him say he was at the ball last night and was, like many others, captivated by my beauty. Could he not just be interested in our furnishings since they are an extension of me?" Briana asked her mother in the hopes her mother would agree and calm down.

"Yes, maybe dear. But I cannot ignore the look in his eye. It was the exact look your father had when he was in his ill spirits. He could be so greedy and so cruel." Her mother shivered and ran her hands up both arms. Just as Briana was about to comfort her mother, there came a crash in the hallway where glass was heard shattering. Both Briana and her mother were transported instantly to the last time glass was heard shattering in their house.

CHAPTER 6

September 1840: Briana could hear his steps getting louder, closer, more insistent as they made their way down the hall. The sound of the door opening down the hall occurred the second Briana sucked in her breath, waiting for the inevitable portion of the night where her father would lock himself in his study to drink and curse his poor luck. The pacing would begin first, followed by yelling and smashing anything breakable that dared to mock his misfortune by simply existing in the same space as him. She knew better than to go near the door to offer any sort of comfort to her father when he was in this mood. A dark and angry mood that was once a rarity had become the mood that encompassed every day of her father's life for the last seven years.

Crash! The sound of a shattering glass bottle echoed down the hall reaching Emily's ears. As she hugged her legs closer to her chest, she reminded herself that as long as she stayed in her room, she would not have to bear any chances of her father's hand meeting her face like it did the last time. Briana flinched as she touched her fingers to the bruise on the left side of her face that was beginning to heal under her makeup. A tear fell down her cheek as she wondered how her family ever got here. Her father had never been an overly happy and gentle man, but he always had a grin to share with Briana when she was younger. Now, her father spent his days gambling away his money and selling the family valuables to pay back debts. Knowing her father was on the path of selling away the family fortune, Briana had removed the most valuable heirlooms from her house and placed them in the care of her best friend Emily, claiming that the house was being cleaned and the family didn't want to risk these valuables being misplaced. Blessed Emily, despite her curiosity, asked no questions and simply took them and kept them safe.

The door down the hall opened again, but this time it didn't close. Briana heard her mother's voice trying to coax the drink out of her father's hand. She squeezed her eyes shut as she silently prayed her mother would get out of the room before her father's mood darkened even further. Her eyes opened wide as the sound of her mother's piercing scream rang through the air, followed by the sound of something hitting the wall. Without a second thought, Briana ran down the hall to see her mother curled up in a ball against the far wall and her father marching toward her with bloodshot eyes and unsteady steps. As Briana stepped into the room, her father's eyes fixed in her direction as he focused all his attention on Briana. She could feel the wave of panic sweep over her as he began taking large strides in her direction. Briana lost all sense of hearing and feeling in her legs. She raised her arms in front of her and braced herself for what was to come next. No matter how many times she endured the pain, knowing she couldn't stop him and couldn't protect her mother left her feeling what she feared the most: helpless.

Briana opened her eyes and let out a shaky breath as she realized she was back in 1851 in the front parlor with her mother. Her mother blinked a couple of times before focusing on her daughter. It seemed they both had been transported to the past and were both left feeling uneasy. Wallace had finished apologizing for stumbling and shattering the teapot and cups he was bringing. "Yes. It was startling to hear, but thank you Wallace for checking on us. I think I'm in need of a lie down, to calm my nerves, you see. And you dear?" Briana could see the wisdom in her mother's words, but she knew there was no way she wanted to close her eyes just now and be haunted by further visions of her father.

"You go ahead. I think I'm in need of some fresh air and may go for a walk to clear my head. I shan't be long and should be returned by the time you awake," Briana responded. As her mother patted her hand and left the room, Briana did not bother to ring for her maid and instead walked straight out the front door and made her way to the gardens a few blocks away from the house. These gardens had been an escape for her most of her life. She loved the calming effect the aromas had on her as well as being aesthetically pleasing to the eye. She took in a deep breath and let out a long sigh. The tension in her shoulders eased as she felt the stress and anger from earlier leave her body. She let go of the painful memories of her father and the anxiety brought on by Mr. Gutterson. She took in another deep breath. There was something about the smell of roses and freshly cut grass that relaxes the soul and the mind. Briana tried to make sense of all that had happened inside with Mr. Gutterson and Lord Edwards' visit. Mr. Gutterson did not hide his social indelicacies and bordered on purposefully rude throughout the visit. He seemed to enjoy her mother's discomfort, but was not malicious or direct enough to be given the cut directly and removed from the premises at once. Briana couldn't figure him out.

Lord Edwards, on the other hand, was a perfect gentleman. He spoke of everything socially acceptable, spoke to her mother in a respectful and caring manner (which isn't surprising, with as much as he admired his own mother), and came to her rescue with Mr. Gutterson on more than one occasion. He did not speak passionately about anything, except his mother, but showed great discomfort with Mr. Gutterson's intense interest in the family heirlooms and decorations of the house.

Briana couldn't think any more about that vile man. She sat down on a bench located at the far edge of the gardens. She always loved this bench. It was located close enough to the Hereford household that she and Emily would sneak away there plenty of times from their nannies growing up. Granted, Jake was usually involved in all such matters that involved skirting his studies to get into a little mischief. She smiled at the memories of happier times before looking around and bringing herself back to the present moment's dilemma. She rested her head in her hands. How had it come to this? They'd been so careful for years not to be found and now the fact that there was some person who may have knowledge or an acquaintance with her father did not bode well. She let out a growl of frustration, not caring about decorum since there was nobody around to hear her. As if the world was set on pushing her discomfort to the brink, there was a soft "Oh! Erhm!" behind her. Briana turned around only to find herself face to face with the one man whom she least expected or wanted to see. She saw the man who had hurt years before, only now she was not some young girl and he was no longer her idol. He was just a man. The same devastatingly handsome, elitist, know-it-all he'd always been, but with a slightly confused look in his russet brown eyes.

"I'm sorry to intrude. I was on my way over on behalf of my mother to see how you both enjoyed yourselves at the ball last night. I didn't expect to find you out here walking the gardens alone. Is everything alright?" Cameron said rather stiffly. He was fulfilling his social duties by coming over, he reminded himself. Why did he feel so bloody awkward standing in front of her now?

"Well, it is a nice day out and I wanted some fresh air. Is that such a rare sight that something would have to be wrong in order for it to transpire?" Briana replied a bit too gruffly. She heaved a sigh. "Sorry, I was just hoping for some time to myself. Between last night and this morning, I have many things to straighten out in my mind."

Here was the opening he needed. He had come to apologize for his behavior last night after the kiss they shared together. He was angry and hurt that the kiss with his mystery woman was not meant for him at all and lashed out at a young lady in a most deplorable manner. Not to mention that lady was Briana who had always been around as a child, always with questions for him and statements that brought a smile to his face. It was Briana who was, for lack of a better description, like a sister... no, like a cousin... a very distant cousin's cousin... with soft lips. Cameron shook his head and took in a breath. He was not accustomed to apologizing and had rehearsed his words all morning to make sure it was done properly.

"I see. Well, I hope that the moment that passed between us at the ball is not among them. Really, I see no reason for you to think of it since I was not the one it was meant for. So, I'd very much like to know that you will not think of the moment any further. I have enough to think about between managing both estates, the tenants, the horses, the finances, and then there's simply fulfilling daily responsibilities of my title. I believe I will forget about it completely by tonight. It's a good thing that I will not be here for the entire season so that I may oversee the work efficiently. I'm thinking another fortnight in London will suffice." Remembering that he had come to talk about the kiss and not work, Cameron concluded by saying, "Therefore, I hope you will spend your time and effort thinking of other things and not that moment between us," Cameron said frankly. There he'd done it. He'd apologized and all would return to normal between the two households.

Briana stood dumbfounded. What did he mean that moment? There were so many moments between them last night. Was he talking about the magical waltz they shared where everyone in the room disappeared and they were lost in each other's arms? Was he talking about the conversation they shared where she felt like herself for the first time that evening? Or was he talking about the kiss that she still felt stamped on her lips? She couldn't forget any of these moments and hated him for saying that he could.

"I thought you were coming to apologize to the poor girl," Jake said as he stepped out from behind a rose bush. "I mean, you should know that you never tell a lady her kiss isn't good enough for you to think about or wish to remember as part of an apology. Really, man!" Jake scoffed as he came to stand in between Cameron and Briana.

"This doesn't concern you Jake. Go home," Cameron said tensely, feeling chided. His eyes darkened to black and the muscle in his jaw twitched. He hated being contradicted or teased in the presence of others.

Briana's bewilderment now turned to bitterness. She was hurt and Jake saw that. He knew she always cared for Cameron but to what depth exactly, he was willing to push her and Cameron both to find out. Did she still care for Cameron or was it just the hurt feelings of a teenage girl? Was she ready to move on to another man?

"Well, since Cameron doesn't seem to know how to appreciate a woman, why don't I take you out today for a stroll in Hyde Park?" Jake asked with a devilish glint in his eye as he shifted his gaze from Briana to his brother. "You do owe me since you gave my kiss to another."

Briana wanted nothing more than to fade into the bushes and leave these two brothers behind, but one look at the stern and condescending face of Cameron, and Briana suddenly wanted to do something reckless. She grabbed Jake by the arm and smiled up at him saying, "You're absolutely right. I never back out of a wager, and if you'd rather I repay you with an outing instead of a kiss on the cheek, then I'm most willing."

"Well love, I never said the kiss was off the table," Jake said as he winked at her. Briana chuckled and rolled her eyes at his words and then caught sight of Cameron. Had his eyes turned even darker than they were before? They looked almost black and murderous. Well, he could stand there angry and judge all he wanted. She needed to get away from him, and Jake had just provided her with a way out, not to mention that she knew they would have a fun afternoon together and her mind would be able to take a break from all the troubles she needed to sort through. "Why don't you go fetch your maid and I'll meet you out front? Do you think you'll need longer than 10 minutes?" Jake asked. Briana shook her head and, with a quick bob to Cameron, headed back in the direction of the house, leaving the two brothers standing in the tense air they'd created.

CHAPTER 7

Briana opened the door to her bedroom and leaned back against the heavy wood as it closed. She let out a sigh. It was only early afternoon and she was already exhausted from all the emotions today. She lifted her shoulders to her ears and rolled them back, then moved her neck from side to side in a manner of releasing some of the tension she was holding on to. She knew she didn't have long to get dressed and decided her hair was fine as is since it would be covered by a bonnet. She opened her wardrobe and settled on a sage green dress with lace at the wrists and soft violet florets on the bust. Lucy helped her with the matching satin slippers and tied the bonnet in a fashion that had the green satin ribbons fall to the side. Briana looked herself over in the mirror, decided she didn't need to pinch anymore color into her cheeks after today's emotional ride, and nodded to Lucy before leaving the room.

Wallace opened the front door and Briana was met with Jake's smiling face. She was happy to see that she would not have to bear Cameron's darkly intense eyes on their outing. She had enough to contemplate with Lord Edwards, Mr. Gutterson, her mother, and the ever-present shadow of her father. She did not need to begin worrying over Cameron's feelings as well. She smiled brilliantly at Jake as she stepped out and grabbed hold of his hand. Her maid, Lucy, a shy and often silly young girl, followed behind without a word.

Jake placed Briana's arm in the crook of his own and began leading them in the direction towards Hyde Park. It was close to a thirty-minute walk to Hyde Park from Warwick Street where the Valmont and Hereford Houses were. Briana breathed in the crisp air and began a conversation about the weather. She loved that with Jake she could relax enough to discuss such trivial things like the weather, fashion, and the latest gossip. He always laughed and jumped into the conversation without reserve.

"I know you always loved the outdoors as much as I did. Even on days like today where the clouds in the far distance threaten rain, you would still smile and stay outdoors for hours, sometimes until the rain actually came beating down," Jake smiled and shook his head. "Everyone else would have the sense to get indoors once the sky darkened, but you wanted to experience everything to the last minute."

Briana looked up and smiled back. Jake was not as tall as his brother, but he still stood taller than most men in London. He was of a more muscular build than Cameron, probably due to his love of the outdoors and his own vanity. Jake was known to be involved in some version of physical activity, using the philosophies of Gustav Ernst and Charles Darwin as motivation. Emily shared with Briana the night before that Jake had done some sort of exercise every day for short periods at a time, like Ernst suggested, since that would make him stronger. He believed Darwin's "survival of the fittest" was easier to attain if one were actually physically fit. She loved that he was just as active as she was, although he probably did more exercise throughout the day than she. Briana's exercise often consisted of long daily walks or going for long horseback rides as a means of releasing energy and enjoying the outdoors. They always had that in common.

Briana's smile widened as she said, "Well, when I have the opportunity to be outdoors with such good company like you and Emily, why would I want to end it and return home? You were always so much fun to be around, and Emily held all of my secrets. Home was never as exciting. "

"With you there, how could it not be exciting? You still are just so." When Briana shook her head in disagreement, he reminded her about the ball. "Remember that I did win our bet for a reason. How many gentlemen were interested in you last night? Come on, how many came to call on you this morning?" Jake said as he lowered himself to eye level. "And Cameron and I do not count."

"If you must know, I received a total of 10 gentlemen callers. Of course they came in waves, but all were very nice and pleasant. It was very strange to be the center of attention," Briana said quietly.

They continued to stroll down the streets of London past the men and women who were out gossiping and reliving the events of last night's ball. They passed by and smiled at Lady Windsmere and Sir Robert Buckingham. Jake stopped to share a few pleasantries about the weather and presented Briana to both of them as a friend of the family. "Oh yes, were you the one in the emerald gown who came and spoke to Lady Worthington about a thread in your gown?" Briana simply nodded as a reply since she wanted to correct the man by saying she wasn't simply speaking to Emily but instead was saving Emily from the boredom she would surely die of if she continued speaking to him. "It's a pleasure to meet you, my dear. You really were enchanting last night." Briana smiled and bobbed her head as she said thank you.

Not wanting to keep them any longer, Jake complimented Lady Windsmere on how lovely the color of canary yellow looked on her and that he hoped to see them again soon at the next ball of the season. Briana was amazed at how easily Jake conversed with whomever he came across. He truly was an effervescent man and Briana found his attitude infectious.

"I think you are by far the friendliest man I have ever met. How are you always this happy?" Briana asked out of pure curiosity.

"Well, I don't see the point in hanging on to ill or heavy

feelings. I find the faster I look out and find something good in the world, the faster I feel better. It's a choice to be always happy, I guess," Jake said as he patted her hand. He knew Briana was not always happy growing up, although he never knew why. Whenever he asked Emily, she would either shake her head or begin to cry saying that it wasn't fair for Briana to be treated in such a way. He hoped that now being back he could help keep her happy on a daily basis. "Speaking of happy, did any of those gentlemen callers give you a sense of happiness?" Jake asked as they entered the gates of Hyde Park. He steered them around a group of older women who were standing in the middle of the path discussing the impropriety of young women tilting up their bonnets (or taking them off altogether) to get some sunlight. Jake nodded his head to them and then turned his eyes on Briana. "Soooo?"

"Well, among all the visitors this morning, the one I was most interested and happy to see was Lord Edwards. He is such a nice man who truly seems interested in what I have to say and making my mother and me comfortable," Briana answered with a soft smile on her lips.

Jake smiled knowingly. "Yes, he is a nice man. He's always trying to make those around him happy, especially the women. He was very close to his mother if I remember correctly. Uses her as a measure for any woman in his life, I believe," Jake said with a soft chuckle.

"He does, and what of it? I think it's sweet that he loved her so much," Briana said defensively.

"Calm down, I didn't mean anything by it. He is older than Cameron, I believe, so I haven't had many occasions to speak in depth with him. Cameron knows him better than I due to both managing estates and political affiliations. We could ask Cameron for more information on him to help you capture his heart?" Jake said with a wink.

"I don't think I want Cameron's help with anything. Especially not matters of the heart," Briana said stiffly. "He doesn't seem very knowledgeable or sympathetic to such things." Briana's voice changed from stiff to broken in an instant.

"You know Cam, he's never quite understood what to do when it comes to emotions. He's too logical for his own good. But he'd want you and any other member of his family to be happy," Jake said squeezing Briana's hand so she'd look up at him. They smiled at each other and thus was the end of her crossness.

"Come, tell me more about what qualities exactly Lord Edwards has that makes him such an appealing suitor for you," Jake said, steering the conversation back to the matter at hand. He needed to find out what kind of man Briana was interested in. After seeing her at the ball, this seemed like a mission he could not give up on until he saw her good and married. He smiled at the thought of dancing with her at her wedding, just like they had done as kids so long ago.

Before Briana could answer, she heard an "Ack! What the… " as Jake let go of her arm and jumped back. Briana looked down to see a leather Spell roll away from Jake's foot. It must have been hit hard for Jake to jump back as he did. A small boy came running up to reclaim his ball. "So sorry, sir. My little brother hit this in the wrong direction. Is your foot broken? Please don't tell my mum!" The little boy was on the verge of tears as he said everything in a single breath. He sniffled and wiped his nose with the back of his hand, leaving a streak of dirt behind. Jake simply smiled and with effort bent down to eye level with the boy. "Not to worry, my boy. My foot has seen much worse from my own brother long ago. But you need to be careful playing such a game with all these men and women about. Now, run along. I don't want your mother worrying about you." The boy smiled as Jake patted his head and stood up. Briana also smiled as she watched the boy run off.

"How is your foot, really?" Briana asked with a knowing smile.

"Throbbing. His little brother has quite the arm," Jake said, shaking his head but smiling nonetheless. "Come, let me sit down a bit to rest it," Jake said as he steered her towards a bench. "I believe you were going to tell me about your Lord Edwards," Jake said as he plopped himself onto the wooden bench off the path. He massaged his foot a few times and then simply stretched out his legs to rest. He looked over expectantly at Briana when she had yet to answer.

"He is not *my* Lord Edwards. He is simply a nice man who treats me with respect and care. He is just as happy a man as you are. His eyes crinkle when he smiles and he looks directly at me when I speak, like he is truly invested in what I have to say. He's not afraid to be vulnerable either. I like a man who can show his softer side and also who gives me courage and understanding to be stronger. He may not be the most exciting man, and is definitely only passionate about his mother and his knowledge of Greek and Roman philosophy. I don't know... He just leaves me with a smile on my face," Briana said with a sigh.

"Well, he seems like a very suitable candidate. Although, I don't think you should set your cap for him just yet. You don't know who else may surprise you," Jake said with a knowing glint in his eyes. Briana laughed at his comment and simply shook her head softly.

"Alright, I'm relying on you to present me with other candidates then. Seems you have an idea of who would be better suited for me, huh?" Briana said with a soft chuckle.

Jake leaned in closer to Briana. "Well, I know you well. And maybe even better than you think. I know it has been some time since we have all been together, but you still seem to be the same Brie I remember from years ago," he said with a grin. As their eyes locked, the heavens gave way to a deluge of rain. Taking them both off guard, they simply laughed at the chaos that ensued around them as man, woman, and child ran toward the park exits to make it home. Lucy came running to Briana as well, exclaiming that they must leave before Briana catches a cold and she loses her position for carelessness.

As they exited the park, Jake was able to find them a coach and gave the driver directions to Briana's house. Along the way, Briana tried to dry her dress as best she could by shaking her skirts little by little. Jake thanked her for the walk and apologized for not looking at the sky and getting her home before the rain. "I was having a great time with you. Also, I was able to consider what I want from a suitor, thanks to you. Even if you think you can do better for me than I can do for myself," Briana said. She smiled as she thought you could always leave it to a man to think he knows a woman's mind better than she.

"I think I do. You need a man who will care for you and respect you, yes. But you also need a man who will push you and encourage you. One who will make you feel every emotion possible and still love you for what those different emotions may look like. You need someone who can balance you and you him. Like you always did with Cameron growing up," Jake said as he picked a speck of dirt off his pants.

"It could never be Cameron. Or anyone like him. You know how crushed I was when I told him my feelings back then and he dismissed them so easily. I could never put myself in a position to suffer that rejection again. Not to mention, he knows me too well. I would never be able to keep from loving him again and, since he will never feel the same, I could never marry him just to feel a sense of security. Also, I could never keep things to myself because he'd figure it all out, that is if he even cared enough to pay attention. No, it couldn't be Cameron," Briana said emphatically.

The coach stopped at the front of Briana's home. "Well, I hope you know how happy we all are that you are back. You know you were missed by all of us, right, not just Emily?" Briana smiled and shook her head in disbelief. "Think about it. Emily may have lost her best friend and sister, but I lost my partner in crime who was always up for adventure. And Cameron, well, although he may not have noticed it enough to say anything, he lost the one person who enjoyed listening to his boring stories or ideas for running the estate in the future. He always relaxed and wore a smile for hours after speaking with you. We were all a little lost without you. Thank you for coming back," Jake said as he placed a soft kiss on her knuckles. Briana sniffled and fought back the tears that were threatening to stream down her face. Jake had never been this open with her before and she didn't quite know what to do.

"Anyway, I hope you will do me the honor of another outing soon. Hopefully, this next time will be without the rain or foot injury," he said with a chuckle.

"Of course, I'd like that. Thank you for your kindness. I've missed you all very much and look forward to making up for lost time with you. Enjoy the rest of your day, Jake," Briana said as she flashed him a smile and accepted the groom's hand stepped down from the coach. As she walked up the steps, she could not get Jake's words out of her head. They had all missed her, not just Emily but Jake and Cameron too. She smiled to herself as she walked out of the rain and into the safety of her home.

CHAPTER 8

The following days passed with a few more visitors in the mornings. Some were women of her age and their mothers along with Emily and Elizabeth, while others were gentlemen come with their fathers or friends with flowers and love letters (she even received a personalized sonnet that was read aloud… the poor man). Although there were some visits that were quite pleasant, there were many others that were awkward. Among them was Lord Blackstone, who wished to introduce his nephew who had come home for a visit from Oxford. He was not much older than Briana, but his mannerisms and style of speaking made him seem almost as old as his uncle. He was a short and portly man, only a few centimeters taller than herself. He wore spectacles that continuously slid down his bulbous nose, and his cheeks seemed to have a permanent blush to them.

For the sake of Lord Blackstone, Briana entertained the two for a full half hour, during which they discussed his fascination with herpetology, particularly turtles and lizards. As soon as Briana asked him how he came to be interested in such a field, Charles spoke for the remainder of the visit, leaving Briana to simply nod along and his uncle to smile apologetically at her on behalf of his nephew. When Charles finished talking about the eating habits of the horned lizard, Briana seized her moment to politely end their visit. "Thank you so much, my lord, for educating me in the field of herpetology. I believe I will never look at turtles or lizards the same way again," she said with a smile while she walked toward the door of the sitting room.

Recognizing the social cue, Lord Blackstone tugged at his nephew's sleeve and stated, "Yes, I don't think I will either. Thank you for your lovely company today, my dear." He patted her hand gently and looked to his nephew who followed suit with a quick bow over her hand.

"If you ever want to learn anything else, you just call on me. I always love to speak with someone as passionate about these creatures as I am. I can also recommend some books for deeper reading and understanding so we can discuss more in depth at our next meeting." He smiled so hopefully that Briana took pity on the poor man and told him to leave a list of book names with Wallace for her to find in their library later on. With one more radiant smile, she waved them off and then collapsed on the chaise nearest her.

When a knock sounded on the door soon after, Briana straightened herself on the chaise and prepared for Wallace's entrance announcing another visitor. She was surprised at hearing the Duke of Hereford's name. Seeing Cameron's form fill the entryway, Briana felt her breath catch. How could this man continue to be so stunningly breathtaking and aggravating at the same time? Briana stood and smiled as he bowed over her hand in greeting. "Your Grace, to what do I owe the pleasure of your visit?"

"Well, I wanted to make sure you were alright after my last visit with you. I left feeling that you were still unhappy with me and that did not sit well with me. I have never known you to be angry with me in the years before you left London. I would not like this feeling to continue," Cameron said as he sat down in a vacant chair opposite Briana.

"I'm fine, thank you. The walk with Jake did wonders for relieving any feelings of anger and disappointment. Honestly, you were correct in saying that we should not give that dance or kiss much thought," Briana replied as confidently as possible.

"Yes, you always had a way of making me feel comfortable in your presence when we were younger. I would really wish that to remain the same now in our adulthood."

"A sort of companionship?" Briana asked, using the word he had used to describe her feelings after she'd confessed her love to him ten years ago.

"Why yes! A companionship like we had before. I'm not sure if you are aware, but it is with you that I was able to discuss many ideas and thoughts I had about the estate and before taking them to my father," Cameron said, leaning back comfortably in his chair.

"Well, I am glad I was of help to you. I simply listened and asked questions like anyone else would," Briana said hoping to end the conversation about the past.

"You did like to ask questions! But, the way you showed genuine interest in my explanations when many wouldn't, especially my siblings, reminded me of how your father would do the same for mine," Cameron said looking at her intently. "I was sad to see that change as your father began spending less time with mine and more with acquaintances from the club."

He was referring to the times and people her father began drinking and gambling frequently with. Breaking eye contact, Briana stared out the window, saying, "Your father was a kind soul for always looking after my father and valuing their friendship, even after my father developed his vices. I'm sure he took our leaving London very hard."

"Yes, why exactly did you leave London so suddenly?" Cameron inquired. When Briana did not answer immediately, he continued, "Last I remember, you and your parents visited us in Surrey. After spending a few days with us, there was an emergency calling you all back to London. You can imagine our surprise when we returned to London only to find that your family moved away. Why did you leave?" Cameron questioned.

"We did go visit you in Surrey. My father was unhappy at running up some debts. and was turning to his brandy more often than to your father for support. I believe my mother and your father hoped getting him out of London would help return him to his senses and happy disposition," Briana replied without censoring what she was revealing.

"He seemed to be happy in Surrey. So why did you leave?" Cameron once again inquired confusedly.

"We left Surrey because father became adamant about the importance of an appointment he had with an acquaintance about a business venture which he did not want to miss." Realizing that she once again shared too much of the truth behind their leaving town, Briana quickly added, "Also, because I forgot an appointment I had with the modiste that couldn't be missed," Briana said, feeling guilty for having lied to him. She couldn't bring herself to share the truth.

"Okay, but if that was the case, you did not have to move out of London. So, what happened once you arrived to drive your family to move away? Especially since your father was beginning to find happiness again while out in Surrey," Cameron pressed.

Knowing she was lying once again, Briana answered, "Unfortunately, when we arrived to London, we also received word that my uncle in Kent had suffered an accident and we were called immediately to care after my aunt and cousin. My uncle passed away shortly after our arrival. Not wanting to leave my cousin without a father, we stayed until my cousin became a man," Briana responded, once again kicking herself for lying to Cameron.

"I see. Where is your father now if your cousin has reached the age of becoming a man?" Cameron asked, looking intently at her eyes. He sensed there was some information she was keeping from him.

"He had some business and decided to also take my cousin on holiday as a reward for ranking top of his class. I hear they thoroughly enjoyed their time in Edinburgh," Briana smiled lightly.

"Well, I am glad to know that your father is well. Did you also enjoy your time in Kent?" Cameron asked, hoping to gain more insight into how she'd spent the last ten years.

Briana smiled once again and simply nodded. Seeing Cameron's eyebrows quirk up in an appeal for more information, Briana responded with as close to the truth as possible. "It was strange for a while since we did not know anyone. With the strain of taking care of others, I had to..." Briana trailed off before she revealed too much of her past again. Remembering the lie she had begun earlier, she continued, "Well, the strain was temporary. As my aunt recovered her health and spirits, my cousin began smiling more often and doing well in school. Afterwards, we began to enjoy ourselves once again with friends and family." She breathed deeply hoping to slow the racing of her heart. How many times she'd lied to Cameron right now she couldn't think to count.

Cameron was grateful to have heard her brief story of her time in Kent and thanked Briana for sharing. Standing, he made his way toward the mantel and looked at the clock. He knew he should be leaving, but had no desire to do so. Turning to face her once again, he said, "Brie, I do hope you know how happy the family is to have you, and your mother, back in London. I do hope that you will also be happy here." Seeing Briana nod her head slowly in thanks Cameron added, "I know we've had our differences lately, but please know that you are family to me, just like Emily and Jake."

Briana felt the pain in her heart once again at being thought of as another sibling, but wanting to be polite, responded by thanking him for his kindness toward her family. Cameron let out a sigh and decided it was time to take his leave. Bowing elegantly, he exited the room, leaving Briana to collapse once again onto the chaise lounge. She was left feeling absolutely exhausted. Who knew lying and forcing smiles could be so draining? Closing her eyes, Briana fell fast asleep.

After a nice nap, Briana awoke refreshed. She knew she had to find a suitable husband sooner rather than later and, with the suitors she had over the last couple days, she had narrowed it down to Lord Edwards. Although he did not stir in her the same passionate response as Cameron did, she knew she could not take advantage of Cameron and his family with everything they had done for her in the past. She also knew, after this last visit with him, she could not lie or keep secrets from him for very long. Cameron would always be special to her, but it was time she moved on from him and looked forward to a future with Lord Edwards and the safety and stability he could bring to her life.

Briana's thoughts were interrupted by her mother who came in to announce that Emily and her mother would be joining them for dinner. Delighted, Briana asked her mother if she could help prepare some of the dishes for tonight in order to ensure some of Emily's favorites would be available. With her mother's blessing, Briana made her way to the kitchen and claimed the sage green apron that hung on the wall nearest the door. Looking over at Cathy, she smiled and declared, "I'm here to request and help make some of Emily's favorite dishes for tonight. Feel free to direct me however necessary." Cathy pulled out her worn notebook of recipes with a smile and together with Briana created the night's menu.

Emily and her mother came over a little early in order to spend some extra time before dinner was served discussing the day's events and the upcoming balls. Emily and Briana were both looking forward to the Great Exhibition coming to London in May. Emily was excited to see the fine jewelry and ceramics that would be on display, while Briana looked forward to the rumored telescope and piano. It was only a couple months away and London was abuzz with talk of what one could expect to see. The excitement and expectation were set very high for such a novel event.

After dinner and more conversation in the sitting room, Emily pulled Briana to the seats on the other side of the room to talk in more detail about all the suitors she'd seen leaving

Briana's house. "Briana, you are amazing, did you know that? The fact that you have only just made your debut and already have so many suitors vying for your hand is astounding. I just hope that you don't rush into anything. Or that you don't get caught up in the heat of the moment with any of these gentlemen and find yourself in a dangerous predicament you can't get out of."

Emily was so serious as she spoke that Briana had to roll her eyes. Growing up, it was always Briana who would rush into everything and Emily who was the voice of reason. But sometimes that voice of reason could verge on lecture. Emily continued, "A dangerous predicament can be saying something as a joke to a close friend and it being misconstrued. I mean, you and Jake were foolish enough to make the wager of a kiss at a ball, but it can also be something as simple as holding a man's gaze for too long, Briana." Since Briana snorted at that, she said emphatically, "I mean it, Brie. At the ball, you and Cameron were locked in such a gaze that I could feel the passion from across the room. You must be careful or people may talk. I mean, of course, I would love for you and Cameron to be together, but it must be done in the right way. You must remember social proprieties!" Emily said matter-of-factly.

Briana simply smiled and squeezed her friend's hand. "I know, Em. I won't make any mistakes. Promise. And, even if something were to have already happened between me and Cameron, it was a complete misunderstanding and nobody saw it," Briana said rather quickly.

Emily's eyes widened to the size of saucers. "What do you mean 'if something were to have happened already?' What exactly did nobody see, Brie?" Emily's hands gripped Briana's tighter than before.

"Just simply that at the ball I mistook him for Jake. And when I went to give 'Jake' his kiss on the cheek as part of our bet, Cameron turned his head and we kissed. It's not a big deal, and again, nobody saw it. Also, it will never happen again," Briana said looking into Emily's eyes. The face of her friend had gone as white as the pillow next to her. She could swear

Emily hadn't let out a breath since Briana started speaking. Briana smiled, "Em, please breathe. It's okay."

"Brie, what if someone had seen? To let something like that happen out of wedlock where there is no relationship between the two of you! I have told you and Jake these games you both play are too dangerous and will get you in trouble one day. But, you both always say I'm overreacting. I know I am a bit prudish, but I just don't want to see either of you trapped in a marriage with someone you don't love due to circumstance," Emily said, letting out shaky breaths and holding back tears. "I love you both so much, but sometimes you are just so reckless and I worry."

Briana looked at her friend who for so long served as a sister to her as well and knew that her words, though conservative and stern, were well-meant. She looked into Emily's eyes and said, "Em, I don't mean to make you worry. Jake and I were just having some fun and teasing one another. I don't wish you to feel uncomfortable or anxious around us. Again, nobody saw anything and so no harm was done to anybody's reputation. Thank you for caring so much for us. I will try to be on my best behavior from now on. I promise," Briana said, placing her hand over her heart. Emily smiled back and sighed in relief. "But, if Jake challenges me, you know I have to accept any bet he makes. We just will come up with a socially respectable prize instead. Or let you pick the prize and save us all from trouble," Briana said laughing.

"You know, that might be the way to do it so nobody ends up in uncomfortable situations in the future. I think if you and Jake had to marry, you would end up strangling each other and then I'd be forced to pick a side and that would be too messy for me," Emily said, finally relaxing back into her joking tone. "But, aside from any concerns I had previously, and out of pure objective curiosity, how was the kiss? Did you know what to do when your lips touched? And also, because I know there once were strong feelings on your part, were you excited or disappointed when you found out it was Cameron and not Jake?"

"Emily! How you surprise me, especially after just scolding

me!" Briana laughed, taken aback. She looked down at her hands before she said, "I don't know what I felt, and of course, I had no idea what to do or what was happening! I was confused at first because I thought it was Jake who was kissing me and I knew that was all sorts of wrong. The kiss was so soft and tender at first that it didn't seem to match Jake's bachelor ways. But then, there was this passion and control to the kiss that thrilled me and I became confused even more because I didn't want to feel that way about Jake. And then, it deepened again to where I forgot where I was and who I was with. It was wonderful!" Briana sighed with a soft smile on her lips and a glassy look in her eyes. "But then, we removed our masks and it wasn't Jake at all, but Cameron! I was in shock that someone as aloof as he could kiss like that. And yet, I was elated that what I had dreamed about years ago had finally come true. I finally kissed Cameron whom I've loved for so long. But, I was angry because this was not supposed to ever happen. Not with him. I told myself to move on from him after he rejected me years ago, and finally, now that I moved on, he kisses me like that. I didn't want it to be him, and so I left with that feeling of anger, confusion, and loss inside me once again," Briana said dejectedly. "Like I said, I promise it will never happen again."

"Whew. Brie, I never knew someone could feel all that in one kiss. It was probably better that the kiss happened with Cameron, though. Was this your first kiss?" When Briana nodded her head shyly, Emily responded, "Well, I think that kiss was probably as amazing as one could hope for in a kiss, even though you were not expecting to truly kiss anyone. But if it had been Jake, he may have thought it funny to pull your hair or something when you were going to kiss him on the cheek, or blow in your face as a way to further his prank. He is so sneaky and diabolical!" Emily said, shaking her head at the thought but wearing a hint of a smile that conveyed the love she held for her rascal brother.

"Oh Em, I love you! And as much as I hate to admit it, you are right. That kiss truly was the best first kiss a woman could ask for, even if it came from the man who you wrote in one of your letters as saying 'No woman could ever be as beautiful as my horse' when your mother pressed him to marry," Briana said through laughs. The two girls passed the remainder of the time laughing and catching up about the various marriages that had occurred while Briana was away from London. They were joined by their mothers who also added to the conversation any gossip they had gathered until it was late and Elizabeth deemed it time to return to their own home. Everyone hugged and kissed good night with promises to see each other the next day. Briana walked to her room and replayed Emily's wise words. She must make sure there are no instances of impropriety that could lead her to marry Cameron, or Jake for that matter. Everything must go smoothly so she could marry Lord Edwards and care for her mother as promised. She slept soundly that night with visions of her tranquil marriage and happy mother without worries.

CHAPTER 9

April 1851

Feeling restless, Briana awoke early in the morning and helped Cathy clean the house. She also went to check the inventory of valuable items they had in the house in order of importance, just in case they needed to sell something soon to keep up appearances. By early afternoon, she was losing her feelings of restlessness and beginning to replace them with frustration at not having heard from Lord Edwards since his visit almost four days ago. Sitting down at her writing desk, Briana looked through the notes she had compiled of sights and conversations that gave her inspiration. She began writing a scene for romance between a man and a woman who meet on a hill overlooking the city. He'd run after her upon seeing her in town simply to ask for her name. Smiling to herself at the sweetness of the scene, she began to bring the gentleman to life by adding descriptions of his looks and mannerisms. Upon realizing that the man in her story bore a striking resemblance to Cameron, Briana crossed out her descriptions and modeled them after Lord Edwards instead. Remembering that she hadn't heard from Lord Edwards since his last visit though made her even more frustrated and once again the story came to a halt. Crumbling the paper in her hands and throwing it into the waste basket, Briana decided to ease her mind with some mending in hopes that, by fixing one problem, she would come up with a solution that would help her encounter Lord Edwards spontaneously so they may get to know each other better. Usually, when writing didn't ease her stress, mending always did the trick. As much as she dreamed of being a writer, she longed even more for a happy marriage and stable life.

While in her room mending a pale blue day dress, there came a knock on the door. Once allowed to come in, Lucy crossed the length of the room and gave Briana a letter. "Mr. Wallace said you'd be eager to be receiving this letter, Miss. I believe it is from Lord Edwards. A fine and handsome gentleman he is," Lucy said, as a blush touched her cheeks. Having realized she'd spoken aloud, she covered her mouth with the back of her hand and bobbed a quick curtsy before leaving the room. Briana let out a soft chuckle at the young girl's bashfulness and went to retrieve the letter opener from the writing desk in the corner of her room she was seated at earlier.

She sat down and began to read the elegantly penned letter.

> *Dear Lady Briana Valmont,*
> *It was such an honor to call upon you at your home. I was very pleased to see how well we got along. My mother always said you can measure a true lady by how she handles herself in small company. She also taught me the value of a well-penned letter to stir a woman's heart. I would like the honor of requesting to call upon you tomorrow for a carriage ride through the city. I will call upon you tomorrow at mid-day.*
> *Affectionately,*
> *Lord Michael Edwards*

Briana couldn't help but smile and blush. It was like he had heard her thoughts and penned his response immediately to ease her anxiety. She quickly penned a response to say that she would be very happy to spend time with him tomorrow. She would eagerly await his arrival. She sent the sealed response with Wallace and then began to fret over which of her dresses would be appropriate to wear that she hadn't been seen in recently. She found a violet dress with white lace fringe on the sleeves and bodice and decided she hadn't worn that one at all since her return to London. Briana sat down to fix the hem which had started to fray again from years of wear and hummed to herself happily, knowing that tomorrow's carriage ride would help bring them closer to a proposal and a happier future.

Cameron awoke the next morning with a renewed sense of tending to his finances and writing letters to his estate manager at the Hereford country home in Surrey. Ever since meeting with Briana in the rose garden and seeing how easily she conversed with Jake, he decided he would not think of that mistaken kiss anymore. It didn't matter that he could still smell the fragrance of her hair whenever he walked by the flower vases in the house, or that he couldn't help but see her mysterious and sparkling eyes every time he saw anything or anyone wearing emeralds. No, he had always seen her as a close friend to the family and would continue to do so. After all, when he looked back on his adolescence, he remembered being followed by Briana and Emily who always wanted him to dance with them, join their imaginary tea party, or read to them. Of course, once Jake came into the room or announced that he would join them, the girls would stop trying to convince Cameron. Briana always wore a big smile when she was joking with or being chased around by Jake. The smile she'd always bestowed upon Cameron was shy and reserved, almost as if she was not sure how to be around him. Unfortunately, it seemed she was the only one who could get Cameron out of his head and genuinely smile. She could make him laugh in earnest and enjoy things outside of his work. Cameron had to admit that Briana was able to bring out a side of ease in him he never knew existed. He felt most like his father when she was around listening to his thoughts, bringing out laughter in him with her questions, and forcing him to take a break when she wanted an adventure but was without a companion. It seems life wanted to send him a message by making his mystery lady from the ball and the young Briana the same person in order to bring joy back into his life. Well, if she and Jake decided to marry, he'd have to come to terms with her being Jake's source of joy. She'd be more than just a family friend to Cameron since he'd have to begin calling her his sister. He scowled at the thought of their marriage and felt his jaw twitch, but simply shook his head and returned to his business.

He had many letters that needed to be mailed out to his estate manager in Surrey but knew he should take the opportunity to get out of the house and visit his mother and sister before they started to hound him for working too hard. He'd mail the letters first and then buy his mother the little lemon cakes she loved so much before visiting. That would earn him a few smiles and would get his mind off of picturing a certain someone and her mass of curls loosely falling down her back as they once did before. Maybe Emily could give him some peace of mind that she would only be staying for the London season and leave again so he wouldn't have such confusing thoughts interrupting his daily life. It was only a kiss for Pete's sake! Cameron pushed his chair back, grabbed the stack of letters, shook his head once more as his eyes landed on the emerald mask he kept on a bookshelf, and like a man on a mission, looked straight ahead and walked out the door.

Briana descended the stairs in her violet dress with matching bonnet and parasol. She had thought taking a parasol when she was already wearing a bonnet was redundant, but Lucy had insisted, saying it was very fashionable. Frankly, Briana didn't want to disappoint the poor girl and carried both. If Lord Edwards had an opinion one way or another, he did not voice it. He simply smiled at her and held his arm out to escort her towards the carriage. It was a beautifully sunny day, which was a rarity here in London, and Briana silently thanked Lucy for insisting on carrying both since the bonnet was a little snug and did not block the sun as much as it should. She stepped up into the open top carriage and Lord Edwards sat across from her. Lucy sat up front with the driver. Emily would be proud of how proper everyone was in this carriage.

As the carriage started to move, Lord Edwards began a pleasant stream of conversation centered around the blessing of nice weather on their outing. He asked after her mother and wished her well. She in turn shared how returning to London and being amongst friends had done wonders for her mother's disposition.

"I am very delighted to find a woman such as yourself whom I get along with well. So often the women of the *ton* are all the same: young, absurdly inane, too shy, or too forward. You are the perfect balance of a woman, which my mother would say is the true measure of a woman. She would love you, although she would probably have said that your emerald dress the night of the ball could have withstood a shawl draped over the shoulders. She was always nitpicking on every woman's attire, but I think you would have rendered her speechless once she came to know you," Edwards said with a radiant smile that lit up his entire face and brought crinkles around his soft blue eyes. Briana thought that soft shade of blue was one of the prettiest colors she had seen. If only she could have been blessed with such beautiful eyes. Honestly, they were lost on a man. She smiled back at him and moved the same curl that always managed to loosen itself from any hairstyle (or bonnet, apparently) and fall across her forehead. Edwards helped tuck it behind her ear and pin it behind the laces of her bonnet.

"Thank you. It's always a mess no matter what I do with it, unlike you who always seems so well-put together and have those beautiful eyes that would make any woman jealous." Briana shook her head at her words.

"Jealous? Of my eyes? That is indeed an interesting thought that I had not heard before. Most likely because that is not something a woman tells a man whom she is just starting to know. But, I find it sweet you think so nonetheless," Edwards said rather uncomfortably, but with a soft smile still on his lips. "I know the kind of woman you are, and thus know that your comment was meant as innocently as it entered your mind. From our few interactions, I have already gathered that you are a gentle woman with no ulterior motives that would make what you said sinful," Edwards said matter-of-factly.

Briana could feel her face flush out of guilt for misleading this nice man. Of course she had ulterior motives! She never thought it was sinful to tell a man he had beautiful eyes, but she knew it was sinful to make a man fall in love with and propose just so she could have access to his money. She felt her face grow hotter and saw his smile widen with pleasure. He thought she was blushing at the compliment he just gave her... how wrong he really was. Could she really continue to lie to a man as nice as he? Did it matter she couldn't lie to Cameron and he was the only other man she'd considered? If one lies for a good reason and it results in stability, safety, companionship, or even love, does the lie become worthwhile?

Before Briana could answer her own question, she was met with a familiar face approaching the carriage. Sitting so high up put her closer to eye level with him than she'd ever been before. He wore an expression she had never seen. It was a mixture of indifference and something else like anger. She schooled her features to match his. As his horse stopped next to the carriage, he touched the brim of his hat and dipped his head in greeting. "Lord Edwards. Lady Valmont." The greeting was said in such a cold tone. It bothered Briana, but seemed to have been missed entirely by Lord Edwards who bowed in return.

"Your Grace, how very nice to see you out on this beautiful day," Edwards said with a cordial smile. Noticing the package of sweets Cameron held in his hands, he commented, "Stopped into the bakery today, I see."

Cameron had to control himself for want of rolling his eyes at the obvious statement. "Yes, I am on my way to visit my mother and sister," he retorted.

Briana could sense the unease and, wanting to alleviate the

tension she felt, she smiled broadly and replied, "Oh, I know they will love them! Of course, they will love seeing you more though. They are never happier than when you and Jake stop by to visit. In fact, it was just a couple days ago at dinner that your mother was wondering when you'd pay another visit. Apparently, you never visit enough," she said as she swatted his hand in mock punishment. Before she could pull her hand away, Cameron had grabbed hold of it and stared at her eyes. The eyes that at first looked indifferent and cold now held a glint of fire and danger. She hadn't seen this look since the kiss at the ball.

"Careful, Brie. We don't want Lord Edwards to think you have lost all feminine sensibilities," Cameron said tersely. The cold tightness of his voice did not match the fire in his eyes. He knew he should not be using her nickname in public, but a desire to demonstrate to Edwards just how close he was with Briana superseded societal manners.

Briana had to look away from those deeply mysterious chocolate eyes. They were not the beautiful color of Lord Edwards, but Lord save her, they could bring her heart up to her throat if she continued to stare.

"Ahem, Lady Valmont?" Lord Edwards said, breaking her stare. She pulled her hand out of Cameron's grasp and turned her attention to Lord Edwards, who was wearing a rather tight expression as well. "I think we should not detain His Grace from his visit to his mother any longer. Shall we continue on?" At Briana's slow nod, his smile returned. He looked over at Cameron before giving a curt bow and waiting for Cameron to return his farewell. He told the driver to continue on and left Cameron rooted to his spot watching after them, his hand burning from Briana's touch. How could she light him on fire that easily with a simple touch? No woman had ever affected him this way, and he had grown up with her! This was madness. If he didn't get ahold of himself, or ahold of another woman for that matter, things were only going to get messy. No, things were already messy. Ever since the ball, even before the kiss they shared, he wanted Briana. But wanting a woman did not equal marriage, and as much as he wanted her,

Cameron knew he should be looking for a wife that would be able to carry out the roles of a duchess. Although Briana was not the wild girl from their youth, she was still not quite what society would deem acceptable for the position of a duchess. Pity. He took a few more deep breaths to cool his body off and then, with one more glance at the carriage down the street, he urged his horse on in the direction of Hereford House.

Glancing back, Briana saw the elegant backside of Cameron as he rode off. Letting out a breath she had been holding, she turned her attention once again to Lord Edwards and began discussing the Greek poetry she'd read yesterday evening. Seeing his eyes crinkle once again, Briana knew he was no longer upset with her. An hour later, Lord Edwards and Briana had circled around and were on the road back to her house. They had enjoyed the remainder of the carriage ride with sporadic small talk about the upcoming balls. But, for the most part, they rode in silence. Briana thought he was mad at her for holding Cameron's hand earlier, but just then Lord Edwards broke her thoughts by saying "It is nice that we can sit in companionable silence like this and don't feel the need to fill every moment with idle chatter. Not that I think our conversations are idle chatter, you see." Briana slowly nodded her head in confusion. "I see you seem dazed. Maybe it's from too much sun. Your home is in sight and I recommend you go lay down for a spell."

"Thank you, Lord Edwards, I will. I'm sorry for any discomfort I may have caused you earlier, what with my interaction with the Duke of Hereford earlier. I meant nothing by it," Briana said ashamedly.

"It's alright, dear girl, just be careful with your behavior. You are too comfortable with that family and if you continue to treat him and his brother as you do, there will be talk of you being disingenuous or worse. I would not like to see your reputation besmirched in such a fashion. Also, I could not keep company with a woman of such a reputation. I hold propriety to the highest esteem and like to believe you do the same," Lord Edwards said this in a kind yet firm tone that made

Briana believe would be one a loving father would use with their child as a gentle scolding. Briana nodded in response, thoroughly ashamed.

"I understand. Thank you for your kind and gentle reminder. Having grown up with the family and then being parted for so long, I think we all sometimes revert back to our youthful interactions. I will remember your words today and heed them well. Thank you, Lord Edwards, for a lovely outing," Briana replied as the carriage stopped in front of her home. Lord Edwards exited the carriage and helped her down. With a quick bow and words of repeating another outing sometime soon without the interruptions of another gentleman, he was back in his carriage and down the street before Briana could respond. Turning around to step in the house, she knew she would have to call on Emily soon to discuss her date. What with Cameron coming up in discussion with Jake and then coming face to face with her on her outing with Lord Edwards, she needed reminding of why it's important to stay her course. She could not get pulled down into the dark abyss that are Cameron's eyes and begin the slew of mind games she'd experienced as a young girl loving someone who did not return her affections. She was an adult now and would fall for a man who would have the same level of affections for her as she for him.

CHAPTER 10

Having decided to meet Emily away from the chance of running into either Jake or Cameron, at half past noon Briana found herself atop the beautiful chestnut colored mare named Honey she borrowed from the Hereford stables. She had needed two men to help her settle herself onto the horse, but was now elegantly waiting Emily's arrival. How she really detested having to ride sidesaddle. It was more work than necessary. Despite these negative thoughts, there was nothing that could compare to the feel of the wind on one's face while riding. She smiled as she saw Emily approach the stables with her maid trailing behind her. Briana felt a slight pang of envy as she saw how beautiful her friend was. With her classic looks of blond hair and beautiful blue eyes she'd inherited from her mother, it was no wonder she was never at a loss for a suitor. She would not be in the dire situation Briana found herself in now. No, Emily could simply bat her eyes and she would have the sheer luck of meeting the perfect man for her in an instant, especially since Emily was by far the most proper lady of her acquaintance. Emily's lips curved up softly into a smile as she pulled her horse to a stop beside where Briana was waiting.

"Brie, I am so happy we were able to do this today. It feels like ages since I last rode. I know you wrote in your letters that you went out for a ride almost daily, but with all the events mother had me attend alongside her, I was lucky enough to ride once every two weeks. I hope it is not too crowded in the park so we may speak more freely. You seemed agitated in your note after your outing with Lord Edwards yesterday," Emily said as she grasped Briana's hand in companionship.

Briana sighed and replied, "I too am happy you could join me. I seem to have gotten myself a scolding from Lord Edwards yesterday and it has left me feeling rather confused and misjudged." Briana gave her horse a soft pat with her whip to move Honey forward. Emily followed suit and the two began their ride to the park for exercise and conversation, expertly maneuvering around any other riders if necessary.

Once they finally decided to break, Briana led them to the far end of the park. It was indeed less crowded and, with more trees available at this end, there was a bit more shelter from the sun and the dust that could be kicked up by walkers and riders alike. "So, tell me what happened. From the letter you showed me, he seemed to be interested in you. He has called on you before and was a polite gentleman, especially when next to that vile man Mr. Gutterson. You also seemed interested in him as well. What could have possibly gone so wrong in one outing that you feel this anxious?" Emily probed.

"Oh, Em. We really were getting along and learning more about each other. He even said that I was the perfect balance of a woman and that his mother would have loved me, but everything changed when we ran into Cameron," Briana said softly.

"Cameron? When did you see him?" Emily asked as she pulled her horse to a halt. She wore a look of confusion that quickly faded into a different emotion as she squinted her eyes and said, "What did he do?" The menacing look was quite comical and out of place on one who generally wore such a serene face. Briana always laughed at it whenever it made an appearance during the years of their childhoods.

"Well, nothing really. He was on his way to visit you with pastries and I told him he should visit more since I know your mother says he doesn't visit enough. But when I swatted his hand, he held mine and wouldn't let it go at first. He had the same look in his eyes that he did at the ball when he was so angry. Lord Edwards scolded me afterwards for being too familiar with Cameron. He said I need to keep my distance from your family. But I could never do that!" Briana said in desperation. "Doesn't he understand that we have all just been reunited?"

Emily reached over and gave Briana a hug. Smiling at her friend, Emily said, "Oh Brie, I wouldn't be able to stand being parted from you again either. I'm sure Lord Edwards wouldn't keep you away from us. I think he's just protective of you and wants to make sure you know that he is serious about courting you. He wants the same seriousness in return. When Cameron is around, I think it's fair to say that your attention is diverted." Emily shrugged and gave a shy smile as she said the final words, knowing her friend would deny it vehemently.

"What? You can't say that when you haven't seen me in ten years!" Briana said with a laugh. "Believe me when I say that I have left any illusions of me and Cameron behind."

"Oh, have you?" Emily asked with a knowing glint in her eye. She knew her dear friend was trying so hard to believe her own words, but the sadness that lay behind the conviction was all too telling.

"Em, I tried to be strong and confess my feelings to Cameron in the past and he dismissed me as easily as he put on his shirt that morning. I cannot relive that pain. I promised myself to never love someone who does not love me. So, it is nice being with Lord Edwards who seems to like me just the same as I do him. It is not a love affair, but the companionship is mutual and there is room for stronger emotions to develop with time. He is also able to provide for my mother and me in the future, which is all I could ever want. You recall me explaining the tough situation my father was going through trying to reconcile his debts when we left London. It gave a great deal of pain to my mother and I as a result. I need to know that we won't suffer like that again, even if my father takes to gambling again," Briana replied with a look in the direction of a couple walking past arm-in-arm. She smiled at them before catching the eye of her friend.

"I understand your need for security. I am glad to see you all have managed well over the years. I know I haven't seen your father yet, but hope he is well. As for Cameron, if he didn't notice you then, I think he would have to be blind not to notice you now. He was so young then that I don't think he knew anything besides work and living up to my father's expectations. Although he is much the same, he has changed in many ways as well. You may want to remember that the next time you are in his presence. What may have been ignored in the past may not be so easy to ignore now," Emily said with a knowing smile. "Remember what Lord Edwards said and take it to heart as much as possible. I do remember the heartache of the past and agree that putting some distance between you and Cameron may not be a bad thing. You don't want to risk your heart, as well as his – especially knowing that Lord Edwards is a nice man who would view your marriage in the same fashion. There would not be any emotional struggles or moments of passion that could suddenly change everything."

Briana nodded, knowing that Emily spoke the truth. She knew it would be best to limit her time with Cameron, but she couldn't help that he would be in her presence from time to time given the close relationship of their families. The families had always done everything together. Even when her father began drinking heavily, Emily's father was always there to take care of Lord Valmont if anything should happen. The ability to play carefree was easy when you had an entire family to run off to if necessary. They really were like siblings growing up. Briana chuckled at the memory of a prank she and Jake pulled on Cameron one day when she had left her parents arguing in the house. Emily stared confusedly at her.

"You know, if you continue laughing to yourself like that, the *ton* will begin to talk," said a deep voice from behind Emily. As Briana looked up and Emily turned around, they were surprised to see Jake on horseback wearing his lopsided grin. "In order to protect your name, Emily and I must know what you were laughing at." Jake brought his horse to a halt alongside Emily.

"Hello Jake! I was just remembering the time we hid Cameron's artist notebook and how he spent all day searching for it. Do you remember that he even went to look in the stalls and came back covered in mud from digging?" Briana asked Jake and Emily with a smile. She motioned to the trio to move further into the park toward the shade.

Jake turned his horse to follow the women and said "Gosh, were those sketches horrible. I can't believe he ever thought those sketches would be helpful to anyone. He was so mad! Wasn't it you, Emily, who told him to look in the stalls? He never suspected you since you were always so cautious. He never thought you would be in cahoots with us. But, why was he digging in mud, though?" Jake asked as he dismounted and allowed the horse to munch on the grass.

Briana followed Jake's lead and motioned to one of Emily's grooms to help her dismount. Before the groom was able to approach Briana, Jake already had his arms extended to help her down. She allowed him to place his hands at her sides as she placed hers on his shoulders. Once she was lifted off the horse, Jake took a step back to maintain the socially appropriate distance between the two. After Briana's feet touched the ground. she answered Jake's questions, saying, "Actually, that was me. I heard Emily tell him to check the stalls and I told him that I saw you bury it just outside. I didn't expect him to dig for it himself," Briana said with a slight shake of her head and another muffled laugh.

"He was determined not to let father down and prove his worth, so of course he would not have stopped searching until he found it. Although I enjoyed myself then, that time did not compare to the time we adhered all his boots to the walls and ceilings with fish glue. Remember, Emily?" Jake said laughingly. "I don't think I have ever seen such a comical face. His nose was scrunched up and his eyes were the size of saucers!" Jake exclaimed, doubling over in laughter. Briana knew it was not a gentlemanly display of emotion, but they too couldn't help laughing in the same manner.

"How it was that I got in trouble alongside you both when

I didn't participate in the deed still eludes me. I don't know who was more upset, Cameron or his valet. Mother was livid as well. Remember how she insisted we help remove the shoes from the walls and shine the boots? Jenkins was appalled by the idea of having us help and then was simply annoyed at the horrible job we did shining the shoes," Emily said with a smile and a smothered laugh. For as much as she prided herself on being a voice of reason among her family and friends, she could never quite stay away from the adventures of Jake and Briana.

"Thinking back to these times, your mother was a saint for allowing me to visit your house on a daily basis," Briana said with a soft satisfied smile that left a sparkle in her eyes. She looked over to Emily and then to Jake and counted her blessings that she was now reunited with those of her childhood. These friends that she felt were more like family members to her. Living away from them for so long were the darkest years of her life. Having family to reminisce with and who desire to spend time together making new memories was something she would carry into her future family. Her children would play jokes on each other and spend time outdoors together just as they had. Jake caught her eye and opened his mouth to say something, but at that moment a gust of wind blew and carried Briana's bonnet off her head and up into a nearby tree. In shock, Briana turned to see Emily holding her bonnet firmly on her head with her hands.

"Well, that's unfortunate," Jake stated with a chuckle. "Although, the face you are making now bears a striking resemblance to Cameron's during the 'Great Shoe Show of 1838.' Would you like some help getting it down?" Jake asked with a wry smile.

Briana blushed and looked away more frustrated with the bonnet than with Jake's teasing. She turned to size up the tree and the three men available to her. Jake was the tallest among them but, if her memory served, he had a fear of heights that he never let anyone know. She was not able to reveal his secret phobia in front of others. She nodded and replied, "Yes, if one of the groomsmen would do me the favor of retrieving my bonnet, I would be much obliged." She looked at the groomsmen who shared baffled looks with each other. Neither seemed keen on the idea of climbing up the tree.

"We can assist you ma'am, but it may take a while since the bonnet landed on a branch that is quite removed from the trunk itself," one of them said while the other nodded. "Not to mention that some of these branches may not be able to hold our weight," stated the second groomsman, who was a bit more portly in stature. The two men looked at each other and began motioning to the horses nearby. With a nod, one of the groomsmen retrieved a riding crop from the horse and returned to face the tree. Without a word, he reared his arm back and threw the riding crop towards the tree branch cradling the bonnet. It hit the side of the bonnet but simply served to lodge the stubborn piece more into place along with the riding crop.

The second groomsmen decided to try a different tactic and, wrapping his arms around the tree, shook the tree vigorously in the hopes of dislodging the bonnet. Alas, all that came from that endeavor were fallen leaves and a frustrated groomsman. Briana heaved a sigh and, removing her gloves and handing them to Emily, began to approach the tree.

"Brie, what on earth are you thinking? I've seen that look before on your face and I never like the results." Emily said this in such a matronly fashion that Briana couldn't help but chuckle. That did not seem to be the correct response since Emily pulled her back by the hand. "Don't tell me you wish to climb this tree? Briana, we are in public where anyone may come upon us. Think of what everyone would say seeing you up there."

"Well, that's why I have you two to be the look-outs. We all know that I am the fastest climber among us and that branch cannot withstand the weight of these gentlemen. So, my dear Emily, unless you are volunteering to climb up in my place, you just help keep people away and I'll make sure to come down quickly." Briana turned once again to face the tree. It's true that the branch bearing the bonnet was further removed from the trunk, but Briana was able to find a path in her head that should work quickly and easily.

"Brie, my dear, can't you simply buy a different bonnet? Or take one of the many that Emily or my mother have? I have to agree with Emily that this is not a very safe or ladylike decision," Jake said, staring down at her with worried eyes. They were the same worried eyes he had always given her when they were younger and she wished to climb trees or brick fences. It was one of the sweetest and honest looks she'd seen in Jake.

"I'll be fine. Just like always. I need this bonnet. It's special to me since I have had it for many years and do not wish to spend money to replace it. Please, just stand at the bottom in case I need your assistance in any way." In truth, this bonnet had no sentimental value, but the reality was that Briana did not want to spend money on a new bonnet since that would be less money they could rely on later in case of emergencies. With that in mind, Briana placed her booted foot in the hand of one of the groomsmen and with a boost began to climb. Although she knew she should not be enjoying herself, she couldn't help but feel the serenity that comes with the nostalgia of pleasant memories.

With every step up she took, she found her way with ease. Looking down at the concerned faces, she gave them a reassuring smile and grasped the branch that held the bonnet. It was thinner than the others and creaked with any added weight. She had climbed on thin branches like this before in her past, but she had been a young girl then. Now, as a woman, she hesitated for the first time since stepping toward the tree. She took in a deep breath and held it. She couldn't seem to exhale for fear that any added sound would wreak havoc on the tree branch and her tightly-wound nerves.

"Brie, please be careful!" Emily called from below. She was wringing her hands together while also looking around to make sure her dear friend would not be discovered in such an unladylike position. Briana was stabbed with a pang of guilt for putting such a good friend through the stress. She had to get this bonnet into her hand and climb down safely as soon as possible to end this awkward situation. She lowered herself into a sitting position and began to shimmy her way across the branch, ignoring the creaking sounds of refusal.

Briana let out a sigh of relief as she reached the end of the branch and saw that the bonnet and the riding crop were an arm's length away. She could do this! She would reach out and retrieve both and put this moment of discomfort behind her. She really was nervous about the branch she was on. Did it seem like it was dipping lower? And were the creaking sounds getting more frequent and louder? She stretched out her hand and grazed the long strings of the bonnet. She needed to get closer somehow. Shimmying forward a bit more she attempted the movement again and this time made contact with the bonnet. Just as she tightened her grip on the bonnet, she heard a snap in the branch. She looked around for something to hold onto, but found herself falling the long distance to the ground instead with the bonnet in hand and the riding crop falling beside her. She noticed that Jake had moved away from his initial post next to the trunk of the tree and was now running to catch her as she fell. She was too stunned to yell, but heard a scream below that must have come from Emily as well as a man's voice call out her name. Jake wasn't going to make it in time, and even if he did, would he be able to catch her in time? Briana closed her eyes, bracing herself for the fall that seemed inevitable and found herself making contact with something strong yet soft.

"What the blazes do you think you're doing?!" a deep voice shouted near her ear. She slowly opened one eye and then the other. Her mouth formed a soft O as she was met with Cameron's face. His eyebrows were drawn together so tightly and his eyes were wide and black as sin. The muscle in his jaw was twitching faster than she'd ever seen and the lips of his mouth had disappeared into a strong line making the dimples that were usually on display on either side of his mouth invisible. His skin that normally had a nice color to it looked as white as his cravat. She'd never seen this face or heard that tone of voice from him, even when he was mad at her for participating in his brother's pranks as children. He tightened his arms around her body until she squirmed.

"I had to get my bonnet," Briana stated matter-of-factly. She was trying to appear as prim and proper as she could while being held in Cameron's arms. She felt her body's temperature rising. His face was so close that she could smell the lemon tea on his breath as he spoke to her. She wanted to kiss him again. To feel the strong lips over hers taking control until she was weak in the knees and her lips melded into his. She knew a kiss would never again happen between them. "You can put me down now," Briana said again in as stern a voice as she could. Cameron didn't bother looking at her. He simply turned to Jake with her still in his arms.

"And you allowed her?" If Briana was feeling warm it had to be in part from the steam that was radiating off of Cameron. He was seething so much so that the colorless face was now taking a turn towards shades of red.

Although Jake was just as tall as his brother, he cowered under his stare and shrugged his shoulders, saying, "What? As kids, Brie was always the best climber. She knew she could get it down faster than any of us could. Plus, we knew the branch was thin and couldn't stand too much weight." As soon as the words left his mouth, Jake regretted saying them. He averted his gaze from his brother's as did the two groomsmen.

"You knew the branch couldn't stand too much weight and you still let her convince you climbing a tree would be a good idea?" Cameron said through clenched teeth. "I could strangle you right now, Jake. Have you no common sense? She could have been killed. I don't care how good of a climber she thinks she is," Cameron said.

Briana squirmed once again trying to get out of Cameron's arms. "I am a good climber. I got the bonnet, didn't I? And..." The look she received made her stop talking midsentence. His eyes were still furious, but his arms released a bit and he gently brushed his hand over her arm a couple of times. Briana saw that gentle touch reach his eyes before the gaze hardened as quickly as it had changed.

"It is one thing for you to climb trees as kids. It's highly improper for a grown lady to be up in a tree," Cameron asserted once again with a tone so cold it seemed at odds with the fiery heat of his body.

"It's no more improper than the way you're holding her now in your arms. In public, if I may add. I'm sure Briana would be mortified if this scene got back to Lord Edwards since she seems to be accepting his courtship in earnest," Jake said with a grin and glint in his eye. His lips quirked up a bit more as he saw his brother close his eyes in acknowledgement of the logical statement.

Cameron knew he should put Briana down but he couldn't bring himself to let her go quite yet. He lowered his head to hers so that their foreheads touched. "Don't ever scare me like that again." He lingered there for an instant longer and then returned her to her feet. Briana knew her feet were touching the ground, but her world had completely shifted. She could see Jake and Cameron talking, but the shock of being in Cameron's arms seemed to have some lingering effect on her hearing. She shook her head once. Twice. She heard Cameron say, "Take her home, Jake. She's had a shock and people are starting to make their way over. We don't need people staring or asking questions about how she came to be in this state in the first place, now do we?"

"She's okay. We'll walk a bit more until you're steady, okay?" Jake said, looking down at Briana. He looked thoroughly ashamed and worried. Briana simply nodded as Emily came to her other side and took hold of her arm.

"No. Now, Jake." Cameron growled and held his brother's eyes until Jake nodded in agreement. Without a glance to Briana, Cameron spun on his heel and, before taking a step away from Briana, was brought to a halt as he saw Lord Edwards approaching. "Hmph. What do you see in that dullard anyway?" Cameron asked. Did he truly want a response?

"He's a gentleman who is always caring after others," Briana said quickly before turning a smile to Lord Edwards. "Lord Edwards! It's so nice to see you. It was such a beautiful

day that Emily and I couldn't help but come for a bit of air."
She could feel the tension rising in Cameron's body once again
as he stood next to her, arms touching.

"Yes. And I do believe you got more air than you bargained
for, my dear." Lord Edwards said as he bowed stiffly over her
extended hand. His eyes met hers and she could see something
akin to disappointment within them.

Briana felt herself flush. Had he seen everything? Did he
know that it was her decision to clime the tree? Had he seen
Cameron holding her? Touching his forehead to hers? Did he
know about the heat that stirred within her while she was in
his arms? How she longed for him to kiss her? She cleared her
throat and began "Truly, the bonnet flew off my head and into
the tree…"

"No matter the reason, a woman who is serious about
marriage should not behave in such a manner. Falling out of
trees and resting in the arms of a man is inconceivable. I do
not care how many times you claim to only think of these two
gentlemen as your brothers, your behavior is highly
inappropriate and your reputation is as good as ruined." Lord
Edwards said, not meeting Briana's eyes.

"What? How is my reputation ruined if nobody has
witnessed anything except for us? I know I was wrong and
will never do something so reckless again in my life. Can we
not move past this incident? Please?" Briana pleaded. She felt
Cameron's arm clench with tension once again. He was
holding himself back from saying or doing something and
Briana knew he was not happy about it.

"My dear, I just do not know what to make of your
behavior. It was not only reckless, but confirmed a lingering
doubt I had about your seriousness to marry. Or maybe you
have your sights set on another?" Lord Edwards said, looking
towards Cameron. "Your Grace, what do you make of Lady
Valmont's behavior?"

Briana turned her eyes up at Cameron. She didn't know
what she wanted him to say in this moment, but she hoped
that the tender affection he had conveyed a moment ago while

she was in his arms would once again appear. Instead, Cameron replied, "I am in agreement, Lord Edwards. It was dangerous and highly unladylike. If the lady I was courting behaved in such a manner, I too would call her marriage potential into question... as well as her mental health." Cameron looked down at Briana with such a cold glance she was surprised snow hadn't started falling from the skies that instant. She really needed to stop getting her hopes up and seeing moments with Cameron as something romantic when in truth he simply saw her as a nuisance he must take care of due to family ties.

Briana straightened her posture and pulled her shoulders back. She took a step away from Cameron and towards Lord Edwards. When she stumbled over the fallen riding crop, she told her body to reach out for him rather than Cameron and when he pulled her up towards him, she ignored that fact that she had seen Cameron reach out to her as well. Briana smiled and said, "Thank you, Lord Edwards. I want you to know that I am neither deranged nor unsure of my desire to marry. In fact, this debacle has made it abundantly clear to me that life is short and my seriousness towards marriage to a man who would be present to care for me with all his heart and keep me from ever needing to have such notions has never been stronger."

"Well, I'm glad to hear you say that. I would definitely never let you out of my sight, my dear. If ever you had an emergency, you know you could rely on me to not only solve any problem, but to do so in a manner that your reputation would never be called into question." Lord Edwards replied as he gave a pointed look at Cameron and then at Jake. Cameron's scowl deepened so much that Briana thought it would be permanently etched into his face. Jake, on the other hand, seemed to be enjoying the exchange and wore an amused expression on his face. He nodded slightly in assent to Lord Edwards before turning apologetic eyes towards Briana. As much as he seemed unconcerned with the situation, she knew that the feelings of guilt he felt were more than anyone else present since he knew Briana had climbed that tree simply to keep his fear of heights from being revealed. He was a coward and his childhood friend was now suffering from it. He would definitely work hard to repay her kindness and show her the care she truly deserved.

"Come, my dear. I will take you home. Can you ride or would you like to walk? I can ask my groomsmen to take the horses back," Lord Edwards asked as he placed a gentle hand at Briana's elbow. She saw Cameron's quick step forward and then backward before turning her attention to Jake.

"I think I would like to walk if that's alright. Jake, would you take Honey back and keep Emily company? I'm afraid I don't have the strength to ride, and since I borrowed Honey from the Hereford home, she must be returned," Briana asked quietly. At Jake's nod, she turned, looped her arm through Lord Edwards's, and walked up the path without a backward glance.

The rustle of the wind shook a few leaves free from the tree above. Without moving, he simply dusted them off his shoulders and let out a puff of smoke. So, she now had two rich men she was stringing along. He would be able to use her rash behavior of climbing up the tree as blackmail for sure to make others lose respect for her, but it would be nothing to sharing information about how the Duke of Hereford held her lovingly and she blushing and inching her face toward his as if asking for a kiss out in public. And all this was witnessed by Lord Edwards who is courting her as well? If this information didn't ruin these families, what will? All he would have to do is use this to his advantage and get the money that was stolen from him by that lousy drunk of a father she had.

There was a time when her father helped him win more money than he thought possible, mainly because he was so bad at gambling, which left Gutterson with the ability to win against others he usually lost to. It never seemed to matter how much Valmont lost at gambling since he had enough money to stay afloat, which made him the perfect person to go into business with. Gutterson snickered as he thought about the past. He knew once he gained more money, he would be able to have the same amount of prestige as those of the titled gentlemen and women of the *ton* and would never be looked down on again.

Gutterson watched as Lord Edwards escorted Briana away. And he looked on as Cameron clenched his fists tighter as he fought for control of his body. Oh yes, the Duke of Hereford was definitely more attached to the Valmont girl than he let on. "It will all come to light soon enough, and with her father out of the picture, I will be able to get even more money than I dreamed!" He tossed his cigarette down and stepped on it. He took joy in imagining it was the face of the Valmonts as all their dreams and future happiness were squashed as his was years ago. Licking the sides of his lips and grinning menacingly to himself, he set off in the opposite direction to ponder his next move.

CHAPTER 11

Dorian Gutterson was a man who came from new money. His father was a stern and angry owner of a textile mill who always resented being looked down upon for making his money instead of inheriting it. His mother was the daughter of a vicar from the countryside of Ipswich. She was a silly, absent-minded, genteel woman who seemingly wanted nothing more out of life than to accumulate ornate things that one could only describe as gaudy to the members of high society. Much to her husband's chagrin, she'd be so attracted to these objects that she'd often purchase the same objects multiple times having forgotten her previous purchases, thus leading guests to find such things as gold-plated and jewel encrusted vases in the washroom and randomly placed outside in the garden. His mother even put some of her objects in the kitchen due to lack of space. He'd grown up as their only child, ignored by his parents and angry with how his father was treated as lesser than due to his desire for a better life.

Gutterson did not miss how members of high society, those of old money, laughed at his parents for their ridiculous and uncouth behavior. Despite their fortune, his parents did not behave like those who were raised with a fortune. They did not place small amounts of food on their plates at a time, entertain many guests, have excellent table manners, and were not able to discuss multiple topics of conversation.

When Gutterson was nine and twenty, his father lost the mill due to a large fire that could not be controlled. Seeing his life of comfort ending, his father arranged a marriage between Dorian and Miss Petunia Simpton, who also belonged to a family of new money after establishing themselves in the steam engine industry. Discouraged that his future fortune was gone with the last bit of ash, he agreed to the marriage and, after courting Miss Simpton for a matter of four months, was able to live a life among the *ton* simply off her money.

Petunia was a quiet and sickly woman who never cared much for marriage. All she ever wanted out of life was to make her parents happy, since she felt she'd always been a burden to them with her weak constitution. She would spend most days indoors sewing or at the church praying for a healthier life. Gutterson, who never was much of a religious man, found her frequent trips and prayers useless, but encouraged her to go so that he could enjoy the time to frequent the gentleman's club to socialize and invest in various underhanded business ventures.

Gutterson and Petunia lived out the first month of their marriage in this manner, separated most of the day and only coming together at night. Petunia knew everyone expected her to be with child as quickly as possible to continue the work her father had begun. Making sure to limit her daily activities to maintain her strength so she may fulfill her wifely duties, she was happy to discover herself with child by month's end. Shortly thereafter, Petunia and Dorian began sleeping separately in order to prevent any discomfort to her during her pregnancy. Neither of them seemed to mind being separated. Once Petunia gave birth to a lovely girl, whom they named Abigail, the two settled into a comfortable existence without spending much time together except for the weekly dinners they would host with family. While Petunia made sure to care for Abigail as best she could, her sickly condition continued to worsen over the years, leading to the hiring of a governess to raise and teach Abigail. Gutterson made sure to spend some time with his daughter daily, but since she was not the son he'd hoped for, he spent most of his time out of the house enjoying the wealth he'd now secured and all the new acquaintances he'd begun making of the entitled class.

By the time Abigail made her debut to society at the age of fifteen, Gutterson had spent most of the family fortune to pay off his gambling debts. Feeling the sense of urgency and the gripping fear of losing his position with the titled gentry, he made it his mission to marry his daughter off to the first wealthy man he could find. He spent time and money to provide his daughter with the best dresses and accessories, hoping she would catch the eye of many. When weeks into the season Abigail began being courted by an earl, Gutterson thanked the heavens above for his luck.

Petunia helped her daughter plan a beautiful wedding and Gutterson more than happily fulfilled his fatherly duties of walking Abigail down the aisle and preparing a fitting dowry, despite their finances. Knowing that he could rely on his daughter for financial support helped set Dorian's mind at ease. He soon returned to business ventures he would gamble on in the hopes of increasing his wealth only to see his fortune dwindle away with every loss. When Petunia fell sick with tuberculosis and passed away, Gutterson's gambling debts had risen to the point where the fortune he'd gained access to from his marriage was gone.

Turning to his daughter and her husband for support, Gutterson began asking for assistance until he was able to win back his losses and rebuild his fortune. Unable to see her father hurting and falling to gambling out of a sense of depression from losing his wife, Abigail convinced her husband to provide her father with an allowance for a time. It was during this time that Gutterson made the acquaintance of Lord William Valmont, who would frequent the same clubs and engage in heavy drinking to pass the time. Dorian spent no time at all in forming a friendship that could be turned into a partnership for one of his business schemes. Using Valmont would be easy and would help him establish himself for life among the elite.

After six months of supporting her father and watching him lose all the money he was given only to ask for more, Abigail disowned Gutterson and cut off all ties with him. In six months, Gutterson's life was completely gone. He spent the next fortnight meeting Lord Valmont for drinks late into the night, encouraging him to give into his desires of imbibing to forget about the obligations he felt he had to carry. Valmont would speak about the wonderful feeling of brandy as it burned his throat and drowned out the nagging voice of his wife always worrying about his looks, the confused look in his daughter's eyes when he didn't live up to her expectations of a great father like His Grace, the Duke of Hereford. It was obvious that Valmont was a man with demons that played on his insecurities. With the desperation of a stray dog tearing at scraps, Gutterson sunk his teeth into Valmont.

With daily emphasis on a better life for both of them, he convinced Valmont to invest a large sum of money on converting an abandoned stable house just outside of London's East End into an apothecary shop. He would be the brains to run the business venture specializing in exotic herbs and remedies from the Far East to serve as a cover for the opium den he was planning on setting up. All he needed was Valmont's money to make it all come to fruition, but then Valmont grew a conscience to be a better man to his family and pulled out of the venture all together. Gutterson was left with the little money he was able to gain from gambling and a solitary desire for revenge. He would make Valmont cower to him, stripped of his money and family name, just like he'd left Gutterson. Using Briana and her gentlemen seemed like a perfect way to bring the Valmont family to destruction.

CHAPTER 12

Cameron awoke late the next afternoon with a splitting headache. He had spent most of the night at White's trying to forget the events of the day before, especially the protective feeling he had towards Briana. He'd stumbled back to his bachelor lodgings on Brook Street well past midnight. As much as he told himself he'd feel just as protective if it were Emily in Briana's place, he knew it was a lie. The truth was that Briana was stirring a whirlwind of emotions within him that he did not know how to handle. He was plagued all night with images of her falling out of the tree as well as the surprise in her eyes when he'd held her. The feel of her body in his arms radiating heat all the way down to his loins made any chance of a good night's sleep impossible. Damn, how he wanted her. He knew that he wanted her more than any other woman he'd known, but he also knew that she wanted a nice and proper gentleman as a husband and that would not be him. He shook his head as if that would banish his thoughts, but alas to no avail.

He was sitting slouched in his favorite chair located next to the fireplace in his study. He'd loosened his necktie, removed his jacket and vest, had undone most of the buttons on his shirt so his chest was left exposed, and had apparently kicked off his shoes throughout the night. It was this vision that greeted

Jake as he walked in the door. "Man, you reek of whiskey. And I don't think you can rub your temples enough to erase whatever is on your mind." Jake clapped his brother's shoulder and then proceeded to sit in the dark red velvet chair opposite him. When Cameron's response was nothing more than a grunt, Jake chuckled. "Tell me, are you upset about Briana climbing the tree or her pledging her commitment to marrying Lord Edwards?"

"She did no such thing and well you know it." Cameron sat up and growled at his brother. "She merely stated that she intends to get married. She did not at any point accept a marriage proposal from that dullard. Now, if you have nothing else to say, leave me to nurse this headache in peace." Cameron sat back against his own dark red velvet chair and draped his right arm over his eyes.

"Well, I think she is all but ready to accept a marriage proposal from 'that dullard' as you call him. That is unless someone better proposes marriage to her first. I wonder if there is such a person. She's a good girl. Maybe I could be that man," Jake said with a knowing grin on his face. Cameron sent him a dark scowl. "Or, maybe not..." Jake chuckled.

Cameron stood up and walked to the fireplace, resting an arm over it as he continued to rub his head with the other. "I did come with a message from Mother, as much as I hate to break up this brotherly moment. She wanted me to tell you that we are all attending the opera tonight. She asked that you escort Briana while I escort Emily. Do clean yourself up ahead of time. We wouldn't want Briana and her mother to think you've fallen into a barrel of whiskey." Jake once again clapped his brother on the back and walked towards the door. "I'm interested to see what adventures are in store tonight. It's never a dull moment when Brie is around. See you tonight, Cam."

Cameron could not fathom attending an opera with loud singing and having to engage in small talk with others at the current moment. He knew he couldn't turn down his mother, and despite his attempts to forget his feelings, he wanted to see Briana again. He knew his time was limited now that Lord Edwards was courting her, but he wanted to talk to her. He felt like he had not gotten the chance to check on her well-being for the last ten years and wanted to make up for that as best he could. It was after all, the kind and gentlemanly thing to do. Friends often check on each other, do they not? And with that, he yelled for his valet to begin readying him for the night's outing.

Briana was jolted from her concentration by a knock at the door. She had been deliberating her actions from the day before and replaying the feel of Cameron's arms since she awoke that morning. She had tossed and turned all night thinking about how coldly he dismissed her in front of Lord Edwards, but yet looked at her in such a way that made her head spin. Since she found herself restless, she had awoken early that morning and did what she always did when anxious: pace back in forth repeatedly across the length of her bedroom, write a pros and cons list on the stationary she kept in the writing desk across the room, written a few more scenes in the romance novel she was working on, and then picked up her thread and needle to sew anything she could get her hands on. It was now at the sewing part of her routine that she determined that as much as she wanted Cameron, Lord Edwards was the better choice of the two since she could be secure in his feelings for her. Hearing a knock at the door, Briana called in the direction of the door for the person to enter.

Lady Darby entered followed by Cathy who held a rectangular velvet box in her hands. Briana continued mending the mint green silk stockings she had worn a few months ago in order to reuse them later in the week. She thanked God above that the rip on the stocking was on the underside of her foot and out of plain sight. Seeing her mother, Briana set the mending aside and gestured to the space next to her on the window seat. Her mother sat down and immediately took Briana's face in her hands, turning it this way and that way.

"My dear, you look exhausted! Did you not sleep well? Why do you have such dark circles under your eyes? This will not do. We are to attend the opera tonight with His Grace and his family. What will they think? Cathy, get some rose water and cloth for me please." Releasing Briana's face, she watched as Cathy bobbed her curtsy. The maid was never one to be at a loss for words, but since she said nothing now and simply stared at Briana, it had been obvious that last night's lack of sleep had really taken its toll on her appearance. Cathy caught herself as soon as Briana gently smiled. She left the room immediately in search for all the rose water she could find to help the poor mistress.

"I'm sorry to have concerned you, Mother. I'm afraid I was plagued with nightmares all night and never quite fell into deep sleep. But, you look like you wanted to discuss something. I saw Cathy carrying a velvet box as well. Is everything alright? Is that a set of jewelry you would like me to sell or to hide away for safekeeping?" Briana asked, concern coating her voice. She had been keeping track of the finances and everything was manageable for now. Her mother shouldn't have to sell any jewelry for the moment.

"No dear, there is nothing for you to sell. In fact, I have paid to borrow what is in the box from a jewelry merchant in town a few days back. He was elated to know that they would be worn by the season's Incomparable at the opera tonight. Darling, open it." Violet handed her the box and smiled broadly at the sudden intake of breath that came from Briana. "These are Caribbean Emeralds which are rarely seen outside of the islands. There will be so many of the *ton* present at the opera tonight that we must keep up appearances, and what says we are more than financially secure than wearing rare emeralds? Not to mention, walking in on the arm of the Duke of Hereford will further erase any possible doubts." Briana's mother was grinning more than she had the night of the masquerade ball.

"Mother, these are gorgeous! They are too much though for someone like me, no? I don't think I can do them justice. The fact that they are borrowed makes me all the more nervous that something may happen to them. I can't wear these, Mother," Briana said as she tried to pass the box back to her mother.

"Absolute poppycock! You are the season's Incomparable and you will wear these emeralds and continue to stand out so that Lord Edwards, who I have been told has confirmed his attendance for tonight, will propose marriage sooner rather than later." She took her daughter's chin in her hand gently. "You are a wonderful woman, and you will look wonderful wearing these emeralds. End of discussion, my darling."

As Briana opened her mouth to reply, Cathy opened the door and carried a tray with a jug full of rose water and various strips of cloth. "I didn't know how much to bring for the poor thing, but with eyes like that, I thought to myself she may need multiple sessions of letting the rose water-soaked cloths lay on her eyes. Here you go, love," Cathy said as she lay the tray down on a nearby table. "Now, you don't have much time to waste. You go ahead and lie down. I'll be here to help you replace the cloths until I see your eyes and skin restored to their normal glow. Then, we will set out to ready you for the opera tonight." Briana opened her mouth once again in protest, but was quickly bustled to the bed and had two strips of cloths on her eyes before she could say anything. The cool water worked quickly to relax her, and before she knew it, she had fallen asleep.

"Don't you worry. I will wake her up and have her ready in complete splendor. Emeralds included," Cathy said as she smiled and winked conspiratorially to Lady Darby who in turn nodded her thanks and left the room to begin her beauty regimen.

In the carriage, Emily and Briana sat arm in arm and discussed what they knew about tonight's soprano. Briana had taken them all by surprise when they had seen not only her gown for the evening but also the Caribbean Emeralds. Any doubts she had earlier about not doing them justice vanished the minute she heard Cameron's breath catch before he held out his arm, saying that she looked just as stunning as she did the night of the masquerade ball. He'd smiled down at her with the same fiery look in his eyes as that night after their kiss. She glanced over at him to see if he could possibly know her thoughts, but he was quietly looking out of the window seemingly oblivious to her thoughts and desires.

They arrived at the opera house and waited in the carriage line before stepping down at the front steps. Jake stepped down first, followed by Cameron, who turned and helped both Emily and Briana out of the carriage. He once again presented the crook of his elbow and waited as Briana gently placed her hand into it. He readjusted her hand by looping it further through his arm, and with a satisfied smile, led the party inside the opera house.

As they entered their box located stage right, Briana quietly followed behind Emily to sit in the first row of four chairs. They were followed by their mothers sitting at the end of their row and by Cameron and Jake, who sat in the remaining two seats in the second row of chairs. Briana was aware of all the stares and glances she received as she walked in with the Duke of Hereford. One of the main social advantages to owning your own opera box was that everyone could take note of your arrival, while in turn you could take note of everyone's clothing, jewelry, and tawdry activities from up above. Briana had never been to the opera before, since she was so young when leaving London. Now, she simply had to continue to play the part of complete elegance. Her dress was a deep shade of crimson and had a fit that was tighter than most in the bodice, not because Briana wanted to draw attention to her bosom but because the dress was one she hadn't worn in years. Thankfully, it was not so low cut that would be deemed scandalous by the *ton*. The lower cut of the bosom drew one's attention to the emeralds that lay delicately draped around her neck. She fingered them nervously as she caught the attention of the gentleman in the neighboring box.

"Quit fidgeting. You look very fetching tonight, darling."

Briana could feel the hot breath on the back of her neck before the voice even started. The soft purr in Cameron's voice sent shivers down her spine. "Not at all like the reckless girl from yesterday with leaves in her hair. An image I am still recovering from, might I add. Why don't we try to keep ourselves planted firmly on the ground tonight, shall we?" Cameron said with a chuckle. Briana turned around to scowl at him, but that was a mistake. His face was close enough that she could see the laughter in his eyes and the indentation of his dimples as his smile broadened. He was closer than she expected and felt her breath catch. To onlookers, the distance between them would look innocent enough, as if he were explaining what to expect of the upcoming opera. To Briana though, he may as well have been sitting in the same chair as her, taking in the same breath. She locked eyes with him and cooly nodded her head in his direction before turning around once again and glancing over at Emily who had been using her opera glasses to scan the persons in attendance.

Leaning over slightly, Briana asked her companion, "What exactly, or should I say who exactly, are you looking for?" When Emily simply gave a slight lift of the shoulders, Briana hmphed. She picked up her own opera glasses, ones that were given to her as a gift from an older woman she cared for five years ago. The golden glasses adorned with diamonds fit perfectly in her small hands and completed the look of elegant refinement needed for such an occasion. The lights flickered once, twice, then went dark. With the opera house in the dark, the curtains were raised and the stage opened up to a beautiful pastoral scene with the night's soprano sitting on a stone bench. She wore a loose fitting, white gown that when paired with her red hair made her look rather angelic. As she began to sing, the opera house quieted as all were enraptured by the beautiful songstress who sang of a childhood love she wished would return. "Isn't she lovely?" Emily whispered. Jake was the first one to answer in the affirmative, followed by Briana and her mother. Briana leaned forward captivated by the emotions the music swayed within her. The story was not unlike her own, since it followed two lovers once separated and now reunited to either be joined in love or continue on their separate paths. What would the lovers choose? Would they choose different than she? The male protagonist was as haughty and seductive as Cameron, which meant that Briana was constantly aware when Cameron leaned forward, and especially aware when his breath would catch when the lovers were drawn together in a passionate kiss. Was he reliving the kiss they shared as well?

CHAPTER 13

When the lights of the opera house came back up, Briana needed an intermission more from Cameron's close proximity than she did from the opera. Glancing over at Emily, Briana was surprised to see her friend staring at the stage with a tear running down her face. Reaching out and taking Emily's hand in hers, Briana asked, "Why Emily, whatever is the matter? Do you not like the opera?" She looked at her friend's face with clear concern.

"It's beautiful. I'm sorry, I seem to be overcome with the emotion of two people finding one another again. It's such a beautiful story and I hope the lovers can overcome their hardships and be together. I'm fine, really. I was just moved," Emily said, wiping the tear from her face with a handkerchief she kept tucked in her reticule. "Come, shall we go the ladies room and freshen ourselves up?" Emily asked, tucking the handkerchief back into her reticule. Briana gave a smile and stood up.

Cameron and Jake had already been on their feet since their mother and Lady Darby had stood up immediately when the lights came on to greet a dear friend in the passageway just outside of their box. Cameron offered Briana his arm and asked if she would like him to fetch her a refreshment while she was in the ladies room. "Yes, thank you. That would be lovely. Maybe one for Emily as well since she was overcome with emotion during the opera?" Briana asked, smiling up at Cameron. He reassured her that it would be his pleasure and led the foursome in the direction of the ladies room. Leaving the ladies to their business, Jake and Cameron went to fetch the refreshments and greet friends and acquaintances along the way.

Once they had made their way back to the spot where they left Briana and Emily, Cameron smiled as he was able to get a full view of Briana's backside. The bodice hugged her perfectly and accentuated her slender shoulders and tiny waist. He remembered the feel of her in his arms the day before and knew under that skirt lay perfectly shaped hips that gave way to a nice round bottom. Adjusting his vest, Cameron took three deep breaths. He really needed to get himself together before he took her right there in front of everyone. Jake glanced over at his brother. "You look rather 'overcome with emotions' yourself, Cam. You sure you don't need some time in the men's room, you know to splash some water on your face or what not?" When he received the squinted side-eye look from his brother, Jake chuckled. "I'm simply saying these operas can be a bit stifling with all the people and the body heat they radiate." With a wink at his brother, Jake turned back around before saying over shoulder, "Since you're no longer flushed, let's join the ladies." Cameron simply shook his head at his brother's audacity and followed behind letting Jake weave their way through the crowd and make any small talk necessary along the way.

As they reached Briana and Emily, Cameron was unhappy to see Lord Edwards among the gathered. Thankfully, he was not encompassing all of Briana's attention as she was able to converse with him as well as Lord Burfel, Lord Blackstone, and Lady Turner equally. Since the space at Briana's right was already taken by Lord Edwards, Cameron expertly placed himself to her left and touched her elbow in order to gain her attention. As she turned her brilliant smile on him, Cameron almost forgot the glass of champagne in his hand. Clearing his throat, he handed her the glass and let his fingers touch hers for a second as she reached to take the glass, keeping his eyes locked on hers the entire time. He heard Lord Burfel turn a question to him about his estate in Surrey, but Cameron had no desire to answer at the moment. This brought a confused look to Lord Burfel's face who began playing with the monocle he always carried on his person. It was not until Briana gave him a fixed look with a subtle smile that he dropped her gaze and answered Lord Burfel. Jake made a comment about how the scenery in one of the pastoral scenes reminded him of their family home in Surrey, which inspired them to talk about the necessity of visits to the countryside.

"It's good for the mind and soul," said Lady Turner.

"As well as for one's health," said Lord Blackstone, remembering his late wife. He looked over to Lord Edwards who he knew would be thinking of his late mother and their last trip to the countryside in the hopes of reviving her spirits.

"It is also good for running away from prying eyes, wouldn't you say, Briana dear?" asked a low voice that sounded disgustingly dripping in a sugary coating. It was the voice that made every single hair on the back of Briana's neck stand on edge. She knew her father was on some level of friendship with this man before he left and for that she decided to remain cordial despite her discomfort.

"Well, Mr. Gutterson, I do not know why you would ask me. But I believe some people may like the quietness of the countryside to the watchful eyes of the *ton*. In fact, Lady Turner, hasn't Lady Phillips left London recently after saying that she had had enough of the London Season?" Briana asked, expertly steering the conversation to safer topics.

Lady Turner nodded in response and began to answer before being cut off by Mr. Gutterson. "Well, it seems that you don't mind having the eyes of all the *ton* on you, Lady Valmont. You are doing a splendid job in holding your title of the season's Incomparable. Your father would be proud of the elegant woman you've become," Mr. Gutterson said again in a honeyed tone that squeaked every now and then as if in irritation. He lowered his eyes to the Caribbean Emeralds that hung elegantly from Briana's slender neck. He continued to lower his gaze over her ample bosom that was emphasized by the slightly lower cut and the emeralds. With his eyes lingering, Mr. Gutterson smiled at her obvious discomfort before returning a placid look on his face and saying in a dark tone, "Despite the elegance you carry, how do you think your father would feel about so much of you being on display? The emeralds are unique and I assume fetch a pretty fortune. Would your father approve of such lavish behavior? How could you afford such a necklace without your father near, I wonder? I simply ask, my dear, to serve as a father figure to you in his absence and have you think a bit more about your behavior for his sake," Mr. Gutterson said with a slight bow in her direction.

Cameron could feel every muscle in his own body grow taut, but it did not compare to the lioness standing beside him. Although she stood ram-rod straight and the tips of her ears were beginning to turn red, she gave Mr. Gutterson a curt smile at his bow. "I thank you for your concern, Mr. Gutterson, though I find it misplaced. I am sorry that you have mistaken any of our encounters or my conduct as lavish or wanton, but I assure you that I am neither of those things," Briana said as she took a drink from her champagne hoping to calm her nerves. She felt both Lord Edwards and Cameron move in closer to her on both sides, as if creating a protective shield around her. She could feel the eyes of everyone around her since their conversation had reached the ears of others nearby with every sentence from Mr. Gutterson getting louder and louder. Did he want to create a scene?

"I think you've said enough, Gutterson. I don't think anyone will think you rude if you excuse yourself now," Cameron said in a rough tone. Briana knew he was keeping his anger in check for her and she was touched by his coming to her defense. She made the mistake of looking over at Lord Edwards who seemed to be avoiding her gaze. Gutterson licked his lips and smiled again in her direction. It was a smile that did not reach his eyes, leaving them to turn a stormy and cold shade of gray. Nervously, Briana took another, longer swallow of her champagne. She had just gotten the champagne glass but it was now more than half empty.

"I was simply speaking as a father in the place of an old friend. I know I would have some serious words with my daughter had she dressed and behaved in such a manner for a simple title. Of course, my precious Abby would never dream of gaining admirers in such a manner. She's such a good girl to her dear Papa. I only wished the same for dear Briana here. My dear Lady Worthington, tell me don't you think your friend's dress is not quite as fashionable and refined as your own?" Gutterson said as he turned to Emily, who simply stared back with wide eyes in unabashed shock. She was saved of answering by her brother Jake who, by placing a hand on her arm and giving a slight shake of his head, silenced her.

"Mr. Gutterson, I think you may not have had the same opportunity to look upon the beauties this London Season has to offer us younger gentleman. It seems you are simply stuck in the past ways, old chap," Jake said with the ability of speaking in a genial and yet final manner of tone. Lord Edwards and Lord Blackstone nodded their heads in agreement while Cameron, Emily, Lady Turner, all remained rather frozen in their spot trying to figure out how this terribly uncomfortable scene would finish. Briana met Cameron's eyes and seeing the disgust and anger in them, took a longer swig of the champagne.

Lord Burfel cleaned his monocle and said, "The past is but a door that leads to the future."

Ignoring Lord Burfel completely, Gutterson maintained his attention on Jake and replied, "Maybe so lad, but I felt it must be said. Also, Briana dear, you may want to slow down on the champagne. I think we all know that your father's drinking habits were not a secret, and you don't want people saying that the apple doesn't fall too far from the tree, now do you, dear?" Mr. Gutterson said as he reached over and gave two quick pats on Briana's gloved hand before he found his hand arrested mid-air by Cameron.

Pulling his hand back and seeing the redness reach Briana's face, Gutterson smiled as he heard the whispers from others around him commenting on the scene and how the Valmonts always dress in such unnecessary excess. He knew those around them were watching Briana's embarrassment rise and were taking pleasure in it, just like he was. He knew he had planted the seed of doubt in the heads of many tonight and soon she would feel as isolated and desperate as he had. "Well, take care dear. Remember your self-worth. Even if your father is away on holiday with his nephew, you are still his daughter." Gutterson gave her a wicked smile, and with a bow to all present, simply faded into the crowd to leave Briana listening to the whispers and avoiding the scrutiny from all present.

The lights flickered to alert the audience that intermission had come to an end, and with that, everyone gave one final glance in Briana's direction (some were sympathetic like Lord Blackstone and Lady Turner, while others were calculating and full of malice like most of the younger ladies present). Briana remained rooted to her spot, unable to move from the myriad of emotions she was feeling. She was angry and embarrassed, feeling both the cold shiver of shock radiating through her body as well as the internal fire of rage that had ignited deep in her core. She felt hot and dizzy. The room seemed to be getting smaller with every blink of her eyelashes and she found she could no longer breathe easily on her own. Her legs felt weak and she immediately reached for Cameron's arm to steady herself.

"Lady Valmont, you look unwell. Come let's step outside and get some air. You've had a shock." Lord Edwards moved to take Briana's free arm and steady her, but she unconsciously dug herself deeper into Cameron's side. Michael met Cameron's steady gaze. "All she needs is some time to get her breath, Hereford. If she leaves now, people are going to talk."

"People are already talking, Edwards." Cameron said curtly, dropping the honorifics as Lord Edwards had done.

"She needs to go home in order to steel herself for whatever battles she will have to face tomorrow."

"Please, I need to get out of here," Briana said to nobody in particular but looked up at Cameron with tears in her eyes.

"Fine. Then I will take her home. Come, my dear." Lord Edwards said as he held Briana's hand to help her steady herself. Once she was steady, he pulled her gently on her arm so her body was touching his side. He then let go of her hand and placed an arm around her waist in order to guide her out toward the line of carriages waiting outside. Briana looked over nervously at Cameron.

Feeling like his most valuable possession was about to be lost to him forever, Cameron stepped forward and pulled her toward him so she stood face to face with him. He expertly moved her to his side and placed a protective arm around her while never releasing her hand. "Since she came with me in my carriage, I fear it is my duty to see the lady home. Jake, please let Lady Darby know that Briana had a headache and that I agreed to send her home in my carriage. I will send another carriage for you to escort Mother, Emily, and Lady Darby home." At Jake's quick nod and a reassuring smile for Emily, Cameron proceeded to the doors with Briana on his arm still shaking and with skin warm to the touch. She looked up at him with eyes that conveyed her gratefulness and he felt like in that instant he could win a war simply for that look again. Together they made their way to the awaiting carriage, moving with the ease of one body.

Holding her hand, Cameron was relieved to see she was no longer shaking although her body continued to radiate heat. The look on her face was no longer that of shock but was now replaced with anger. He squeezed her hand reassuringly and helped lift her up into the carriage. Giving the driver directions to Warwick Street, he followed in behind her with one fluid movement, never letting go over her hand. Briana had seated herself toward the middle of the seat, expecting Cameron to take the seat across from her, but when he sat down next to her, she was too shocked to move. His tall frame was pressed into the corner of the carriage and his strong thigh rested perfectly against Briana's. Rapping on the roof of the carriage, Cameron let the driver know that they were both in safely and ready to drive on. Giving Briana's hand a tight squeeze to get her attention, he didn't have to ask how she was to know her feelings and said, "I am sorry for not getting you out of such a situation sooner."

Briana could see the anger and guilt in Cameron's eyes. She lifted her gloved hand from his and caressed his cheek with her knuckles. "It was not your fault. I should not have baited him so. I couldn't help but engage. The things he said about my father." Try as she might, Briana could not hold back the tears that had threatened to spill down her face for the better half of her conversation with Mr. Gutterson. Without a care for her silk gloves, Briana placed both hands over her eyes and began to sob. Cameron gathered both her hands in his and removed her gloves, placing them in his jacket pocket. He gave her his handkerchief to use instead. Overcome with emotion, Briana did not even register the exchange but continued to weep and wipe at her tears.

Cameron gathered Briana's sobbing form into his arms and let her cry into his chest. He stroked her back and made "shushing" sounds in an attempt to soothe her. The steady beat of his heart, the steady vibrations of the timbre in his throat, and the warmth of his arms served to calm her enough to take gulping breaths of air. "That's it, love. I'm right here. You're okay," Cameron said softly while tightening his embrace, melding their upper bodies together until there was little to no space between them. He held her like this for another few minutes until the tears had stopped and her breathing had returned to normal. Briana pushed against his chest slightly with her hands to be able to get a better look at Cameron. "I'm alright now, thank you. I'm sorry you had to leave the opera early on my account. You and your family may have also been indirectly exposed to rumors and scandals now because of me, so maybe it is best if you all keep your distance from us for the time being," Briana said as she pulled herself further out of his arms and settled herself back in her seat.

Cameron raked a hand through his dark locks and gave Briana a look that seemed to convey thoughts of disbelief. Shaking his head so that one lock fell onto his forehead, he stated, "You are not thinking clearly. Why on earth would I, or my family for that matter, keep our distance from you when you have only just come back to us? As for any scandal you think you may have brought on us, I'm sure we can handle it. This situation gives me even more reason to extend my stay in London." Taking her chin between his thumb and the knuckle of his index finger, he turned her face toward him and said with authority, "I am the Duke of Hereford, and though you may not think so, my title holds more weight than you may realize. I have been mulling over staying in town for another fortnight or so and this confirms it."

She didn't want to trust him and let him know just how much she loved and needed him. He knew too much about her past already from what she'd accidentally told him earlier of her father's debts. She could try and avoid him like she'd done years before and recently, but now he knew her mind and would go after her. Or would he? Did she want him to chase her if she were to accept another man? She'd thought if she could keep him at bay, she would be free of him. Now, as she looked into Cameron's eyes, she sat transfixed, unable to even contemplate departure.

"You look confused? I thought you would be happy to hear about my new plans to remain in London for another fortnight or so." Cameron touched Briana's arm and winced as she jerked it away.

"I... I am happy you want to stay here with your family and..."

"With you!" Cameron interrupted. He seized her hand and gripped it tightly rendering her incapable of pulling away. She looked up into his deep brown eyes, the ones that had begun to haunt her dreams with their depth and shrewdness. How could she continue lying to this man?

"Cameron, you don't really know me. You don't have any idea where I've been these last ten years or what I've had to do to keep my family together. You don't even know what I'm truly capable of. I'm not the woman you think I am." Briana looked down to hide the tears she felt stinging her eyes. She couldn't cry again in front of this man. She couldn't cry about her past and about the horrible deeds her father did to her and her mother. She was stronger now, right?

"I think I see who you are better than you do." As if to better make his point, Cameron grabbed Briana from behind the neck and kissed her passionately. His tongue urged her lips apart to allow its entry. The distance between their bodies no longer existed. Briana's train of thought vanished into the fuzziness of delight. Her vision began to blur and despite her attempts to remain logical, she knew she was his.

Breaking apart from the kiss in a last attempt at trying to keep him away, Briana whispered, "I don't want to see your name ruined. I was taken off guard tonight, but I can handle Mr. Gutterson on my own in the future. You all don't need to protect me."

"There you go trying to push us away again. Trying to push *me* away. I told you, there will not be a line drawn between us tonight." As if to make his point, Cameron grabbed Briana by the shoulders and crushed his lips to hers. He was angry and demanding, his lips seducing her body and mind to yield to him. His hands left her shoulders and came up her neck just as he titled his head to deepen the kiss. His tongue traced her bottom lip encouraging it to open so his tongue could enter and join hers in the wicked dance it so desired. Briana's hands came to rest on his chest for a second before they balled into fist on his vest as she pulled him closer to her. They pressed closer in a heat of passion, with a need to become one with each other. Later, they would think about the dictates of society. Later, she would put up her guard once more. Later, he would begin to analyze again.

Lost in each other's arms, the carriage was burning like a freshly stoked fire. Cameron removed his jacket, never once breaking their kiss. His hands traced her cheeks, her neck, and her collarbone. His lips soon followed the same path. Briana's eyes remained closed as she let out a soft moan of pleasure as his lips passed over each new area of her body. She didn't know what was happening, and even though part of her brain knew they should stop she couldn't bring herself to say the word. Cameron's lips traveled lower, passing by the emeralds which seemed to be a nuisance now, and resting on the tops of her breast. "This dress is cut perfectly for occasions like tonight, wouldn't you agree, love?" Cameron said in a husky town. Briana simply moaned in response. "You have no idea how much I've wanted you." His hand moved up her side until he was massaging her breasts through her dress. His other hand came around to lift her up and onto his lap. Briana's eyes grew wide at the sensations coursing through her body. She was aware of a deep need building within her as she met Cameron's eyes once more.

"Cameron?" Briana whispered. She wasn't quite sure what she wanted to ask him. All she knew was that she was feeling things for the first time and didn't know what to expect. Cameron kissed her again, just as passionately as before, but there was no anger behind this kiss. There was simply a desire that drove them to possess as much of each other as they could. Cameron's hand, moved to her knee and then traveled down her leg until his fingers dipped under her skirts. She could feel his hand trace the length of her inner calf, the back of her knee, and then her inner thigh. She was on fire and wanted more. Of what exactly she didn't know, but she ached for his touch.

His fingers found her mound of curls and played with her until she could feel a wetness in between her thighs. Before Briana could register what she was feeling, his fingers slid into her and she screamed his name. He kissed her hard and thoroughly, exploring her mouth as another finger slid in to join the other. She felt full and brought her hips to match the rhythm he set as he played with her. She was going to explode. Everything in her felt like it was going to rip apart.

"Cameron! Oh my God! What are you doing to me? I want… I need… Oh, God!" Briana screamed out yet again through gritted teeth. She was trying to be quiet given their location, but really didn't know how much more she could control herself. Cameron laughed huskily and urged her on to complete her release. He'd take care of himself later. Briana shut her eyes tighter as a jolt of pain shot through her. Cameron slowed the rhythm of his fingers, but didn't stop. Once she opened her eyes and her hips began moving faster he picked up the pace again until Briana was driven to oblivion and collapsed against him with complete release.

Cameron removed his fingers and using the abandoned handkerchief from earlier wiped his hand before placing his arms once again strongly around Briana. Briana in turn brought her arms around his neck wanting the closeness they had moments ago. "I can't believe we just did that," Briana whispered as she buried her face into the side of his neck, suddenly very shy. His hand came and tucked the stray curls that had fallen out of place behind her ear. He kissed her softly on the cheek and then on the lips.

"You have no idea how incredibly enchanting you are. You've bewitched me since I saw you at the masquerade ball, my emerald of the night. I want you more than I've wanted anyone before. Say you'll be mine? No lines between us, remember?" Cameron said as his fingertips caressed the side of her face.

Briana was elated. All these years of loving him and now he was saying that he wanted her just as much. She wasn't sure if he loved her, but there was passion there and he did care for her. She would be able to live safely and comfortably with him and her mother would be taken care of. He also had a title and respectability to protect her from any slanderous allegations other may throw her way in the future. She nodded her head vigorously.

"That means you no longer have any feelings for that dullard, Edwards?" Cameron said teasingly. "I'm not willing to share what's mine, you see."

"Of course not! I never had any feelings more than companionship. Nothing like what I feel when I'm with you. I will let him know soon," Briana replied as the carriage came to a stop in front of her home. Briana kissed Cameron's cheek and moved to lift her arms from around his neck in order to break the embrace.

"No, wait. Let me stay like this. Just for a bit longer," Cameron said as he tightened his arms a bit around her waist. He smelled her hair that always smelled faintly of roses and vanilla. He had not expected the night to end this way, but he was sure that he needed Briana more than any woman he had ever met. She fit so well in his arms and understood his mind in ways others never could. She was innocent but lit his body on fire more than any mistress ever had before. He needed to officially end things with Serrafina tonight.

With a sigh, he pulled Briana's arms from around his neck and kissed the inner palms of both hands. "Come, love. Let's get you home. I believe you've had enough excitement for one night." Settling her back on the seat, he straightened his clothes before stepping down from the carriage and extending up a hand to her. Briana followed suit by straightening her rumpled dress as much as she could and righting her hair in much the same way before grasping Cameron's hand and stepping out of the carriage onto Warwick Street.

"Thank you, Your Grace, for escorting me home and for, umm…" Briana said awkwardly not knowing how to finish her sentence. "I mean, thank you for making this night end better than it had begun," she said, smiling up at him brightly.

"It was my pleasure," Cameron said with a self-satisfying smirk and wink. "I'll call upon you tomorrow. Don't give Gutterson another thought and sleep well." Raising her hand, he bowed over it and placed a light kiss upon the knuckles. Briana nodded and walked up the steps to the door before turning around and saying goodnight so she could look at him one more time. Smiling and then shaking her head as in disbelief that he was there, she gave him a wave and entered the house. Although his body was still seeking release from tonight's events, he needed to take care of Serrafina first. Giving directions to the driver, Cameron climbed back into the carriage for what he hoped to be a rather easy conversation with his mistress. He would continue to provide for her until she found a new benefactor of course, but he hoped it wouldn't be long.

CHAPTER 14

The sunlight streamed through the window and fell upon Briana's face. Trying to turn her face away from the light to sleep a little longer, Briana buried herself deeper in the covers. She'd dreamed of Cameron over and over again. She'd dreamt of his hands and his mouth, repeating every word he'd said to her the night before. She touched her fingers to her lips and realized she was smiling and could feel heat rising to her cheeks. He wanted to be with her. He wanted to be with her! No longer concerned with the sunlight, Briana threw off the covers and went to look at herself in the mirror. Surely she looked different today. She felt like a new woman that was more beautiful, elegant, and confident than she had ever been. She would see him again today and she wondered if he'd see this new woman too. Catching sight of the mass of unruly curls in the mirror, Briana set out to ready herself for the day and Cameron's visit. She'd never been this happy. Smiling and humming to herself, Briana began by washing her face and picking out the soft lavender gown to be worn with the new cerulean blue sash she'd bought a couple months ago. Cameron didn't say what time to expect him, but she'd be ready and waiting for him soon nonetheless.

Briana was done with breakfast by nine in the morning and was sitting in the front parlor reading Shakespeare's play, *A Twelfth Night*, to pass the time. Lucy was in the corner of the room working on her stitching when Wallace announced a visitor. Thinking that it was too early for Cameron to visit, Briana assumed the visitor to be either Emily or Emily's mother. Setting aside the play and smoothing out her skirts, Briana sat on the cream colored couch and rang the bell for a new pot of tea to be brought for her guest. Lucy too, put aside her stitching and moved to a chair closer to Briana. As soon as Briana let go of the bellpull, Wallace opened the door and Briana looked up to see Lord Edwards stroll into the room before executing a gentlemanly bow.

"Good morning Lord Edwards, what a lovely surprise!" Briana said as she stood up and gestured for him to have a seat at the chair to her right. He wore a dark blue jacket with a cream colored vest that matched his trousers. He sat his top hat down on the table in front of him as he sat down and crossed one leg over the other. Briana readjusted her skirts once again after sitting and saying, "You have perfect timing with your visit. I've just rung for some tea and biscuits."

"I'm happy to see you were home. I was walking in this direction and thought I would take a chance to visit and see how you were feeling today after last night's events. I know you suffered quite a shock with Mr. Gutterson during intermission," Lord Edwards said with a worried look on his face.

"I'm better now that there is some distance between us. I am lucky to have friends like yourself and those of the Hereford household by my side to help combat any gossip or rumors that may rise. I want to think he meant well as an acquaintance of my father's, but some of his comments and the look in his eyes left me very unsettled," Briana confided as she shuddered at the thought of Mr. Gutterson.

"Yes, the nerve of that man! My mother would have been

appalled that a man would behave in such a manner in front of everyone and create a spectacle. You handled yourself very well, my dear. I'm only sorry that I was unable to escort you home and was only able to check on your well-being this morning," Lord Edwards said, searching her face to make sure she was truly okay. Briana was touched by his obvious concern. "I felt very uneasy about you going home before your mother and leaving instead with the Duke, who was so angry that he was involved in such a display."

"No, I think you've misunderstood him. He was really very caring on the way home and let me give way to the emotions I withheld in front of Mr. Gutterson." Briana's mind was filled with visions from the night before. She recalled how sweet he'd been holding her hand and then holding her in his arms while she cried. He'd rubbed her back and soothed her until she was calm. Then he'd kissed her and turned her world upside down.

"Hmph. I should hope he let you cry. My mother always said that a true measure of a woman was how she did not give into her emotions in public and how she does in private. I would have liked to have been that shoulder for you, but alas I can only hope he was as gentlemanly as I would have been," Lord Edwards said gruffly, looking away from her to hide the envy in his face from Briana.

Although Cameron had been caring and warm while soothing her tears, she wouldn't necessarily classify everything else that happened in the carriage as "gentlemanly." At least, she was sure Lord Edwards would not think so. Briana smiled at the thought. She was feeling her face flush as visions of Cameron's fingers and the feel of his lips on her body raced through her mind. She averted her gaze from Lord Edwards and took a deep breath to calm her racing heart and said, "Of course he was. He was also very attentive... and firm in his saying that the gossip would not ruin our relationship, of course." She couldn't help but add with a sigh, "He was amazing."

Lord Edwards did not like the dazed look that entered Briana's eyes and the soft smile that only treasured memories can bring to one's lips. Briana was falling in love with Cameron and he knew it. He also knew that Cameron still kept a mistress, which would not be fair to Briana. He did not want to hurt her by saying so, especially since she had not shown any indication in pursuing him.

"Was he speaking of the relationship between your families, or the relationship between you? I know you have said you are serious about marriage, but is he?" Lord Edwards could see that he surprised her with his questions, but he had to know if a confession had been made in order to decide his next move. He knew Briana would make a wonderful wife for him and wanted her to know he would treasure her, whereas someone like Cameron may not.

"He was speaking of our families, of course! I... I don't know if he is looking for marriage right now, but he knows he will have to eventually to carry on the family title. Our families are very close and we've become closer as friends since I have returned to London." Briana rambled, unsure of what type of answer she should provide Lord Edwards. It wasn't like Cameron proposed marriage last night. He didn't even propose to officially court her either, but their relationship had taken a drastic turn and she was ready to pursue him. She had to let Lord Edwards know in a gentle manner, right?

Briana was given a chance to gather her words when Cathy bustled in through the open door holding a tray with a fresh pot of tea, a plate of freshly baked muffins with butter and jam on the side, and a plate of biscuits. She placed them down on the table that sat directly in front of Briana and had been hosting the Shakespearean play and Lord Edwards' hat, both of which were removed by their respective owners as soon as Cathy entered the room. Seeing that Briana looked a little flushed, she asked if all was well. Briana nodded in reply and thanked her for the tea, saying they would ring if they needed anything else.

Grateful for something to occupy her hands as she delivered her thoughts to Lord Edwards, Briana began to pour the tea. She remembered that he did not like milk in his tea but did like a little bit of sugar. As she passed him his tea, Briana glanced toward Lucy who was watching her surreptitiously under the guise of working on her stitching. Returning her attention to her visitor, Briana said, "Honestly, Lord Edwards... I know you have been courting me fairly openly these last couple of months, but last night with how Cam...I mean, the Duke of Hereford was with me, I've been thinking... " Briana was unable to finish before he cut her off.

"He has a mistress." Michael revealed before looking to Lucy who had dropped her stitching and opened her mouth to protest.

In a stern manner, Lucy said, "Now, Lord Edwards, you know it's not fitting to discuss such a topic in front of a lady like this. I'll ask you to please refrain or..."

Briana held up a hand to stop Lucy's protest. Taking a deep breath, Briana said, "Lucy, let him continue. I believe it is important for me to hear." Shaking her head in disagreement, Lucy returned to her stitching while keeping her eyes, and ears, trained on Lord Edwards.

Clearing his throat, he continued speaking. "I know it is not proper for me to say it in such a manner and to such a proper lady as yourself, but I had to tell you. He has made it pretty well-known that he intends to continue seeking such pursuits outside of his marriage when the time comes. Unless he has told you otherwise. Has he mentioned her to you?" Lord Edwards asked, feeling sorry and ashamed that he was behaving in this cruel manner.

Briana dropped the biscuit she had been buttering on to the carpeted floor in shock. She shook her head from side to side in response to Lord Edwards' question. A mistress? Why was that so shocking for her to hear? Of course, he would have a mistress. It was only normal for a bachelor like him to have one, right? She could overlook his having a mistress as a bachelor, but would he really continue to have one as a married man? She could not accept that life, no matter how much she loved him. "No he hasn't. But... what if he loved his wife?" Briana asked, voice breaking slightly. She stood and walked to the fireplace across the room under the guise of repositioning an ornament on the mantle.

"Well, all married men love their wives, especially how indispensible they are to running the house and managing all the social affairs. I don't see why the Duke of Hereford would be any different." Lord Edwards answered thinking about the other prominent marriages he knew of. "Although, I don't know if that would be the honest and comfortable life you would want."

"No, I don't think so..." Briana answered, keeping her back to Lord Edwards. She could feel the tears pricking at her eyes. She could not be the kind of wife to share her husband, no matter who he was or what form of love they shared, be it passionate or otherwise.

"I'm sorry, my dear. I know you are close with the family and felt that you may have some feelings for the Duke, but I wanted to provide you with this insight that you may not have had otherwise." Edwards stood and crossed the room until he was standing directly behind Briana. He turned her to face him. "I see that I have overwhelmed you, so I will take my leave. Please know that I hold you in the highest regard and will always be near to care for you if you'll let me." Raising her hand in his, he bowed elegantly and dropped a light kiss over her knuckles. His clear blue eyes looked cloudy with concern seeing the tears in her eyes, tears which he knew he caused. "I'm sorry again," he said, giving her hand a gentle squeeze before dropping it, striding back across the room to pick up his hat, and leave. Briana was able to last twenty seconds before she gave in and allowed the tears to stream down her face. Lucy quickly moved to her side and held her, rubbing her arm and saying not to believe Lord Edwards since she was sure the Duke cared for her. Telling Lucy that she wished to be left alone, Briana made her way up the stairs to her room.

She had known from the start not to get her hopes up when it came to Cameron, but after last night she had and now the cloud she had been floating on had suddenly disappeared and she felt herself crashing back down to Earth's reality. She knew she needed to talk to Cameron, but couldn't bear the idea of facing him yet. She needed to get control over her emotions first and remember that her main goal was not falling in love with Cameron, but to marry a man with enough fortune to provide for her and her mother since her father had left them. Since he had not made his whereabouts known to them in ten years, he was not likely to be contacting or coming to their aid in the future either. Briana laid on her bed face down and cried into her pillows until she fell asleep.

Early afternoon had Cameron making his way from his bachelor lodgings on Brook Street to Warwick Street to visit Briana. He had not gotten much sleep the night before, and it was not solely due to his longer-than-expected conversation with Serrafina. The minute he was in bed, his mind was filled with images of Briana. The feel of her breasts in his hands and the taste of her skin as his lips explored every part accessible to him was enough to drive him mad. He would feel a tightening in his loins as he grew harder and harder until sleep was near impossible. It wasn't until taking a cold bath that he was finally able to sleep.

Thankfully, he had been able to leave Serrafina on good terms. Although confused at first with his decision to end their relationship, Serrafina understood that theirs was not one to last forever. Like old comrades, they spoke of the past months together with smiles and laughter. In many ways, Serrafina had been a confidant to Cameron and it was bittersweet to see her go. She had asked him if he could introduce her to another man in want of a mistress. He gave her two names, one of them being a recent widower in his forties and the other being of a close friend in his thirties who had been growing tired of seeking out different women but was not quite ready for marriage. Lastly, they discussed his growing feelings for Briana. Although Serrafina knew it to be love, Cameron was still dissecting his own heart and mind to determine the name for what he was feeling. He insisted that it was desire like none before and that he wanted only her, in whatever way possible. Knowing that Cameron was always careful with his words, choosing them with as much precision as a valet would give to his master's ensemble, Serrafina simply smiled and nodded slowly. With a shrewd look and cunning grin, Serrafina said in a melodic voice, "I'm afraid, *mi amore,* that I will see you happily married before the year is through. That girl has your heart more than you know." Cameron simply smiled and shrugged his shoulders in return before planting a light kiss on her cheek, thanking her for the drinks, and walking home.

Now, as a free man without any entanglements, he was ready to see the woman who had been the star of every dream he'd had for the past month that she had been in town. He was ready to become one of those bumbling idiots and officially ask to court her. He knew he had to return to Dalton Place, his country estate, within the next few weeks. Not only was it where he lived for most of the year, but it was where he preferred to be. He never stayed in London for an entire season, five months was much too long and too busy. Instead, he would participate in the first couple months before returning to his quiet and routine life out in the country. Would Briana go with him? Surely not without being married. Was he ready to marry her? With her father being out of town, who should he ask permission if he did choose to marry her? Maybe he should track her father down just in case since he still provided for them, even if he was not an upright and present father.

Reaching the steps to the Valmonts' townhouse, Cameron looked up at the door and took a step forward. First, he would see how she was feeling today, and then he would ask Briana directly for permission to court her. Although, with the events of last night, he may have skipped ahead already in his planning. He knew she wanted him as much as he wanted her. It was obvious in her kisses, her moans, and every time she said his name. Even in public, she had a certain musical tone to her voice every time she said his name and smiled up at him. Yes, he needed to court her and claim her as his before she accepts a marriage proposal from someone like Edwards and is lost to him forever.

Adjusting his jacket, he knocked on the door and greeted Wallace like an old friend. Wallace ushered him in and directed him to the small table in the middle of the foyer where gentleman callers usually left their cards, hats, or gloves in order to be announced. "Hello, Wallace. I've come to call on Lady Briana to see how she is feeling today. She knew I was coming, so she is probably expecting me. Could you let her know I have arrived?" Cameron asked, placing his hat and gloves on the round table in the entrance.

Wallace smiled and replied, "I will have to fetch her, my lord. Seems she retreated to her room after her visit with Lord Edwards this morning. You are welcome to wait in the front parlor while I let her know of your presence. Would you care for any tea while you wait?" Wallace asked politely.

"No thank you, Wallace. I'll just wait in here then," Cameron said as he entered the parlor and made himself comfortable in the same chair that had been occupied by Lord Edwards earlier that morning. Picking up the book Shakespeare's *Twelfth Night*, Cameron began reading from the page the book happened to open to. He'd read a good five pages before Wallace returned to announce that Briana was in bed with a headache and would not be able to see him. Did she suddenly change her mind about him? Maybe she regretted what transpired between them in the carriage last night. Were her feelings for him as sure as he thought they were? Had something happened earlier with Edwards? How could she not come to see him?

Baffled and feeling wholly unsure of where they stood, Cameron left word with Wallace that he would be back tomorrow to check on Briana and that he hoped for her speedy recovery. Leaving the parlor, Cameron looked toward the stairs Wallace had indicated earlier and pictured Briana asleep in bed. He hoped it was indeed a headache Briana was suffering from and not a change of heart.

Briana watched him leave the house from her bedroom window. She saw him pause as he reached the last step in front of the house and look up, as if searching for her. Quickly moving away from the window, she sighed in relief as Cameron gave up his search and made his way down Warwick Street. She knew she should have seen him and asked him about the information Lord Edwards shared with her this morning, but she could not bring herself to face him. She knew she was still emotional and puffy in the face from all the crying. No, she'd meet with him another time. She knew he would be attending the Great Exhibition with his family and hers next week, but she would give herself at least tonight to cry and refocus on a marriage of stability and not love.

CHAPTER 15

May 1851

Feeling miffed at being ignored by Briana for multiple days now, Cameron decided the best way to work through his feelings was to have a heart to heart with the woman who'd turned his life upside down. He needed to know why she refused to see him after that night in the carriage. He'd burned for her and she for him, and yet she had done everything she could to douse the flame before it became the raging fire he knew it could be.

Having been let in to the Valmonts' home by Wallace, Cameron found himself once again waiting for Briana in the front parlor. He'd picked up the latest edition of *The Gentleman's Magazine* to read while waiting. He was so enraptured with the magazine's latest publication of scientific intelligence that he did not hear Briana and her chaperone, Lucy, come into the room. It wasn't until Lucy cleared her throat that Cameron looked up and made eye contact with Briana. His breath caught as he took in the sight of her. She'd been out for a walk and the touch of pink on her cheeks made him think of the last time he'd been the cause of that shade of color on her cheeks.

"Your Grace, I'm sorry to have kept you waiting. I'm glad you had something to keep you entertained," Briana said in a cordial yet stiff manner. She hadn't expected to see him and, having avoided him successfully for the last six days, Briana felt completely awkward and out of sorts.

"Oh, it's 'Your Grace' now, is it?" Cameron replied with a smirk. "Very well. I was hoping you could spare a bit of time for a chat with me. I do think we have much to catch up on."

"Yes, of course. Lucy, can you send for a new pot of tea?" Briana said as she gave a smile to her maid in dismissal.

"That won't be necessary, Lucy. Wallace has just brought this pot to me not but five minutes ago. We don't require anything else and wish not to be disturbed. Thank you." Cameron's tone was that of such authority that Lucy, not knowing what to do in the presence of a Duke, simply bobbed a quick curtsy and left to spread the word to the rest of the staff.

"Are you mad? How could you dismiss her in such a way? Imagine what she will tell the staff. It's not proper for us to be alone without a chaperone. Honestly, sometimes I wonder if you don't hear yourself or are just so accustomed to everything following your order?" Briana said as she placed her hands on her hips in displeasure.

"Well, not everything. And since when have you been such a stickler for propriety?" Cameron asked, bristling under her combative attitude. Wishing to calm them both, Cameron smiled and gestured towards the couch. "Come sit down with me. I was not exaggerating when I said we have much to discuss."

Sitting primly on the couch next to him, Briana made sure to leave a good distance between them. She'd already begun to close off her heart and wanted no chance of touching him and reigniting any lingering passion she may have. Pouring herself a cup of tea she asked, "So tell me, Your Grace, what do we have to discuss exactly?"

"Well, Lady Valmont," Cameron said mocking her prim tone, "How about we start with why you have suddenly decided to avoid me after our tryst in the carriage? Try as I may, I am at a loss for answers," Cameron said, holding his frustration in check as best he could.

Surprised that he would begin his visit in such a manner,

Briana stammered as she answered, "I... I wasn't... I wasn't avoiding you. I just was thinking and helping my mother with various activities."

"Mmmhmm." Cameron rolled his eyes in disbelief. Inching closer to Briana he asked, "So, if you weren't avoiding me, where does that leave us now?"

Feeling her composure slipping, Briana took in a deep breath and reminding herself of the mistress he was unwilling to part with, she responded in the only way she could think to do. Squaring her shoulders once again, Briana replied, "I don't know what answer you want from me, but I think we both know that what happened was a mistake. I was very upset that night and was not thinking clearly. Maybe you misread my feelings, and I was too shocked to stop you. We both know that I once had feelings for you, but I did not know what to do in that moment. You know that I am looking for a calm and stable marriage, and I just think we have too much of a history for that to happen. I mean, we're like family, right?"

Cameron could feel the blood in him begin to boil. Was she trying to rip out his heart or just slowly crush it piece by piece? No longer able to control his patience, the muscle in his jaw began to twitch as he said through clenched teeth, "Family? It was my understanding one doesn't do what we did with family. I think you're making a mistake marrying a dullard like Edwards, and I don't understand why. Why are you so desperate to get married that you would accept someone so obviously wrong for you?"

"What makes you say he is wrong for me? Lord Edwards is a good man, and with my father away, I've been left with managing our finances. My mother and I have fought so hard to keep them in a state that would make him relieved when he returns, but my mother is an anxious person who constantly worries about the endless possibilities of what may go wrong. I've been taking care of all the finances as well as my mother since my father has been away. Now it's time for me to find a man I can marry who will take care of us both and help me manage some of this strain. You have no idea how much responsibility I have had to manage in order to keep us afloat due to father's debts. I need to get married, Cameron. That's the whole reason I came back. I know we had a moment, but I need more than a moment. Can you promise me more than lust for the rest of our lives?" Although Briana began her speech in a defensive and haughty tone, she finished rather quietly as the emotional strain she'd juggled for years became evident. She wished he could be the one for her, but she did not have the luxury of waiting until he was ready and willing to commit to her.

Cameron could see the pain in her eyes. He wanted to tell her there was more than lust between them, but the idea of marriage when she believed he could not give her what she needed, would never work. So, Cameron did the only thing he could do. He played the bachelor saying, "Brie, I'm sorry that I didn't know what you've been going through. If you want a marriage simply to cover your father's debts, I do believe I am more than qualified. And yet, since you see yourself as better-suited with Edwards, and all we had was a moment with nothing more for me to offer, I won't stand in your way." Knowing that he was lying to her made Cameron feel like the biggest cad in all of London, but if he'd taken advantage of her, then that was what he was. The shame he felt was overwhelming. He continued, "In fact, I was going to tell you that I've decided not to extend my stay in London and will be leaving in two days' time. I have been letting the country estate to its own devices for far too long and have some of the tenants who are in need of care. Of course, I have a few more reservations about your need to marry any man except me, but I believe those will have to go unanswered. Let me know when the wedding is and I'll be sure to attend, as family, of course." He knew it was cowardly for him to run away, but he didn't think he could stay in London to watch her fall for some other man. He couldn't stay and fall for her more than he already had when she didn't feel the same.

Feeling herself become queasy and the tears stinging her eyes, Briana nodded slowly before saying, "Yes, well, I believe

Lord Edwards may propose soon. I'll make sure you get an invitation. I do hope you have a safe journey when you leave. There is no need for me to say my goodbyes now since we'll see each other in two days' time to attend the Great Exhibition with our families. I shall formally bid you farewell then, and for now simply say good day."

Finding it harder to breathe and feeling like he'd been punched in the stomach, Cameron nodded before standing and folding over into a stiff bow. He exited the room leaving Briana with silent tears streaming down her cheeks.

Two days later, it was time for the Great Exhibition. Cameron had been trying to see Briana as simply a family friend for the last two days and was finding it absolutely impossible to do so. She had not come to his mother's house for dinner the night before, with her mother reporting that Briana had felt fine that morning but was suddenly overcome with a headache and some stomach pain an hour before they had to leave. Had he truly misread her that night in the carriage and put her in a situation she did not want to be? Was it truly a mistake like she said? Did she not harbor the same feelings of desire for him as he did for her? Curling his fingers into a fist by his side, Cameron clenched his jaw. It's not like it mattered much anymore since he was leaving town as soon as he could. He'd have to see her today and prayed that he could keep himself in check.

Turning down Warwick Street, he could see both families waiting outside. They had decided to ride together, knowing that the crowds on the street would be horrendous. Although the exhibit was set to last until October, and the families had hoped to attend on opening day, knowing that many would come to hear Queen Victoria's welcoming speech and be among the first to see all the wonders on display made them wait a few weeks before seeing the exhibit with slightly fewer crowds. He had also been looking forward to the event and was thankful his mother wanted to attend later rather than earlier. If it was truly as grand an exhibit as expected, he would likely attend again at a later date as well.

Cameron stepped down from the carriage and greeted everyone present. His mother was the first to step forward and give his hand a squeeze. She was elegantly dressed in violet and carried a parasol instead of a bonnet. She'd heard that the exhibit was in a palace made of glass, but insisted that having to maneuver through the crowds outside the palace would mean being in the sunlight for extended amounts of time and her skin must be protected. Cameron obediently helped her up and into the carriage, followed by Lady Darby and Emily, who'd been speaking with her mother about a charity she would like to attend the following week. Closing the door behind Emily, Cameron purposefully left Jake, Briana, and himself to ride in the second carriage provided by the Hereford household. He made sure to sit beside Briana so that he may talk to her more easily along the way and assess her mood and feelings towards him. Although he had ended their last conversation with pretending that he had no deep feelings for her, he couldn't help but think about her and care for her. He only hoped that he could manage some time alone with her one last time before leaving town.

As the carriages made their way toward Hyde Park, Briana was amazed to see the amount of people walking the streets all heading to the same place. London had always been overcrowded, but the crowds today were on another level entirely. The exhibit was bringing in visitors from around the globe, and the carriages in the streets were moving at a snail's pace. It was a lucky thing indeed that he was able to purchase day tickets early, knowing there would be a set amount of tickets printed for the first weeks.

"You can't be that amazed already. We have yet to see any of the exhibit's wonders," Cameron said teasingly in Briana's direction.

"How can I not be? Look at this crowd. And this is only the first day. Imagine what it will be like if ticket prices decrease later on and all social classes are able to attend. To know that there are people here from around the globe all joining us to see such displays of science, art, and culture is astonishing," Briana said, never once looking away from the crowds.

"And to think we can come multiple times until October," Jake intoned with a voice that was also filled with awe. "I'm assuming we are going to leave the carriages outside of the park, yes? I doubt we will be able to move through the crowds much better than we are now."

"Yes, we'll have to walk, but there is a lot to see, so I don't think it will be a problem," Cameron responded. "Brie, make sure you stay close to me so we don't get separated."

"I'll make sure to stay close to all of you, so don't worry."

"You'll be on my arm at all times, understood? There are too many people here and it can be very easy to lose you in the crowd if you are not holding on." He'd spoken before even realizing his words.

"I can just as easily be safe on Jake's arm as well. You should really accompany your mother, right?"

Cameron cleared his throat and responded, "Yes, well, I'll accompany you and Emily, and Jake can accompany our mothers."

"Gee, thanks Cam." Jake snickered.

Cameron simply grinned back and nodded his head to say "you're welcome!" Once Jake turned his attention to the crowds again, Cameron leaned over slightly again and whispered to Briana, "We need to talk. I want to make sure you are alright since our last conversation and I intend to keep you on my arm so I can get a few answers to questions I have. It's important for us to return to normal before I leave."

"Normal? I'm not quite sure what that is with you anymore, and I wasn't avoiding you... I just wasn't feeling well and didn't want to get anyone else sick," Briana said primly as she looked out toward the park that was coming into view.

"Right... Well, since you are here now, I'll take my chances. We won't be leaving today without me sharing what's on my mind. You'd do well to do the same," Cameron said steadily with a volume only she could hear.

147

The carriages pulled up to Hyde Park and Jake was first to get down in order to help the ladies in the other carriage, leaving Cameron to take care of Briana, much to her chagrin. He had taken the time to examine her in the carriage, but was so fixated with trying to read her face that he hadn't yet taken in her ensemble. She wore a seafoam colored dress and matching bonnet. He had seen Emily tie it for her before they left, so hopefully there would not be a chance of it blowing away. He could feel her warmth as she placed her hand in his and stepped down. Without skipping a beat, Cameron looped her arm through his and guided them to the rest of their party who was starting to make their way into the park.

The wind blowing in the air helped alleviate some of the heat accumulating under one's clothes, which Briana was very thankful for. The crowds that had amassed were moving forward toward the entrance at a snail's pace. Cameron led the party with Briana on one arm and Emily on the other. He politely steered them around the tourists that had come from different countries to gain further insight into various world cultures. Jake followed closely behind with the mothers.

Cameron heard a collective gasp from the ladies as they looked upon the glass structure ahead of them. Though the crowds barred some of their view, the building was so impressive that it stood tall enough to house and incorporate the several elm trees that were left untouched. The curved ceiling of the entryway seemed to touch the clouds with its height. The grandeur of the amount of glass used was well worth the given name of Crystal Palace. With the sun's rays that peeked through the clouds reflecting off of the glass, the Crystal Palace was enveloped in a halo which served to further elevate its majesty. The flags circling the roof presented all the various countries with items to be displayed.

As they came closer to the front entrance on Kensington Gore, Briana could hear the clicking of the turnstiles as each person deposited the entry fee of a pound a head. There was a mixture of murmuring, gasps of wonderment, and loud exclamations of "Mama, look over here!" and "My word!"

from kids and adults alike. Cameron led them first to the left where they first saw various spices from Trinidad and Tobago. They continued down the British Nave to see a large crystal glass fountain with full-sized elm trees behind it. Briana, who was captivated by the enormous fountain, let out a soft "Oh!" and, forgetting her determination to remain solely cordial with Cameron, patted his arm with her gloved hand and pointed to the intricate details of the base of the fountain. Her eyes the size of saucers matched the round shape her lips had formed moments before, and Cameron couldn't help but grin at her enjoyment. Taking in a deep breath, Briana smiled as the perfumed water from the fountain reached her nose. The sense of awe was further amplified by the music coming from an organ being played overhead on the secondary level. The lovely notes from the organ as well as the perfumed water created an almost spiritual experience causing all that entered to freeze, enthralled as they were in the peaceful and magnificent sounds.

Once Cameron and Briana began to feel the push of the crowd, they turned left at the fountain to continue down the British Nave. Emily and Lady Darby stopped to get a better look at the ormolu mounted dressing case with its silver-gilted accents that added to the word carving's majesty. Jake and his mother found their attention drawn to the tempest prognosticator which involved twelve leeches in bottles who would become agitated by an approaching storm and cause a small hammer to strike a bell in order to alert for the likelihood of a storm. With everyone's attention on an exhibit, Cameron and Briana were left to their own devices.

Wanting to extend their time together, Cameron pointed to continue down the British Nave on the other side of the crystal fountain. She could see the banner for India in the distance as Cameron began to steer them in that direction before she could respond. The collection of artifacts they saw were things that ranged from spices to weapons to howdahs on stuffed elephants, which he had only read about and never thought to lay eyes on. Wanting a closer look, Cameron stepped closer to examine the intricate detail of the howdah to see how the bed remained intact while on an elephant's back. Amazed by its majesty, he turned to ask Briana for her thoughts only to find that she had slipped away to examine Koh-i-Noor, the world's largest known diamond. Stepping beside her, Cameron found himself just as transfixed by the diamond's size as Briana was. Both reached out automatically hoping to touch it, but as Cameron's warm fingers met with hers, she jerked her hand away and looked into Cameron's soft eyes. He smiled sheepishly at her and she had half a mind to smile back. She couldn't. She had to end things now before she lost her heart to him even more. She would not share her husband with another woman, no matter how much she loved him.

"Sorry. I didn't mean to startle you," Cameron said with a glint of passion in his eyes, "but it seems we both have the same interests in mind." She knew his words held a double meaning. When Briana made no acknowledgement of his words, he continued, "I've come by often to see you since the night of the opera and it seems you've taken ill many times or you've been out. That is until our recent conversation. Do you feel yourself recovered?'

Briana smiled tightly and said, "Yes, thank you for your concern. It must have been some passing illness. As you probably noted at our last visit, my energy levels and resolve are back to normal." She could not meet his eyes for fear that he would see through her deception. She wanted to tell him her concerns and fears, but knew nothing would come of it. Also, being out in public was definitely not the place or time for discussing mistresses and levels of intimacy. Briana once again turned her attention to the large diamond in front of her and, after asking a question to the exhibitor, listened quietly to his answer and the follow up questions from Cameron. He always had a thirst for knowledge and seemed to ask questions others wouldn't think about. Once Cameron felt satisfied that all his questions had been answered, he continued to move them from country to country, all the time trying to engage her in conversation. He asked her about her thoughts on the artifacts: Which were her favorites? Was she enjoying herself? What was she most looking forward to seeing? Briana, reminding herself to remain reserved, answered his questions as tersely as possible with the occasional glance his way: Her favorite so far had been the Koh-i-Noor diamond. Yes, she was enjoying herself. And she was looking forward to seeing the stained-glass windows upstairs and the hand painted pottery and vases from China.

Coming to the end of the corridor, Briana felt herself relaxing in his company. She truly was enjoying herself, and since the conversation was focused on the exhibit, it was easy to forget about what was between them. Briana asked for refreshment before continuing on to see the collection of stained glass located on the second floor. Making their way back to the crystal fountain, Cameron steered them behind it toward the Boy and Swan fountain and the large gates leading to the refreshment rooms. Leaving her to sit in one of the cool, open-air refreshment areas, Cameron left and returned twenty minutes later with a Schweppes carbonated mineral water. Briana smiled obligingly at him as she took the offered drink and continued to look around in quiet amazement, especially at the large elm trees that had been incorporated inside the Crystal Palace.

The two sat in companionable silence for some time until their drinks were finished and the beads of sweat that had begun to pool on their brows dried. Taking the glass from her hand and setting it on the tray nearby, Cameron offered his arm once again and asked with a hopeful voice, "Would you like me to continue to escort you upstairs so you may see the stained glass and the exhibits from above?" Briana knew they should wait for the rest of their group, but she was enjoying herself so much and, being such a lover of the way the light plays on stained glass, she nodded her head as eagerly as a child would when receiving an offer of candy. She stood and smoothed out her skirts before taking his arm and winding through the crowds toward the set of stairs located in the corner.

Reaching the top, it was a relief to find it not as crowded as the floor below. Despite there being more space, Cameron continued to hold his body just as close as he did when they were downstairs amongst the throng of people moving elbow to elbow. He knew he should maintain his distance, especially since he had made up his mind to leave and she had made up her mind to pursue Edwards, but his body had other ideas. Trying to maintain her sense of propriety, Briana moved aside to put a little distance in between them. Without missing a beat, Cameron stepped with her and lowered his head to whisper in her ear "You look very beautiful with the light of the stained glass falling across your face."

"Thank you, but can you please give me a bit of space?"

"I find that very hard to do when you look at me like that."

"Like what?"

"With that look in your eyes that scream of your inner frustrations and passions. You say I misread your feelings in the carriage, but you have the same look in your eyes now as you did then." Cameron caressed the inside of her wrist subtly hiding the touch from view.

"Stop it. Do you have no concern about reputation? Have you forgotten that I am an unmarried woman? One who is being courted by another man, mind you," Briana said indignantly. She knew she should not have said that last part, but honestly, she needed to remind him more than ever that he was not the man for her.

"Well, for a man who is courting you, he sure is a fool for not being with you now. His loss is my gain. I enjoy our time together, although right now is nothing to your company in a carriage," Cameron said in a husky tone and leaning his head closer to her ear so the vibrations from his voice reverberated all the way from her ears, down her spine, and to her toes.

He was playing with her as if she was a new toy. Is this how he acted with *her*? His mistress? Briana felt her cheeks begin to flush. She was feeling warm and knew it had nothing to do with standing next to the stained-glass windows and the sun's rays shining through and onto her arms. How dare he? Pulling her arm out of his and straightening her spine Briana, spat out in a hushed tone, "We've already discussed that night. It was a mistake and we both know it. For a rake as yourself, what happened between us may be commonplace to you, Your Grace, but I assure you it is not for me. Once again, you are misreading my feelings."

"Oh, am I now? Why are you so breathless if not out of desire? Admit to me that you wanted what happened between us as much as I," Cameron said as he pulled them deeper into the far corner under the guise of looking at and discussing the architecture of the building. "I never wanted a woman more than I want you. I want to be able to kiss your lips, your neck, your shoulders… I want you beside me every day and under me every night," he nearly growled in her ear with a wicked tip of his lips as he looked into her eyes. He knew she wanted him too. He could see her longing for him as he leaned in closer to her. He wanted to kiss her now in front of everyone and claim her as his. His wicked smile widened as her body leaned in to close the minimal distance between them. Gently turning them so they were mainly hidden from view behind the giant curtain used to separate the exhibit from the stairs, Cameron's lips brushed against her ear as he murmured her name. His lips traced down to her cheek and to her jawline before finding their way to her lips. His kiss was feather light and with the slightest hint of friction that made her feel off balance and cling to his arms for support. With a tilt of his head and a hand finding its way to the back of her neck, he deepened the kiss, his tongue joining hers in a possessive need that made Briana feel all the passion and desire she felt in the carriage all over again.

Briana felt her body engulfed in the fire of passion he had stoked within her. He had begun this intimacy in the carriage weeks ago, and Briana had forgotten how much her body craved his touch. He was only kissing her and already she felt herself shiver with the delight of anticipation. He made her feel more womanly then she ever could have imagined. She could feel his desire pressed against her through their clothing and knew she was weak. The resolve she had before was wavering. She loved him so much and wanted to be with him. He pressed her back into the wall and, when a moan began to escape her lips, he swallowed it with lips so forceful she could swear they would bear his seal for the rest of her life. Cameron's hand strayed to trace the length of her side down from her neck to her breasts to her waist as he focused his eyes on hers and whispered, "I've wanted you ever since I saw you at the masquerade ball before I even knew it was you. After that kiss, I knew I had to make you mine. You say you want someone to help manage your finances. I'm more than capable and can offer you pleasure that Edwards can't. Say you'll be mine. I can give you everything you ever wanted. Tell me anything you want and it's yours."

He'd said the words Briana needed to bring her back out of the passionate daze she'd been in. He couldn't give her everything she wanted because what she wanted was for him to love her and only her. She'd told him she was looking for someone to marry to help her manage everything, but hearing him say that crushed her even more. She wanted his love and she needed to hear those words from him. She wanted a happy marriage with him. All of these desires were not things he was capable of. With anger rising anew, and a strangled cry escaping her lips, she pulled out of his arms once again and said with a mutinous look in her eye, "You can't. I will not be your new mistress." Her voice was flat and cold. Why did he have such a hurt and confused look? "Yes, Cam, I know you have a mistress. It's not necessarily a secret with you being such a sought-after bachelor. Isn't that your intention? You say you want me and for me to be yours, as if I'm some sort of object you can own or something to check off a list."

"I want to be with you. I want to care for you and provide for you. I want to hold you at night and wake with you in my arms in the morning." Cameron said in a baffled tone that was tinged with a slight chuckle of disbelief. Was she so obtuse that she did not understand the depth of his feelings for her? Here he was practically declaring his feelings for her to the world and she was throwing it in his face.

"I believe those are the same things a man provides to a mistress, no?

"Brie, you're really testing my patience here. I never mentioned the word mistress to you. Why are you fighting this? I know you want to be with me as much as I want to be with you. What is so wrong with my proposal?" Cameron huffed, raking a hand through his hair in frustration.

"This proposal will only result in ruining my reputation. Do you not understand the importance of the situation I'm in?"

"I can give you everything you want. When we are together like this," Cameron reached out and stroked the side of her face, "I can make you happy."

Briana couldn't help but fixate on his words "When we are together like this..." Yes, this was the only type of relationship he could give her; he couldn't return the love she had for him. Her anger had suddenly been replaced with a cold detachment that left her with eyes devoid of emotion as she said, "That's not everything, and I feel sorry that you think it is. Thank you for your proposal, but I refuse. As I have already told you, I have decided on Lord Edwards, so please, just let me go." Turning on her heel, she took two steps before he grabbed her hand and stopped her. He kissed her once again hoping that would bring her to her senses and she'd realize how stupid it was to deny her feelings, but instead she wrenched herself free once again. With tears streaming down her cheeks, she yelled, "Don't!" She didn't care if there were people that heard her yell, they'd probably think she was telling someone nearby not to touch one of the artifacts. She needed to get away from him before she really lost herself to her emotions.

"Where are you going?" Cameron hissed with anger and hurt.

"Away to rejoin members of civilized society. Please, leave me alone," Briana said with shaky conviction and a wavering voice. She felt small and broken, contrasting with the feeling of being a goddess she'd felt moments earlier. Without a second look at him, she ran off hiding the tears streaming down her face as best she could. She bumped into a man as she was coming down the stairs, but with the sobs she was choking down, she had little voice to express her apologies. She needed to get to the ladies' room as quickly as possible and hoped there wouldn't be a long line to wait. The man, who bowed to her in response, smiled at her back as he watched her flee. He glanced back up to where Cameron was standing with hands on his hips and chuckled to himself. Mr. Gutterson couldn't help but take satisfaction in seeing members of both the Valmont and Hereford families in such misery, but this was just the beginning. With a little skip down the stairs, he was lost amongst the crowd once again.

CHAPTER 16

Cameron stood wondering where and when everything went wrong. He had done everything in his power to ensure that he would make her happy, and yet she was incapable of seeing it. He told her he'd give her everything and that he only wanted her, and yet, she spoke of mistresses and ruined reputations. How could she not see that he was a man who was making a commitment to her? He would never dream of making Briana his mistress because she was so much more than any mistress could ever be. She'd always been the most important woman in his life, even before he realized how much she'd impacted his life. This woman was his goddess who he wanted to worship and love every day, and yet, she saw his love as something to be scorned with disgust. What was he missing? She may have looked disgusted with him toward the end of their conversation, but her body had responded with complete pleasure to his kisses and caresses. Yes, she wanted him as much as he wanted her, without question. The heat of her pressed against him was still radiating in his loins as he gulped another breath of air to calm himself. How could she go from hot to cold so quickly?

"There you are!" Emily peered in front of him and tilted her head to the side as she tried to find his gaze. "We were looking everywhere for you. Jake is with the mothers getting refreshments. Where is Brie?"

"I believe she was headed in the direction of the ladies' room. At least, that's what she said over her shoulder as she ran away from me." Cameron sat on the bench opposite the stained glass and rested his head in his hands.

"Cam, what's wrong? Did something happen?" Emily lowered herself elegantly next to her brother on the bench and placed a hand on his shoulder. A lock of blonde hair fell into her eye as she tilted her head once again to try to meet Cameron's gaze. Tucking the hair behind her ear, Emily cleared her throat lightly before calling his name once again.

"I don't understand. She says she can't accept my love, that she can't accept me." Cameron's eyes finally met Emily's while his body remained slumped over in a very ungentlemanly manner. His eyes were as dark and stormy as the emotions twisting inside his heart in battle with his mind's memories of his most recent encounter with Briana. Sighing and shaking his head in disbelief, Cameron uttered, "She talks about wanting to get married, but when she receives a proposal, she refuses. How can she be so dense and rash? I can give her everything she could want and care for her." Sitting up straight and taking Emily's hands in his own, Cameron stared directly into his sister's calm blue eyes and said, "Em, you know I would take care of her." The earnestness in his voice was heartbreaking.

"Of course, you would. But Cam, did you tell her you love her? Did you even use the word marriage at all in your proposal? Promising her anything without using words of love or marriage, what was she supposed to think?" Emily said as a soft reproach.

"She's supposed to think that I bloody love her, that's what," Cameron said under his breath. "We've known each other for so long and she was always the one who was able to bring me out of my shell. I've never felt more at ease and happy than when I'm with her, even ten years ago before I truly realized. She left without a word back then, taking with her all the laughter and balance she'd given to me, and now that she's come back, my life has been a whirlwind of emotions I never thought I would feel."

"She is one to bring out a person's true nature since she is able to make everyone around her feel at ease just by the look in her eye or by her toothy smile. Despite this, she isn't always at ease with herself, especially when it comes to love. Don't you remember her confession to you before she left?" Emily asked.

"What confession? You mean when she told me that I was handsome and she found herself caring for me?" When Emily nodded in response, Cameron was quick to snort in derision before saying, "She was only fifteen at the time and cared for me like a brother or cousin."

"I can assure you she has never cared for you like a brother... *or* a cousin. Jake maybe she thought of as a brother, but not you. You completely dismissed her, saying she shouldn't mistake companionship as love and that she shouldn't fall for every handsome man who gives her attention," Emily said, planting her hands on her hips and shaking her head disapprovingly.

"Well, she shouldn't. I still stand by the advice I gave her then. It was sound and well-meant. I fail to see how any of this has bearing on the current situation," Cameron said as he stood up in exasperation.

"You basically went and made her a proposal based solely on the fact that you find her attractive and care for her, which was exactly what you admonished her for earlier. Of course, she remains guarded with you since she is not looking to make the same mistake. She wants words of love from you, Cam, the same ones she was hoping to receive back then," Emily said with a soft smile on her lips and a pat on her brother's arm.

"So, since I did not use the word 'love' during our conversation, she thought I was proposing for her to be my mistress? I give up. I told her I'm leaving town and maybe that is the best thing I can do for her. Please, Em, take care of her and let her know how much I care for her. She won't talk to me now since she is too angry and hurt. Could you talk to her?" Cameron said pitifully.

"Of course, Cam, but I think leaving town is a mistake. I think you have to make it clear to her that you love her and want to marry her. I'll fetch her and calm her down. Will you be waiting in the refreshment area or will you all move around too?" Emily asked.

"Well, I know that the crowd around the Trophy Telescope will be fading, so now is the time to see it while everyone else is looking elsewhere. Shall we meet there?" Cam asked. Emily nodded her agreement while Cameron said he would speak to Jake and the mothers in order to begin a path to the telescope. Feeling a sense of loss and hurt, but a sliver of hope, Cameron began to move down the stairs to meet up with his brother while Emily took a turn to her left toward the ladies' rooms. With Emily's help, he'd be able to set the record straight about his feelings and proposal.

Briana let out a final sigh as she once again smoothed her skirts and checked her face in the mirror. The redness around her eyes was now faint and her breath was steady enough for her to face everyone again without hinting at what had occurred up above. Stepping out of the ladies' room and moving aside to the little space available, Briana let another woman enter the now vacant spot. Looking around, she could not find anyone from her party. It had been some time since she left Cameron and she knew the others would have wanted to finish seeing the bottom floor of exhibits before moving to the top. Being already at the far end of the main passage, Briana decided to try her luck and see if anyone ventured toward the technological inventions. She remembered Cameron was most looking forward to seeing the Trophy Telescope and that Jake wanted to see something called a voting machine that automatically counted votes as they occurred. Setting out in that direction, Briana reminded herself to make as little eye contact with Cameron as possible and focus on the exhibit in order to enjoy herself in front of the party and not cause a scene like she almost had upstairs.

After stopping to look at a few more artifacts and jewelry that caught her eye along the way, Briana came to the gathering in front of the telescope. Looking to her left and to her right, she found her eyes meeting Cameron's. He stood tall enough that he could see her over the heads of many in the crowd. He wore a gentle smile that did not quite reach his eyes. Making her way to the rest of the party, she stood between him and Jake in silent awkwardness until Cameron broke it by asking after Emily. Confused, Briana replied that she hadn't seen Emily and assumed she was still with everyone else while she was in the ladies' room. There was a moment of quiet panic that passed through the party as they all began to look around amongst them.

The Dowager Duchess was the first to break the silence by asking Cameron where she went since he was the last to have seen her. "She was going to meet Briana in the ladies' room and then join her as we all met here in front of the telescope. Since Briana made it here to us, I assumed it was because Emily passed that message along to you." Turning his worried gaze onto Briana, he said, "Did you not see her?"

"No, she never came to the ladies' room. Well, not that I saw. I made my way here, remembering that you and Jake discussed wanting to see the telescope and the automatic voting machine while we were waiting outside to enter. Do you think she got lost amongst the crowd?" Briana responded as she began a sort of nervous dance, moving her body slightly back and forth trying to see past the people in front of her. Of course, being shorter of stature was of no real help in this situation.

"Oh Cameron, we have to find her. There are so many people here. What if we can't reunite with her until we are outside?" Elizabeth asked while nervously wringing her hands. "She looked fine before she parted from us to meet Cameron and Briana upstairs, right? You don't think she fell ill due to the amount of people in here? Maybe she was overheated and stepped out?"

"Why don't we split up once again and search around to see if we can find her." Cameron's authoritative voice sent Jake to the hall of machinery and the mothers toward the ladies' room on the other end of the palace in case Emily got confused. Since the mothers would pass all of the exhibits along the way, Cameron decided he and Briana would walk through the larger exhibits outside of the palace to see if Emily ventured that way. They would all meet at the entrance they came in earlier in an hour. Having received their orders, everyone began to move to their given locations without a word, eyes and ears alert for any trace of Emily, be it a glimpse of her dress or her voice as she spoke to the people around her. Briana gave Elizabeth's hand a quick squeeze before separating.

"Do you really think she went outside? You know Emily isn't the type to stray away from a group like this," Briana said quietly over her shoulder in the case that the mothers were still nearby.

Cameron, following behind her instead of beside her due to the amount of people gathered around, responded, "No, I don't think she would either. I just don't know where she would be if not with you."

Briana continued moving forward quietly as her eyes darted all around her. If her eyes had been fixed before while taking in all the exhibits earlier, it was nothing compared to the sharp and worried gaze in her eyes now. Finally stepping out into the open air, Briana did not wait to take Cameron's arm as she should have, but continued to move and weave in between people who stood either looking and discussing the exhibits or simply enjoying the slight breeze in the air. Coming toward a large gathering around an enormous lump of coal, Briana found herself face to face with Lord Edwards. Reading her panic, he asked if he could be of assistance until he saw the foreboding look on Cameron's face.

"What has happened that you both wear such serious countenances while in such an extraordinary place such as this?" Lord Edwards asked as he gestured about him.

"Emily's gone missing. We can't seem to find her anywhere," Briana responded, her voice wavering on the edge of tears.

"Have you checked upstairs or in the hall of machinery?"

Edwards asked quickly. After receiving confirmation that the remainder of the party was searching them now, Edwards offered, "Maybe she went back toward the entrance having been overheated and decided to wait for the rest of you on one of the benches outside."

"Right, let's head back that way and pray one of the others have found her," Cameron replied with a tilt of his head in Edwards direction. He meant it a pleasant manner but still dismissing Edwards, which is why he was surprised when Edwards followed behind them as they made their way back into the palace and through the throngs of visitors.

As everyone reunited at the entrance, Her Grace was no longer the only obviously worried mother. Lady Darby had also begun wringing a handkerchief nervously with eyes that no longer seemed to fix on anything in front of her. Jake took his mother's hand and then gently patted Violet's hand with his other.

"She's not here, Cam. We need to get the authorities involved since we can't seem to find her on our own," Jake said quietly to his brother. Cameron looked at him and then to his right and received a nod of agreement from Lord Edwards.

"Yes, I think we must. Why don't we get everyone back to our carriages and make our way back to the house where we can send word for an officer from the Metropolitan Police and make sure Emily didn't find herself home before the rest of us," Cameron replied as he and the other gentleman moved to get the carriages and help the ladies in with as much speed as possible.

Once in the carriages, it was still crowded in the streets and the traffic was slow moving, which did nothing to alleviate the fears and worries of the party. Lord Edwards, who had not come in a carriage of his own but instead decided to walk, joined Briana and Cameron in one carriage while Jake joined the other, seeing how his mother would not let go of his hand for fear of losing another child.

The carriage ride back was quiet and tense as everyone tried to look amongst the crowd for Emily, hoping she would be seen walking back to the house or in a passing carriage of a friend who had offered her a ride home. Alas, once they reached Warwick Street, there was still no sign of Emily. Briana looked up and down the street three times as everyone else made their way up the front stairs and into the Hereford home. How could her friend simply vanish into thin air? She felt wholly responsible since Emily had been in search of her before disappearing. "Where could she have gone?" Briana mumbled to herself as she ascended the stairs and joined everyone else in the front parlor.

For having just arrived, the scene before her was already one from a poorly written melodrama. Jake had removed his jacket and loosened his cravat, disposing of them carelessly across the back of a nearby wooden chair he now sat in. He had the same nervous gesture as his brother of raking his hands through his hair, except Jake would follow that gesture with a rubbing of his eyes. Her Grace was lying with an arm thrown over her eyes while Lord Edwards stood near and patted her other hand reassuringly. Lady Darby was pacing up and down the room shouting nonsense about Emily tripping and falling into one of those "horrid foreign machines at the exhibit" or, even better, the possibility that Emily was "trampled to death under the feet of a mob making its way to the retiring rooms after tripping down the stairs." Cameron, all the while, stood as straight and rigid as a rod in front of the mantle. He showed no signs of worry or stress except for one button he had undone at the top of his collar and a lock of hair that fell across his forehead as a result of the owner's hands coming into contact with it moments before. As Briana took in the scene and decided what role she was supposed to take in such a situation when she herself was trying to keep her emotions at bay, Lord Edwards cleared his throat and spoke, "May I suggest, while we wait for the servant to return with the officer, we gather as much information about what we know about Emily and her possible whereabouts before the authorities arrive?"

With a feeling of purpose, Briana took the seat opposite Lord Edwards and on the other side of the reclining Elizabeth and began gathering the list of information that would be shared to the officer once he arrived. With as calm a voice as possible, Briana stated, "She was wearing a yellow gown with dark blue florets lining the bodice and giving way to a large bow on the front of her waist. She carried a matching bonnet in her hands, having removed it once inside the Crystal Palace for a better view of her surroundings."

"Yes. Right. What else?" Cameron asked with an encouraging and grateful look at Briana. He was trying his hardest to remain composed since, as head of the household, it would not do for him to lose control and run out of the house to search for Emily himself like a madman. No. he had to be logical and calm in order to keep everyone else around him from falling apart. He was thankful that Briana understood that about him. Others may have seen him as being cold and aloof, but not his Brie. She was just as much a goddess of control as she was a goddess of passion, and he was going to make sure no harm came her way. For as much worry as he was feeling for his sister's disappearance, he knew that if Brie had gone missing, there would be no way in hell anybody would be able to keep him even remotely in check.

"She was most looking forward to seeing the Koh-i-Noor and the Daria-i-Noor diamonds found in the India exhibit. She spent a long time there and spoke with many of the visitors around her about their beauty," Jake offered.

"Were any of those visitors around her anyone of value?" Lord Edwards asked politely. When he was met with blank looks by all, he added, "Anybody she valued as a well-known friend and may have left the exhibition with?" Hoping some clarity would come from his suggestion, he was met instead with shakes of the head except for Her Grace, who was now half lying and half sitting up as if she remembered something.

"Well, she did seem to speak to a gentleman nearby for longer than the others around her, but since he had his back to us, I can't say with certainty who it was. Did you happen get a better look at the man, Violet?" asked Elizabeth, thus bringing Briana's mother to a halt in the midst of pacing and mumbling to herself.

"I... I... can't quite say. Although there was something diff... well... odd in Emily's countenance when she was speaking to him," said Lady Darby in a small and shaky voice.

Before anyone could probe her for more information, the servant who was previously sent to fetch a member of the Metropolitan Police appeared with the officer closely behind him. The officer was a tall man with sharp eyes and a well-trimmed mustache. He was dressed in a black uniform with a high collar, eight silver buttons down the front that accentuated his broad chest, and a belt that with a silver buckle to complete the ensemble. On his arms were three bands indicating his rank of sergeant in the police force. He still wore his officer's cap that was rounded at the top with the Metropolitan Police shield on the front and a strap that fell just on top of his chin. Looking around the room, the officer removed his hat and bent into a stiff bow in the direction of Cameron and his mother. Raising himself back to his standing position, he pulled a notebook from his pocket and began his introductions and questions.

"Good evening, Your Grace. My name is Sergeant Bixley. I understand that a person of the family has gone missing. Is this correct?" He walked over to stand in the center of the room in order to see everyone at once. He made eye contact with each person before locking eyes with Cameron as if expecting His Grace to take the lead in discussing the day's events.

"Yes. My family, along with Lady Darby and her daughter, Lady Valmont, went to the Great Exhibition in Hyde Park. We arrived a bit later than we anticipated, around a quarter to eleven due to the crowds of visitors in the streets," Cameron said as a means of walking the officer through their day.

"And was Lady Worthington with you most of the day, Your Grace?" the officer asked. When Cameron shook his head, the officer inquired, "May I ask who you were accompanying and who was accompanying your sister and mother?"

Cameron bristled at the impertinent question and stiffly

responded, "I accompanied Lady Valmont and my sister for a part of the exhibition until the two ladies were interested in different artifacts, leading me to accompany Lady Valmont throughout the exhibition while my brother Jake stayed and accompanied our sister, our mother, and Lady Darby." Cameron's eyes met Briana's and she could sense the amount of blame he was placing on his shoulders for having selfishly left his brother with so many to watch over. The officer glanced up from his notebook to see the exchange, but immediately turned his attention to the Her Grace and to Jake.

"Where in the exhibition did you spend most of your time?" Officer Bixley was no longer writing in his notebook but was instead looking at his hands, as if checking to see if there was any dirt he'd collected under his fingernails. Briana felt the blood in her veins begin to boil. How could an officer of the law be so unconcerned and disconnected with finding a missing person? Couldn't he even try to have some empathy for the visibly worried Elizabeth?

"We spent quite a while at the Belgium and India exhibits. She was very taken with artifacts of jewelry from India and the statues from Belgium," Jake answered in place of his mother.

"Would you like to take note of what she was wearing? Or even what she looks like so you may know who you are looking for?" Briana asked in a haughty tone. Her impatience with the man was evident and she knew she was crossing the lines of social propriety, but honestly, how was this man to find Emily if he didn't know what she looked like? He wasn't asking any questions of value. Briana stood and left the seat on the left of Elizabeth. Walking closer to the far window, she crossed her arms over her chest and let out a disgruntled humph until she saw Lord Edwards appear by her side and give her a reassuring smile and quick pat on the arm.

Without even a glance in Briana's direction, Officer Bixley replied in a flat voice, "Yes, I will need that information eventually." He looked up from his nails to address Elizabeth and asked, "Your Grace, did your daughter seem to enjoy herself during the exhibition?"

"I believe so, yes. She smiled throughout and spoke with those around her about the amazing artifacts she was viewing." Elizabeth was sitting as still as Cameron was standing, both aware that their title would not allow for histrionics of any kind. Despite her body's composure, there were tears quietly streaming down her face as she asked the officer, "Do you think she ran away of her own accord?" When she received no answer, she sniffed and looked away stating, "Emily would never do that. She would never willingly cause her family such anxiety. Someone had to have taken her." As a sob escaped from her throat, Lord Edwards returned to her side and offered her both his handkerchief and a glass of water from the table in front of them.

Officer Bixley made no comment to Her Grace's claim of a possible hostage situation. He once again looked at everyone in the room before turning his attention to a piece of white lint that appeared on the leg of his uniform. He walked around the room silently nodding to himself and smoothing the corners of his mustache.

Looking over at Lady Darby, who had stopped pacing the floor but was now biting her lip with such nervous energy that Jake was afraid she'd make herself bleed, Jake brought back the previous conversation they were having before the officer's arrival. He stood and, walking toward her, asked, "Lady Darby, didn't you say you saw Emily speaking to a gentleman while we were looking at the Koh-i-Noor diamond?"

"Umm… y… yes, she was. I couldn't see his face, though, since his back was to me. I really think… well… she was fine when she returned to us, though. Maybe she seemed a little tired… She was very quiet." Briana's mother caught her eye and the panic in them let her know there was something her mother was hiding. The panic was the same look she has when she is afraid someone knows the truth of their financial situation and would soon let all of London know.

"Hmm… thank you for the information." Officer Bixley did not ask any other questions, which confirmed Briana's belief that this officer would not be the one to find Emily. She could not trust that his reluctance in gathering information about her best friend would suddenly change or lead to an epiphany. She watched as Officer Bixley sat down in the now vacant chair on the left of Her Grace where Briana previously sat. He then reached for his notebook and scrawled a few words before closing it and placing it once again in his pocket.

"Should we tell you what she was wearing now?" asked Lord Edwards. "We made sure to refresh our memories of her attire before your arrival, thinking that it would be good for you to have in case you find strips of the fabric along the roads."

Before Officer Bixley could respond, there was a sharp and loud inhale from Briana's mother. Her eyes had widened and her face had paled. Briana crossed to her mother and, before asking her anything, saw her mother's lips form her father's name. Her mother knew something and it was connected to her father. In order for Briana to get the information she needed, she had to find a way to excuse them from the room. Turning back to the room, she announced, "It seems my mother needs a moment to gather herself in the midst of all this. Please excuse us." With her mother's hand in hers, she made her way to the door only to be stopped by Cameron's voice.

He had been quiet for some time now, piecing together all the information that had been shared with the officer as well as his conversation with Emily about Briana and her feelings. She had disappeared after that conversation and, for the life of him, he could not help but think he was responsible. Now, there wasn't anything else he could do except help and protect those present to ensure they also wouldn't disappear. Seeing Briana and her mother reach the closed door, he opened his mouth and said, "You may use the room next door. I don't want anyone leaving the house until Emily is returned, even if that means walking to your house next door. Come, I will make sure the room is empty of any servants so you may rest in peace. Jake and Lord Edwards, please give Officer Bixley all the information you can think of in regards to my sister." After receiving a nod from both gentlemen, Cameron crossed the room and opened the door for both of the Valmont women.

He led them down the hall and into the room next door while trying his hardest to make out the whispers between the two women. Glancing back at them, he could see Briana's face no longer carried the concerned smile she had previously worn, but was now clouded in confusion.

The room was dimly lit with the two oil lamps located in the room and the few sconces on the wall. Cameron had brought them to what had been his father's library but now served as a place his mother went whenever she most missed her husband. Knowing he should leave the two women alone after showing them to the settee and plush chairs in the middle of the room, he began to reach out to Briana's mother to help her take her seat. Thinking better of it, he turned to leave the room. He didn't make it more than two steps forward before Briana said aloud, "Mother, what do you know? You mouthed father's name to me and you are more panicked than I have ever seen before. What is it you know?"

CHAPTER 17

Violet sat with a glazed look in her eyes as she stared off into the distance. She knew there were many things she could share with her daughter, but having to come to terms with the fact that her husband had left them because he didn't love her enough had been heartbreaking. She knew there was nothing she or her daughter could do that would convince him to come back to them, but she was scared of his reaction if he got word that the sister of the Duke of Hereford had been taken because of them. Would he be angry or had he completely washed his hands of anything having to do with them? If he had, she didn't think his acquaintance was made aware of that fact.

"I think Emily was talking to a man that knows of your father's true whereabouts," Violet said in a quiet voice.

"What makes you say that?" Briana asked, noting the pallor and wrinkles of her mother's face. Had she always had those lines in between her eyebrows?

Briana's mother shifted nervously in her seat before saying, "Your father spoke of an acquaintance he would often drink and gamble with. He described him as a man whose reputation was very important to him, so he was always looking for ways to bring him more notoriety and a higher status."

Briana tried to recall any mention of her father's friends in the journals she had read over the ten years in order to try to locate him or when it came to addressing some of his previous financial decisions. She couldn't think of any, but if she could get back home soon and reread those journals, maybe the man would be referenced. She looked away from the spot on the wall she had trained her eyes to focus on while speaking to her mother. She didn't want her mother to see her own panicked eyes, so Briana made it a point to stare out the windows.

"So, what made you think Emily may be speaking to this man?" Cameron said quietly, causing both women in the room to jump. It seems they had both forgotten about his presence, but there was something they were hiding and he'd be damned if his sister was hurt because of it. He could see the shock and annoyance in Briana's eyes, almost as if she didn't think he should be present during this conversation. He knew she was also trying to make sense of the information her mother was slowly sharing and he wanted to go to her in comfort, but now was not the time. They both needed to get as much information possible to save Emily. There would be a time later on when she would have to be completely honest with him, and he couldn't wait to shake her for keeping a single thing from him.

Briana's mother broke through Cameron's thoughts as she stood up and walked to the mantle. She brought a nervous hand to her lips before saying, "He used a walking stick that was curved at the top and had some sort of jewel in it. I remember your father being envious of it since he believed it gave the untitled gentleman more status than his own title of Earl. In a drunken fit one night, after he hit me, he tried to take one of my rubies, yelling that he would have a grander walking stick made. Of course, I tried to calm him down, and remind him that we were already stretched thin financially, but you remember how he was in those moments. He hit me some more, and after exhausting himself, fell asleep with the ruby in his hand. I was able to hide it later, but he never asked for it again since he soon purchased other things instead that an untitled gentleman could not." Briana's mother looked at her daughter with the haunted eyes she always wore after remembering her father.

"Oh, Mother. I'm so sorry. Why didn't you call me for help?" Briana asked, tears brimming over.

"My dear, you had just recovered from the bruises he'd given you the week before. I couldn't very well wake you up in the middle of the night and take the chance of him hitting you as well. What kind of mother would that make me?" Violet said as she wiped the tears from her daughter's face.

"Mother, you shouldn't have endured all that alone. But now he is gone and we are safe. The important thing to focus on is Emily. Do you remember the name of this man? Or anything about what he looked like? Or anything about what information father shared with him? Think back to your conversations with father. Could he have told you something when he was in those moods that you've forgotten?" Briana asked. She knew she was asking her mother to unlock years of repressed hurtful memories, but if there were any more answers her mother could give, she needed to do this for Emily. Especially if she was taken as a way to get some attention or revenge on the Valmont family, Briana did not have the time to be gentle with her mother.

Violet began to shake her head in reply. The trembles that were originally found only in her hands were now working their way down her body. She opened her mouth and with a brittle voice said, "I think that man was trying to convince your father to go into business with him, or make some large gamble together? I'm not quite sure, but I remember your father coming home one night after drinking and he looked different. Of course, he was still loud and stumbling throughout the house, but he wasn't angry like usual. He took my hands and told me that everything was going to change soon now that he was going to bring us more money than we could dream. I thought it the ramblings of a drunken man, counted my blessings that he was not in a violent mood, and helped him to bed without questioning him any further. He was always so obsessed with money, having it and not having it…" Briana's mother trailed off.

"I know. By the time I was fifteen, he was pushing me to consider marrying any wealthy man nearby. He didn't care about my feelings. He just wanted money at his disposal again. And now that he's gone, I'm fulfilling the role he wanted of me." Briana said with angry tears stinging her eyes. As one escaped the corner of her eye and made its way down her cheek, she dashed it away quickly. This was not the time for her to cry about past hurts. She needed to stay focused on Emily. Once again looking at her mother, she asked, "Mother, do you think something went wrong between father and this man? Did he take Emily, knowing how close we are with the Duke of Hereford's family in order to get money from us?"

"We have nothing to give, though, with the amount of debt your father left us in. You've been managing the finances, but in ten years, we've only managed to pay off very few debts."

"But this whole time you've been dressed in fine clothes, wearing beautiful jewelry, and making everyone around you believe you are fine. You've been lying and pretending that you are all well and that your father has recovered from his drunken ways. All so we would believe you still had the same social status as you once did, that you still belonged among the elite. Why wouldn't he or any of us think otherwise?" Cameron was seething as he spoke with a gravelly tone that had a sharp bite to it, revealing his anger and hurt. Turning to Briana, he said, "You told me that your father was away on business, as well as travelling with your cousin, and so you have been managing financial affairs lately, making you feel burdened. You made it seem recent, but it's been going on for some time now, hasn't it, and you don't actually know where Lord Darby is? Also, you both claim to be so close with my family and never once let us know, or asked for help, when he was attacking you in his drunken fits of rage?"

In a small voice and without meeting his look, Briana simply nodded her head and said, "Yes." She knew he hated her for everything she'd kept from him, and she still had so much she hadn't said aloud to him. He would continue to look at her with those hurt and angry eyes he had now.

"Right," Cameron replied as he turned his back on her to get his bearings. He had to calm down and rein in his temper. Now was not the time to have this conversation. Why did he keep worrying about her and forgetting about Emily, who was the victim of all these lies? He had to get the conversation back on track. Without a glance at Briana as he passed her, he stood in front of her mother and asked in a stern and penetrating voice, "Where did Lord Darby and this acquaintance meet? Do you recall?"

Briana could see the tears streaming down her mother's face as she looked at Cameron. She knew her mother was overwhelmed and that she was on the verge of losing herself to her emotions, but before Briana could intervene, her mother responded, "I'm so sorry, Cameron. It's all our fault. I can't remember the name of the place. It was just some old drinking hall in Bethnal Green near the old stable yard that's abandoned now." Briana couldn't help but wonder if her father made any more mention to this place in his journals. He was so excited about it that he must have. She turned to share this information with Cameron, but he gave her the cut direct as he walked past her and toward the door.

"Wait! Cameron, where are you going?" Briana asked as she grabbed his hand to stop him from turning the knob.

"I'm going to find my sister and I would appreciate it if you remove your hand from mine."

"I want to help. I think I could find some information in my father's..."

"Yes. I'm sure you do want to help, but I'd have to trust you first, and since you never thought to confide in me enough to help with your situation, I don't think you know what exactly honesty and trust look like. I'd rather work on my own." Seeing the hurt on Briana's face, Cameron couldn't help but feel a bit of guilt. He understood why she kept her family's status a secret, but he couldn't help but feel hurt that she'd made him fall for her as a means to get a proposal. And yet, she had pushed him away recently as well and declared her intent to pursue Edwards, which made him both angry and sorry for the man in question. He couldn't process his feelings right now. Sighing and running a hand through his hair, he said in a matter-of-fact manner, "I'll let you know when I've found her." He opened the door and slammed it shut behind him without a backward glance. He had some information now to go off of and needed to share what he'd learned with Officer Bixley.

Briana stood looking at the door with Cameron's words repeating in her head. Never before had words felt like such a slap to the face. She knew she'd hurt him and that he was worried about finding Emily, but she never thought his words could cut her to the bone so easily. Briana heard her mother's sobs and sniffling from across the room. Taking a deep breath to steady herself, Briana returned to her mother's side. Lady Darby had collapsed once again onto the settee with her head in her hands.

"Mother, let's go home. We've given Cameron all the information we have and you are overwhelmed. You need your rest so you can support Her Grace tomorrow." Briana stroked her mother's back until her mother's sobs quieted into silent tears running down her face. "There, there. Emily will be found and everything will return to normal. Come now."

Not wanting to disturb the household, Briana and her mother slipped out the front door silently and made their way back to their house. Helping her mother ready herself for bed, Briana kept up a stream of reassurances to assuage her mother's guilt. After helping her mother to bed and making promises that Elizabeth would remain a loyal friend, Briana kissed her mother's forehead and closed the door behind her. Releasing a breath she hadn't realized she'd been holding, Briana headed to her father's study to spend the night reading his journals for clues about where he was meeting this acquaintance. If she was lucky, this place could be where Emily is being held and she could save her, return her home, and move forward without any more danger to those she loved.

CHAPTER 18

It was early afternoon now and Emily's arms were beginning to feel the strain of being tied behind her back for such a long time. It had been almost twenty-four hours since she was taken, and she was beginning to lose faith that anyone would find her. She had been sitting on the floor of an empty room at an abandoned inn with both her hands and feet bound. Having been abandoned years earlier, there was no furniture in the room except for a wooden chair in the corner, which was currently inhabited by the vile man who'd taken her from the Great Exhibition. Emily let out a quiet breath as she looked around the room for something to cut the ropes binding her hands together.

The rustling in the chair across the room brought with it a raspy voice, "I know you must be tired after sitting on that hard floor for so long. Why don't I let you have the chair for a while? It can't be that much longer before they arrive." He stood up and, grabbing Emily by the arms, helped her waddle her way to the chair.

"Mr. Gutterson, I really don't understand why you've brought me here. Do you have some sort of vendetta with my brother? Please, I'm trying to understand…" Emily said with a voice devoid of the desperation she truly felt.

Mr. Gutterson's tongue came out to lick both sides of his mouth before laughing in such a way that chills were sent up and down Emily's spine. He crouched down in front of her so his eyes were on level with hers. He then patted her bound hands before stroking the side of her face and replying in a saccharinely sweet voice, "Oh my dear, I have no vendetta with your brother. Now, your father on the other hand was always one to meddle in my affairs, especially where Lord Darby was concerned. I'm afraid you are just an easy means of getting revenge on the two families that left my reputation in pieces."

Emily pressed her back deeper into the chair in the hopes that she could put some more distance between herself and Mr. Gutterson's crazed look. Maintaining a straight back and a strong gaze, Emily knew she was acting in contradictory ways, but for every part of her that trembled in fear came another part that reminded her she must be strong until her family came to her rescue. With a slow blink and noncommittal shrug of her shoulders, Emily replied, "I'm afraid I don't know what you're speaking of, but I can assure you that your reputation will be in more tatters once my family comes for you."

"I hope they do come, as well as the lovely Briana. It would make my announcing our engagement so much easier." At Emily's wildly shocked face, Mr. Gutterson continued on to say, "Why the shocked face? You didn't think I brought you here without a plan in place, did you? No, I know the lovely Miss Emily Worthington of the Hereford line is not so dimwitted." He stepped forward and grabbed Emily by the chin to bring her eyes to his. He could see the quiet hatred lying in her eyes, but true to her upbringing, she was doing a wonderful job of keeping a cool demeanor. With a chilling smile, he said, "What a beautiful wife I will have. I will marry you and be able to take the dowry and all other money your family owes me. Your family stopped me from what I was due before, but now I will be able to get all your assets, and also by taking your surname, my heirs and I will have the dukedom's family name and my reputation will be restored.

As for the Valmonts, I will make sure everyone knows the lies they have spread about their financial standing. They have put on airs long enough and I will have the backing of the earldom's family name to give my words the credit necessary." Letting go of her chin and gripping the armrest instead, Gutterson licked the sides of his lips slowly and, looking Emily up and down, said, "I'm happy I will be marrying such a lovely and submissive lady. It will be important for you to stay just as submissive while I make sure your friend learns her true place. We wouldn't want things to get ugly for you too, now, would we?" Pushing off of the arm rests, Gutterson turned and walked toward the bed and picked up his jacket. He smoothed it out first before putting it on, and then went to smoothing out his hair as best he could without a mirror or brush.

Emily was nauseated. She felt her stomach drop as she listened to Mr. Gutterson talk about her future. Marry him? She could barely stand the sight of the man. How was she supposed to marry such a vile creature who has such horrible plans for her family and Briana's because of some history he had with both families? She needed to buy their families time since she knew Briana would notice her absence sooner than anyone else. Clearing her throat and thrusting her chin defiantly into the air, Emily stated, "I am sorry to disappoint you when you have painstakingly planned such a future for yourself, but I would rather die than marry you. I am afraid I am not as willing a participant in your plan as you may think. So, you may go on and kill me, because I will never marry you. You will never have the earldom's family name and nobody will ever give much credit to anything you may say." She could feel her blood boiling, the rolling of her stomach intensified, and the bile rose up in her throat. She took a deep breath to settle herself and reminded herself she must remain strong. She knew he would not kill her because she played such a strong role in his plans, but keeping him here arguing with her may be the best she could do to make sure he was caught when she was discovered. For as vile a man as he is, she could not picture him to be as dangerous as he tried to appear.

Gutterson, who had been licking his hand and using the saliva as a way to smooth his hair into a respectable look, stopped with his hand in mid-air in front of his face. Turning slowly, he wore the same pleasant smile that he wore throughout the day, the one that did not reach his cold eyes. Without a moment's hesitation, he stalked over and picked Emily up by her arms. Slamming her back into the wall nearby and turning her head at an unnatural angle, he whispered roughly into her ear, "Don't test me, girl. I'm at my wits end and I could kill you easily with a snap of the neck. Your father has already stepped into my business before and led me to lose all my fortune alone to a scamming situation since Darby listened to him rather than keeping his word to me. I am due some retribution from your families and I will damn well get it. My daughter, that damn bitch, has cut me off, leaving me completely destitute. If you push me, I will make sure both your families are reduced to nothing like me before I die, because trust me, I would rather be dead than poor. Don't overestimate your worth in my plans, because I have plenty of other ways to get my revenge and they are all ugly and deadly." As if to prove his point, he squeezed Emily's neck hard enough to leave her struggling for air. "Do you understand now what I am capable of?" After feeling Emily's attempt at a jerky nod, he let her go and stepped back to watch her slide down the wall gasping for air. He smiled viciously before smoothing out the two strands of hair that were now out of place. Moving to pick her up and return her to the chair, his smile broadened as he felt her body shudder under his hands. He gripped her chin again to make her meet his eyes once more before saying, "I like it when you shudder under my hands. It means you know exactly who is in control. I'll leave you now to think about that some more while I go and begin the next phase of my plan by taking a stroll down the London streets and telling all about how the Valmonts have misled us all. It's a good thing I have gathered some formal receipts of dresses Briana has sold off and was able to track down where she found that necklace of Caribbean emeralds she wore to the opera. Oh yes, people will definitely turn their backs on the Valmonts by week's end. Don't worry though. I won't say anything to harm your family's reputation since I would do nothing to harm my future wife." With a caress down the side of Emily's cheek, he turned to grab his walking stick and left her alone in the room, hands still bound behind her back and tears of desperation and anger rolling down her cheeks.

CHAPTER 19

After spending all night searching her father's journals, Briana finally found a clue in one of her father's final journal entries where he made mention of a man with the initials D.G. who wished to invest in a new business venture with him. Running through everyone she knew in London, she was able to identify the acquaintance her mother spoke of as Mr. Dorian Gutterson from the card he'd given Wallace to announce his presence as a morning caller the day after the masquerade ball. Reading the final entries more closely, she was also able to come up with three possible locations near the abandoned stable yard that could be where Gutterson had taken Emily. Her father made reference to a restaurant he visited often with his banker to discuss financial investments that looked promising, White's, where he would go at night for some drinking and gambling or gossip, and a few mentions in his final journal about an inn where he had met with a possible business partner to invest in converting the stable house into an inn and making a profit selling off any remaining horses. After dressing herself in comfortable clothing and walking to the milliner's store under the guise of buying a new hat for the upcoming winter, Briana learned through casual conversation that the restaurant mentioned by her father no longer existed and was now a broken-down bakery that was luckily still in business named Sweet Delights.

Leaving the store, Briana knew she only had one more option to check since women were not allowed to enter White's Gentleman's Club. Now, if only she could get the address or specific location of the inn. Maybe she could just head to that area of town and ask for a list of inns nearby. Could she do that now that the sun was beginning to set or should she wait a bit longer and go under the cover of night? No, she couldn't leave Emily alone for a second longer. Making up her mind, Briana called for a hackney and, as she stepped up into it, asked to be taken to Bethnal Green.

Briana watched as the faces of buildings passed by her view and composed a story in her head of what to say once she arrived at the inn. She knew her story had to be plausible enough for the innkeeper to let her disturb some of his guests. She closed her eyes, wishing she were not venturing into danger alone. She wished Cameron were with her to encourage her and protect her from any harm she was bound to encounter, but she knew he was angry with her and her mother. They had kept secrets from him and had placed his sister in danger, so she could not hold his anger against him.

The hackney came to a stop in front of a row of buildings on the verge of collapse. The streets were dirty and children could be seen with faces as gaunt as a skeleton. Briana accepted the groom's outstretched hand to help her down and, assuring him that she was fine, proceeded to ask the begging children for directions to Sweet Delights bakery, knowing it to be close to an inn. With a sense of guilt for leaving these children who were clearly starving, she gave the children what little money she had with her as a thank you after receiving directions and continued on her way.

The woman running the bakery had wiry red hair and streaks of flour covering the front of her dress. Despite the tumbledown building, dirty conditions outside her store, and lack of customers inside, the woman greeted Briana with a smile. Her rosy cheeks gave her a welcoming countenance, and when she opened her mouth to speak, Briana was pleased to hear a dulcet voice that matched the woman's sweet profession. Smiling broadly, the woman said, "Of course, I know the closest inn! It's just up the street. My sister and her husband run it and would gladly welcome you as a customer for the night. But dear, are you traveling alone? You know this isn't the best part of town and a woman of your class should not be here unaccompanied." The kind woman's eyes grew with concern as she placed her warm hand over Briana's.

Briana shook her head and, with a small smile, replied, "No, I'm meeting my brother and sister-in-law there. They've gone ahead of me and should already be at the inn. Thank you for your concern. We're just passing through for the night. Could you tell me the name of the inn and how far down the street it is? I seem to have forgotten that information, even after my brother wrote it down for me." Briana laughed and smiled again, hoping the woman would have no further concerns or suspicions and give her the information she needed. She was so close to Emily and the more time she wasted, the closer Emily was to imminent danger. With a pat on the hand, the woman told Briana the name of the Blackhorse Inn that was located about half a mile down the road.

"It should be directly across from Monsieur Pelletier's Minks shop. If you see the abandoned fragrance store on your left, you've gone too far. Now, go find your family since it's beginning to get dark outside and it can be very dangerous around here at night for a young lady walking alone. Tell the innkeepers that Suzette sent you and they should accommodate you sooner. Take care, dear!" With another pat on the back and a small loaf of bread, Briana was sent on her way with legs that moved faster than she'd ever known them to do before.

Briana made sure not to make eye contact with anyone as she passed by and continued forward looking for either the Blackhorse Inn or Monsieur Pelletier's Minks. The last sliver of sunlight was fading from view and the hair on the back of Briana's neck couldn't help but stand on end. Her stomach was in knots and her heart was racing. She'd only thought of finding

Emily as soon as possible, but hadn't given much thought to Mr. Gutterson and how they would escape from his abduction. Did she remember to leave a note to her mother about her whereabouts? The sky was dark now and she knew her mother would begin to worry for her daughter, as well as for Emily. Briana knew she should have been reasonable and waited for Officer Bixley to find Emily and return her home safely, but she couldn't wait any longer. With a silent apology to her mother, Briana shook her head and focused her mind on getting to Emily. Together, they would come up with a plan of escape. Right now, the important thing was for Emily to know she was not alone in this situation. Briana would be there for her, just like Emily had been for her when they were younger.

A French accent reached her ears just before Briana heard a door close. Refocusing her eyes on the storefronts across the street, she saw Monsieur Pelletier's sign and with a quick smile to herself she turned around and looked up to see the signage for the Blackhorse Inn. With a couple deep breaths to calm her shaking hands and racing heart, Briana picked up her skirts and stepped across the threshold ready to tell any lie necessary to be reunited with Emily.

"Hello, Miss. How may I be of service this evening?" a portly gentleman with a thick beard and spectacles that slid down the bridge of his nose inquired of Briana. He was joined by a woman of similar stature with auburn red hair that was loosely pulled into a chignon at the nape of her neck. She had the same red tinted hair, rosy cheeks, and warm smile as her sister from the bakery. The main difference was in the studious eyes of the innkeeper's wife. She seemed to be measuring Briana as her husband spoke to her, judging her character perhaps.

"Yes, good evening. I am hoping you can help me by letting me know if my brother and sister-in-law have arrived yet for the night? My brother is an older gentleman of average height with grey hairs at his temples and carries an elegant walking stick. His wife is a younger woman, of similar age as I, with blonde hair and blue eyes. I am supposed to meet them here, but I am afraid they must have been waiting a while," Briana said, trying to remain elegant and calm in order to make her story more believable. It would not do for the innkeeper's wife to discover her lie and not let Briana have a room for the night.

"Ah, yes. I do believe they are here. They arrived a day or so ago. I'm afraid your brother has stepped out for the moment, but I do believe the mistress is resting in her room with a slight headache according to your brother. He asked that she not be disturbed," the innkeeper said with a nod. "He said he would be back by dinnertime and that the two would take dinner in their room. Would you care for a room near them?

"Yes, that would be lovely. Thank you. Is there a way that I can get a key to their room as well? I would very much like to nurse my sister-in-law if she indeed has a headache," Briana asked smiling sweetly.

"I'm afraid we can't do that, my dear. We have to respect our customer's privacy and make it a policy to not give out extra room keys. I'm afraid you will simply have to await your brother's return," the innkeeper replied.

Briana felt the panic rise up in her throat. How could she be so close to Emily and yet have such a major obstacle standing in her way? What could she do to appeal to them to let her in? Praying for the Lord's forgiveness, Briana braced herself for yet another lie. In the most broken voice she could muster Briana said, "I...I...understand. I only hope she and the baby are okay. I knew she had not been feeling well and never told my brother. She swore me to secrecy, but I pray I have not signed her...her...death warrant." Letting her hands tremble, as they naturally have for the last hour or so, Briana made eye contact with the innkeeper's wife whose eyes were studying her closely.

With a worried look in her eyes (the same one as her sister's), the innkeeper's wife asked, "How long has the lass been feeling ill?"

"It's been at least a week now," Briana replied quietly. "She's complained of intense head and stomach pain. She said she was sick for a few mornings as well."

"And her husband knows nothing of this?"

"No. I promised her I wouldn't say. She didn't want him to worry if this was just some passing illness. My brother is one who is prone to worry needlessly and then will behave extremely over the littlest of things," Briana replied.

"Honestly, you women with your secrets will drive any man to behave extremely," the innkeeper muttered under his breath. Not quietly enough, though, since his wife's studious eyes quickly turned to him and made him clear his throat rather gruffly.

Without a word to her husband, the innkeeper's wife took a key off a hook under the desk and motioned for Briana to follow her. "I will take you to her room so that you may care for her. If you will give me some time to check on dinner downstairs, I can come back with a bowl of water and clean towels you can use on her head to help alleviate the headache. Your room will be just across the hall. Do you have any luggage outside?"

"Thank you so much. Luggage? Oh, no I'm afraid my coachman must have gone ahead with it to our house in London. I must not have made myself very clear about stopping here for the night. No bother, I will simply borrow a dress from my sister-in-law."

As the innkeeper's wife nodded slowly in understanding, she unlocked the door and pushed it open to reveal a dimly lit room with a female form lying on the bed. Briana blew out a sigh of relief to see that the form wore the same dress Briana last remembered Emily wearing. Briana turned and, clasping the innkeeper's hand in hers, thanked her once again. She stepped into the room and shut the door behind her before rushing to the side of the bed to make sure Emily was still alive and unharmed.

Emily's eyes fluttered open as she felt a cool damp cloth touch her forehead and her wrists. She heard Briana's voice calling her name gently. She must be hallucinating now after being in the same room for so long and having refused to eat or drink much of what was given to her. Trying to shrug off the cool cloth on her forehead and seep back into a fitful sleep before Gutterson arrived for the next phase in his plan, Emily mumbled for the hallucination to leave her in peace. She needed to save the last remnants of strength she had for when Gutterson returned, and that included her mental strength as well.

"Emily! Em! I am not a hallucination. Now, wake up!" Briana said as she shook her friend by the shoulders. She could tell how physically exhausted her friend was and felt horrible for treating her so forcibly. Seeing how Emily's eyes opened but remained unfocused and their window of escape was diminishing quickly, Briana couldn't feel too sorry about her next move. Briana turned Emily to face her before saying, "Dash it all to hell," and throwing the remaining contents of the water bowl in Emily's face.

"Oh!! What in heaven's name?" Emily exclaimed as she wiped the water from her face and then focused her eyes on her assailant. "Brie? Whatever are you doing here? And why are you throwing water in my face?"

"Sorry Em, but I couldn't get you to see me as more than a hallucination. I've come to take you home. We have to get out of here while Gutterson is gone. He has some sort of vendetta against my family, but I'll be damned if he hurts anyone I care about," Briana said, not ashamed about her less than lady-like manners.

"Oh Brie, you shouldn't have come. He's dangerous and more so than you could have anticipated. He does indeed want revenge on both of our families and he plans to ruin your family name by exposing your financial troubles and lies while using me as a wife to garner a higher role in social circles. He's threatened to kill us all if we get in his way," Emily said as she clutched Briana's hands and hiccupped back the tears that threatened to once again stream down her face.

"Shh. Between the two of us, we'll find a way to either get out of here or stall him long enough for someone to come help us. I did leave my father's journal open on my writing desk in the hopes that someone will see and take it to Officer Bixley for more information. It was the same journal that led me to this part of town and to you, so hopefully there will be someone following my same path that can come to our rescue if needed. Come, calm your nerves so we can devise a plan. How long has it been since he left?" Briana asked her friend as she patted Emily's hand and guided her to take a seat at the foot of the bed.

Emily nodded and, taking in slow breaths at Briana's suggestion, found herself calmer than before. Squeezing Briana's hand slightly, she replied, "He left approximately three hours ago, I believe. My sense of time has been skewed since being trapped in this room," Emily replied.

Briana looked around the room for a way to escape. There was one window located on the far right corner of the wall opposite the door. Unfortunately, the location of their room was too high to simply climb out the window. Maybe if she made a knotted rope with the bed sheets? She'd seen Jake do it when they were younger after he got sent to his room without dinner for breaking his father's prized jade elephant figurine. Looking back, it had been her urging to play a game of tag inside the house even though Emily had reminded them on multiple occasions that morning that they should avoid her father's study. Of course, they had all intention to do so, but when Emily had tagged Briana and Briana had instantly turned to tag Jake, the closest room for him to duck in to just happened to be the study. Jake had managed to stay in the center of the room until Briana's foot caught the bottom hem of her gown and sent her stumbling forward, pushing him into the shelf housing the figurine. Cameron and his father walked through the doors just in time to see the elephant crash and shatter to the floor, little pieces of green jade strewn around Jake's feet. Remembering the roaring voice of the Duke of Hereford made her shake. He was a man who rarely raised his voice, so when he did, it seemed to stop everything around him. Jake had taken the blame and patted her hand as he walked solemnly to his room. He'd seemed so gentlemanly at the time, not so much later on when hunger had prompted him to climb out his window in order to sneak into the kitchen for food. Luckily, Briana was walking home then and was able to pass him food instead, thus saving him jumping down from the second story window.

Refocusing her eyes on the window, she knew the bedding would probably not be enough, not to mention that Emily would refuse for fear of breaking a leg. Briana looked next at the door. If she could guarantee that the innkeeper's wife would venture up to the room with the promised water and cloth for Emily, maybe they could slip out with her under the guise of getting fresh air to relieve Emily's headache. In fact, Briana didn't recall the innkeeper's wife locking the door again after Briana's arrival. Maybe if they moved fast, they could get out before Mr. Gutterson returned. She'd say they were stepping outside for some fresh air to help Emily feel better if anyone asked. With her mind made up, Briana tapped Emily on the shoulder. Was her shoulder always this slender? Had she eaten anything while captured?

"Em, I need you to look at me. The door is unlocked, so now is our chance to leave. We're going to have to move fast. Can you do it?" Briana asked with concern filling her voice.

Emily nodded with grim determination. She felt weak from lack of food and her limbs ached from being bound for so long, but if this was her chance for escape, nothing would stop her. Standing with Briana's help, the two women walked towards the door.

"As soon as we open this door Em, I want you to stay as close to me as possible. We'll say we're getting fresh air to relieve your headache. Then, when we get outside, we will walk quickly to the nearest hackney we can see and head home," Briana said, recounting her plan. "Don't worry. It's not quite dinnertime and I'm sure Mr. Gutterson wouldn't think we'd have such an opportunity. In fact, I would be surprised if he returns within the hour," Briana said adamantly. Turning the door handle, Briana was confused by the lack of pressure needed. As the door opened, she found the reason why. Just as Emily gasped, Mr.Gutterson's angry and thick hands gripped her shoulders and thrust her and Emily back inside the room. The opportunity of escape was now gone.

Tightening the rope on Emily's wrists once again, Mr. Gutterson slowly approached Briana. He hadn't tied Briana yet, but holding a knife to Emily's throat had worked sufficiently well in keeping her rooted to the spot in the room he'd shoved her to earlier.

"Well… well…well. I should have known you couldn't stay away, Lady Valmont. Just how did you find me?" Mr. Gutterson asked in a menacingly curious tone.

Briana refused to show her fear and responded, "It wasn't hard. You're not as clever as you think, especially since I had my father's journals to rely on. You kept stating how close you were with my father. I narrowed down that this was where you were going to start a business, and since you feel wronged, why wouldn't you come back here where everything went wrong and try to rewrite yourself a new future?" Briana tried to appear nonchalant as she spoke, but every muscle in her body tensed as his eyes narrowed in her direction.

"Well, aren't you a clever girl?" Mr. Gutterson's tone was mocking and the menacing edge intensified as he ground his teeth. His thick tongue came out and licked both corners of his mouth, leaving them glistening with saliva. Stepping closer toward Briana, Gutterson continued, "Your father wasn't very clever. He should have known leaving me behind and listening to Hereford would lead him to his death. What a coward. He didn't know the inn we were going to create was to serve as a cover for an opium den. We could have made more money than we ever dreamed, but he wasn't willing to take risks on anything anymore after talking with Hereford." Gutterson scoffed in disgust at the memory.

Briana could feel her temper rising. She was already tense and didn't know how much longer she could behave in a calm, nonchalant manner. Looking over at Emily, Briana could see that, despite her feeling defeated, Emily sat upright in the most proper and ladylike manner with her hands bound in front of her. Briana gained a new sense of strength seeing her best friend refusing to give in to this horrible man.

Gutterson returned to Emily's side as soon as he caught Briana's gaze shift. He continued to berate Emily's father saying, "And, your father just couldn't keep his nose out of our business. You would think a titled man would have more to do than serve as his neighbor's chaperone. Well, since I'm marrying you, my dear, I'll have access to the man's money without having him stop me," Gutterson finished as he ran a finger down Emily's face.

"Don't touch her!" Briana shouted. She couldn't bear to see her friend suffer any more in calm defiance. "Please, I know you're angry, but it was my father who you couldn't trust. I just don't understand why Emily can't be left out of this," Briana pleaded. She'd shortened the distance a bit between her and Emily as she spoke.

Mr. Gutterson stood and pressed Briana's back into the wall. He growled as he said, "I told you not to move. Don't be a fool and make me kill you like I did your father."

Briana's mind went blank as did her hearing. He had killed her father. Her father had been murdered. That meant all these years believing her father had abandoned her and her mother had all been a lie. But her father had argued with her mother and left with a suitcase in hand. She remembered seeing him climb into a carriage and he'd never returned again. Clearing her throat, she asked, "When did you kill my father? Was it the same night he left, having decided to abandon his family forever?" Briana's voice grew with determination despite the tears stinging her eyes. She didn't really want to think of her father, but there was a small part of her that hoped what she'd seen was wrong.

Mr. Gutterson sneered and replied, "Ha! Your father was a coward, remember? For as much as he would get angry and threaten, he'd never be man enough to leave. No, he was meeting me. He'd told me that after confiding in Hereford, he wanted to get himself help for his alcohol addiction and that he couldn't agree to the business venture. He wished me the best on my own, said he was going to become a new man for his family, give up alcohol and gambling completely, and atone for his sins." Gutterson was turning red in the face as he continued to tell the story of what happened to her father.

"But, if he was simply meeting you, why did he have a suitcase with him?" Emily asked from her spot on the bed.

Again, Gutterson curled his lips up into the same vicious sneer as he laughingly said, "Ha! Why, that suitcase was the money he was going to give to the doctor who was going to cure him of his addiction. I believe he planned to visit the doctor after he was done meeting with me, but I wasn't going to let that money go to anything other than what we planned. Since he didn't seem to understand me, I had no choice but to kill him and take the money. It's what he owed me, after all. Don't you agree that a person should keep their word, my dear?" Gutterson asked as he closed in on Briana, pushing her back further into the dresser so she could feel the edges of it digging into her back. Her grip tightened in order to steady herself.

"What exactly did you do to my father?" Briana asked with eyes darker than sin.

Gripping her neck and turning her head into a painful angle as he moved his knife down to the right side of her stomach. Gutterson said, "Why don't I show you instead?"

CHAPTER 20

She could feel the cold of the blade as the sharp tip pressed against her clothing. She'd never been happier to be wearing a corset than in this moment.

"You see, I gave him one more chance to change his mind. To forget about this new version of himself that wanted to lose us both the opportunity to earn money. He not only turned me down, but laughed at my pathetic obsession with money. I've come too far to lose money and have anyone look down on me. When he reached out to pat my shoulder, I dug my knife into his side. It was easy to pour alcohol down his throat later on and leave his body in this area where nobody knew he was the Earl of Darby. And those that did know him would assume he either left town running from a gamble gone awry or died in some drunken state. It was all so easy, especially with the money I took. It wasn't until the money ran out and my daughter, the ungrateful bitch, cut me off that I went searching for your mother only to find you both had moved away. Now, I finally have everyone here that I need to restore myself to the style of living I deserve." To prove his point, he turned away from Briana and looked over to Emily while holding the tip of his knife at Briana's side. Squinting his eyes and speaking in a rough tone, he said to Emily, "Now, I won't have any problems from you both, right?"

Briana shook her head, unable to speak for fear of what he may do next. They needed to get away from him, but he kept them both under such a watchful gaze that escape seemed unattainable. No matter the risks, she needed to at least get Emily free. Taking advantage of his attention being on Emily, Briana straightened her posture and preparing herself for the worst, launched herself at Gutterson with the intent of knocking him to the floor. Unfortunately, her body weight wasn't enough to accomplish that desired effect. Gutterson simply stumbled forward, losing his balance a bit but able to catch himself on the bedframe before completely falling. Briana may not have knocked him down, but she managed to make him drop the knife. It had fallen and slid somewhere under the bed and out of his reach. Briana gave herself a quick mental celebration before seeing the rage on Gutterson's face as he turned his full attention on her.

"Please don't hurt her! She didn't mean to do that, right, Brie?" Emily said panic in her voice.

"I told you how desperate I am. I also told you not to give me any trouble, but it seems you both won't listen," Gutterson replied with a voice as sharp as steel. He was directing his words to Emily, but his eyes were on Briana.

"We'll tell everyone what you did to my father and how you've kept Emily hostage. You won't get the life you want. Not by getting any money from my family or by getting Emily to marry you."

Before Briana could say another word, Gutterson's hands were around her throat. She could feel the air slipping from her lungs as her throat closed with the applied pressure of Gutterson's thick and clammy hands. She tried scratching and clawing at them to pry them off, but to no avail. She could hear Emily scream, but it sounded far away. As everything began to slip from view, Brie vaguely heard a crash and saw a shadow in the doorway.

When Brie's eyes opened, she found Gutterson struggling to get out of an officer's hold. Shouting obscenities, Gutterson swore he'd die before being jailed and poor for the rest of his life. Officer Bixley turned his head and looked over his shoulder at Briana before saying, "Lady Valmont, I'm pleased to see you've returned to us. Your friend has been watching you worriedly. I'm afraid I haven't had the chance to free her wrists from their bindings. Would you mind?"

Briana nodded quickly and stood to cross the room and join Emily on the bed. Before sitting, Briana retrieved the knife from its place under the bed. She didn't pay any mind to the unladylike position she folded herself into in order to retrieve it. What mattered most was that Officer Bixley had not let her down and she would be able to save Emily and return home. She cut the rope bindings around Emily's wrists, and after laying the knife down on the night table, was gathered up into a desperate hug by Emily. Neither woman said anything, but held each other as they cried tears of relief. Officer Bixley was still restraining Gutterson with his own hands and was ready to make Gutterson leave and begin the journey to jail.

"Well, it seems I wasn't wrong in following you, Lady Valmont. I knew you were keeping information from me, but didn't think you'd be able to piece everything together so quickly. You really made my job a lot easier for me," Officer Bixley said with a sly grin.

Briana smiled back and stood to leave with Emily. As soon as they passed by the men, Gutterson grabbed hold of Officer Bixley's flintlock pocket pistol and aimed for Briana's head. "Don't move," Gutterson said tersely. Seeing Officer Bixley move toward him, Gutterson punched him square in the jaw with enough power in his free hand to send the officer in the direction of the floor behind him. Turning his attention back to the ladies, Gutterson reiterated his threat from earlier, "Remember, ladies, if I can't get my revenge and end up dead, you two will be going with me. Looks like it's the end for us all now." Cocking the pistol with both hands, Gutterson smiled with an eerie sense of calm. He continued, "Say your goodbyes, ladies." Briana and Emily grabbed each other close and closed their eyes just in time to hear the gun fire.

CHAPTER 21

Emily opened her eyes and saw Briana's arms still wrapped around her in comfort. She was alive. Oh no! Briana! Had she taken the shot? They had both fallen to the floor after the gun was fired, but never let go of each other.

"Brie? Brie, can you hear me?" Emily asked. Shaking her friend's shoulders roughly.

"Em? Are you hurt?" Briana responded quietly. Briana opened her eyes and both women checked each other relieved to see neither was hurt. "But, what happened?" Looking over to where Gutterson had stood with the gun in his hand, the women now found Bixley standing over Guterson's crumpled form. He'd grabbed the knife and stabbed Gutterson just as he'd fired the gun, causing Gutterson to miss his target and crumple to his death alone.

"Come, let's get you ladies away from this scene and into a carriage. I'll send a message for my men to take care moving the body and securing the scene before I return you both home," Officer Bixley said with a gentle yet matter-of-fact tone. Just as everyone moved to the hallway, they were met with the innkeeper and his wife, who both wore expressions of shock and anger.

"What in the blazes happened here?" asked the innkeeper

motioning to Gutterson's dead body. He was looking accusingly back and forth between Briana and Officer Bixley. He rubbed his chin and said, "This gentleman came with his wife here and they've been fine the last couple days. Then, suddenly this woman shows up claiming to be his sister and all hell breaks loose." His face was turning redder and redder with frustration. His wife patted his hand and tried to calm him.

"Sorry for the inconvenience sir, but this man is no gentleman. He took this lady hostage and tried to force her into marriage as part of a revenge plot. This other lady came to save her best friend with no concern for herself. And I, as an officer of the law, did all in my power to save the innocent. I hope you will forgive the commotion and allow me to do my job in securing the scene and contacting others to collect the body. I want to take care of all this as soon as possible so I can return the ladies home. They've been through more than enough," Officer Bixley finished with a sigh and look of encouragement in his eyes as he looked at Briana and Emily.

The innkeeper's wife moved quickly to the ladies and ushered them down the stairs and into a quiet sitting area near the dining room. She pushed a warm cup of tea into each woman's hands. When both ladies coughed after taking a gulp, she confessed, "I added a spot of brandy into each of your cups. I figured you'd need more than tea to calm your nerves tonight. Drink slowly my dears and know that he can no longer hurt you." She patted Emily's hand before adding, "I'm so sorry that I did not know of your plight when you first arrived. It wasn't until your friend here arrived with such fortitude and concealed panic in her eyes that I was willing to believe something must truly be wrong. I'm usually shrewder and a better judge of character. I'm sorry, again." She lowered her head in shame and her hair caught the glow of the fire, giving her an angelic halo.

"Please, do not trouble yourself. He had many of us fooled. I'm grateful to you for bringing Briana to my room, rather than waiting for him to return. You helped me more than you know," Emily responded and squeezed the woman's hands in return. The innkeeper's wife wiped her eyes before announcing that she would get a carriage ready and also make sure the officer was ready to leave within the hour. Briana and Emily sat side by side holding hands and sipping their tea in silence, both too exhausted and relieved to speak until Officer Bixley came and told them it was time to go home.

Returning to Hereford House was a lively and emotional experience. Officer Bixley was the first to enter the room, but before he could delve into an explanation of how everything was solved and what happened with Gutterson, Elizabeth rushed over and embraced Emily tightly. Both women were sobbing such loud tears of relief that Officer Bixley could manage to only get a word in before being completely drowned out. Lady Darby was not much better. She had collapsed to the floor in tears when she saw Briana follow into the room behind Emily. Hugs and tears of joy were then shared between Emily and her brothers.

Cameron had not moved until Briana walked in the door. He let out a sigh of relief when his eyes fell on her. He'd been holding his breath since the Great Exhibition and Emily's disappearance, but when he'd found out that Briana had gone to find Emily of her own accord, his world stopped. He felt like his heart had been racing for days, and now seeing the woman he cared for brought it to a sudden halt. Emily was safe and Briana was safe. He strode toward Briana and reached a hand out to touch her face before thinking the better of it and said, "I'm glad you are both back safely. What you did was extremely foolish, but thank you."

Briana had been rubbing her neck nervously and, remembering how upset he was the last time they spoke, she simply nodded and mumbled, "You're welcome," before her attention was caught by Lord Edwards who appeared in the doorway. She smiled genially at him and said, "Why Lord Edwards!"

Lord Edwards crossed the room in three quick strides and

took Briana's hands in his. Looking worriedly into her eyes, he said, "My dear! Look at you! How do you feel? To think you rushed out into this on your own. Mother would definitely say that the measure of a woman is patience, my dear. You put yourself in such danger and had us all so worried." Lord Edwards looked her over again shaking his head at the disheveled miss before him. He stopped when he caught sight of her neck. "What on earth happened to your neck?"

Before she could answer, Cameron appeared by her side. She didn't know how he got by her side so fast when he was across the room speaking with Emily. He turned Briana to face him, unconcerned with Lord Edwards' proximity and territorial expression. He ran his fingers over the bruising on her neck before saying, "I'll kill him with my bare hands."

Edwards, who was still holding Briana's hand, looked shocked at the fierceness in Cameron's voice. Seeking to be the one to comfort Briana, Edwards simply squeezed her hand until she was looking at him. "Come, sit down. You need to rest and not talk of killing or being hurt." Edwards sat on a nearby settee and pulled Briana down next to him.

Emily and her mother were sitting on the nearby couch, hand in hand. "As much as you probably don't want to relive what happened, I really wish to know what happened to you and that vile man," Elizabeth said to her daughter. Jake and Cameron moved to stand behind the couch, eagerly waiting to hear what became of Gutterson.

The next few hours were filled with the recounts from Emily, Briana, and Officer Bixley. Emily shared how Gutterson had tricked her into believing that the rest of the family had left the exhibit without her and offered her a ride home in his carriage. She hadn't completely trusted him, but believed since they were in such a crowded area, nothing bad would happen, at least since he never seemed to have ill feelings toward her. It was not until they were in his carriage that he'd covered her mouth with a cloth and she'd woken up inside the inn.

While Emily recounted the two days spent with Gutterson and the plan he revealed to her, Cameron's grip on the back of the couch continued to tighten. To think all this came from a point of such despicable greed. And the idea that he had been plotting to destroy Briana and her mother almost made Cameron forget about all the lies she'd told him.

Briana then shared how she came to find the inn through her father's journals and tried to save Emily on her own until Gutterson revealed that he'd killed her father and tried to kill her as well. It was here that Officer Bixley told everyone how he'd been watching Briana since she seemed to know more than she let on and did not seem like one to stay put. He recounted how he saved the ladies from the gunshot that would have killed at least one of them. Having done his job of returning both Emily and Briana to their families, Officer Bixley excused himself to complete all necessary paperwork.

Feeling the emotional toll of the last few days, Emily excused herself to retire for the night. The exhaustion and relief had finally caught up with her, leaving her limbs feeling much heavier than they were. She kissed her mother's cheek and gave each brother and Briana a hug. With a final squeeze of Brie's fingers in silent thanks, she exited the room and made her way up the stairs.

Briana watched her friend leave and did not know how exhausted she was until she touched her own cheeks to find them moist with tears she had not realized she'd cried. She looked up to find Cameron staring at her with an unreadable expression. Wanting so desperately to hear his voice, Briana said "I'm so happy she's back safely. Now everything can return back to the way things were before." Seeing his eyes turn darker and colder, Briana questioned, "Right?"

"I think it's time you headed home as well. You've also had quite the ordeal," Cameron replied stiffly, ignoring the hurt in her eyes. He wanted to comfort her and reassure her that everything was fine now, but the truth was that he still felt like he couldn't completely trust her. What did that say about him that he'd fallen in love with a woman who could lie so easily? She'd played her role of enchantress so well that any man couldn't help but be seduced by her. He'd fallen for a woman who was honest and genuine. He truly believed she could bring joy to the role of duchess. All the aspects of her he'd fallen in love with were simply a lie, crafted to ensnare a wealthy husband. He couldn't put the image of his strong, confident, cheerful, and seductive *Emerald Goddess* from the masquerade together with this timid and broken woman in front of him.

Seeing Cameron turn away from her nearly broke the last vestiges of strength Briana had to stand on. Nodding slowly as she resigned herself to the fact that Cameron would never care for her again, Briana said, "Yes, of course, you're right. Thank you." She turned and made her way toward the exit. Lord Edwards, who had made it a point to stay by her side since she'd returned, patted her hand and informed her that he would be walking her home and coming by in the morning to check on her well-being. She thanked him and, with her mother's hand in hers, made her way home and to her own bed. Though she hoped the exhaustion would lead to a restful sleep, thoughts and images of Cameron's cold eyes left her tossing and turning all night.

CHAPTER 22

The light that fell across her face early the next morning had Briana saying a silent curse. She had managed to get a couple hours of solid sleep, but that was in no way enough for her body to recuperate. She knew it was time to begin the day and get out of bed, but the heartbreak she was feeling still lingered.

Briana dressed in a pale purple muslin dress with deep violet stripes decorating the skirt. Her bodice was kept simple save for the black lace adorning the bust, which Briana had altered to fit today's fashions. Slipping on her satin shoes, she sat down at her vanity located against the far wall to find a way to tame the mass of curls that hung past her shoulder in an unruly and frizzy mess. Twisting and pinning her hair on top of her head in as close to an elegant coiffure as possible, Briana nodded in the mirror and then stood to make her way downstairs for breakfast.

After a filling breakfast, Briana and her mother sat in the front parlor. They sat together on the settee holding each other's right hand. They'd already shared their relief at being reunited with each other and the fear they had of losing one another. Now, they were sitting in companionable silence. Briana's mother broke the silence first by saying, "What do we do now? We've been hiding for so long from your father that now finding out he was killed just as he was trying to become the man I married..." She trailed off without finishing. She didn't need to finish since Briana knew what her mother was thinking. The idea that there could have been a different version of this family, one that echoed how it had started, was heartbreaking.

Briana nodded sadly and squeezed her mother's hand in comfort, saying, "I know. It would have been lovely." She was lost in her own thoughts of remembering her father before he'd developed his taste for alcohol. He'd been a warm, genial, and lively man who enjoyed literature and horses as much as his daughter. It wasn't until he met people like Gutterson who'd enjoyed gambling at White's Gentleman's Club and won a few games that his taste for alcohol, and change in personality, began. Briana had been seven when she first saw her father drunkenly escorted home by Emily's father. Afterward, his luck with gambling began to take a turn and he grew violent. The father she'd known had disappeared, only to be seen in the rare occasion that he was sober. In those rare occasions with her father, she was happy.

She was brought out of her reverie when Wallace came to the door to announce the visit of Lord Edwards. Both Briana and her mother settled themselves to make sure they were presentable. With a nod from Violet, Lord Edwards was shown into the room. Bowing quickly to both ladies, he crossed and took the chair to the left of Briana. He sat on the edge of his seat and wore a face of determination and concern.

"Good day to you both. I hope you were both able to rest after this horrible ordeal." Although he addressed both of the women, his cloudy blue eyes were fixed solely on Briana.

Briana smiled back reassuringly as she said, "We did, thank you. I appreciate you thinking of us, Lord Edwards."

"Yes, well, I wanted to see for myself and ask you if you were free for a morning stroll." Lord Edwards had a kind smile with eyes that seemed to light up with the hope that Briana would say yes.

Before Briana could give her answer, her mother winked at her and stifled a forced yawn. She smiled sheepishly as she said, "Oh dear, it seems I am still a bit tired. Do go ahead and enjoy yourself, darling." With a smile to Lord Edwards, who had stood and given an elegant bow, Violet exited.

Briana watched her mother leave before turning her gaze back to Lord Edwards. He'd sat down again in the same chair, but she noticed that he'd moved it a couple inches backward in an attempt to maintain a sense of propriety now that there was no chaperone. With an elegant nod and a soft smile upon her lips, Briana replied, "Thank you for the invitation, Lord Edwards. I do believe a stroll would be lovely." Standing and smoothing out her skirts, she made her way to the doors her mother exited through moments before.

Deciding not to venture too far, Lord Edwards directed them to the nearby gardens. As they strolled arm in arm, they talked about the nice morning breeze and the few rays of sunshine that peeked through the clouds from time to time. Lord Edwards had surprisingly little to say other than the little conversation about the weather until they sat down on the bench in the middle of the garden. After asking if she was feeling all right, Lord Edwards revealed his true purpose for taking a morning stroll when he said, "My dear Briana, I wish you will permit me to call you by name as well as my fiancée. I have given much thought, and though I think my mother would have some reservations about your spirited nature, I must say that I think you will find that marriage has a calming effect on a person. I believe we will suit very well together once we settle into our lives and you take on your role as mistress of my house and domestic affairs." Taking her hands in his and gently stroking his thumbs over them in a caress he hoped would convey his genuine feelings, he asked the question he had thought about all night, "Will you do me the honor of giving me your hand in marriage?"

Briana looked at Lord Michael Edwards, a man that was kind and helpful. A man who was very handsome, friendly, intelligent, virtuous, and with whom she'd shared many wonderful outings and conversations. But despite all his wonderful qualities, she'd never felt the same spark she had with Cameron. She could have such a happy and stable life with him as her husband and become the delicate and pious woman he'd wish her to be, especially since they would never have arguments that would leave the other wondering if they'd made the right choice in being together. She wouldn't have the passionate love affair she secretly desired and she knew she would be forced to act in a reserved manner different than her instincts, but he would be faithful to her. She would be happy with a man who could settle all her family's debts and provide for her mother as well, making it so she would no longer have to be rash and live in shame of her decisions. She raised a hand to caress his cheek and to her surprise Lord Edwards brought his lips to hers. It was a nice and gentle kiss, much like the man himself, which lasted only a moment. She smiled at the thought of knowing how gentle he'd always be with her and how much he'd grown to care for her. He'd make her happy, right? She'd have to pretend not to feel so strongly for Cameron, but maybe the pretending will help dull the pain of an unrequited love. There had never really been a chance for them to truly be together anyway, but with Lord Edwards, there was a man who would devote himself to her happiness without any pretense. Nodding slowly as she made up her mind, she smiled and simply said, "Of course."

After his proposal, Lord Edwards wrapped Briana in a quick embrace and place a gentle kiss on her hand before asking when they were going to share the good news with her family. They decided on tonight during dinner. She would let her mother know, as well as Wallace and Cathy, in order to have the dining room and front parlors ready for entertaining. They would make sure to invite Emily's family as well in order to provide a further cause of celebration after the recent ordeal they'd all been through.

Briana dressed in a gown of emerald green and black lace. She'd asked her mother to help her fashion her hair into something different than the normal pinned coiffure she managed on her own. With her mother's help, she was able to smooth her curls into braids which her mother was then able to pin in an intricate design at the nape of her neck. Releasing some curls in the front of her face that threatened to come out on their own later in the night, Briana smiled and felt truly radiant. The only other time in her life she had felt like this was the night of the masquerade ball. She'd spent so much time that day getting ready to find herself a rich husband, and to think that now everything was going to plan. She was happy, right? Smiling at her mother in the mirror, Briana readied herself for tonight's announcement. She knew everyone would be happy, but the thought of a pair of dark eyes that could turn from ice to fire in an instant had her heart beating faster with anxiety. Everything would be fine.

Briana held her mother's hand as the two women made their way down the stairs to sit in the front parlor and await their guests. Briana left her mother there for a brief while so she could check with Cathy and make sure the food was perfect for tonight. She wanted to impress Lord Edwards with her skills of running a household and providing a successful dinner party, even if it was simply family. She knew part of her future as his wife would definitely be to do the same and more for their home. She had to make sure she was the true measure of a woman for him, as his mother would say.

Briana returned to the front parlor and took the seat by her mother just as Wallace came to announce the arrival of Her Grace and Lady Worthington. The women greeted one another and immediately sat to discuss the day's affairs. Elizabeth had heard from Lady Turner that Lady Phillips' grandson had arrived in town and was already being sought after by the ladies of the *ton* and their matchmaking mothers. Apparently, he was a tall gentleman with the same blond hair as his grandmother, but was much quieter than her. His quiet personality gave him a sense of mystery that all the young ladies spent the morning trying to solve.

As the women were moving on to discuss the upcoming

balls and dinner parties for the upcoming weeks, Wallace announced the arrival of His Grace and Lord Jake Worthington. Both gentlemen looked dashing in their dinner coats and soft smiles. It always amazed Briana how similar the two gentlemen were when they smiled, even though Jake's was always a little lazier and mischievous than his brother's. The two gentlemen made their way around the room and greeted each woman individually. When Cameron and Briana were standing face-to-face, her breath caught as she took in the full effect of his presence. As he touched her hand in greeting, the warmth from his body radiated through her. She felt dizzy as he bent to kiss her hand, and when his lips lingered, she felt that spot would never again be the same.

"You look radiant this evening, Brie." Cameron said in a quiet and husky voice. His dark eyes sparkled as his smile grew into a grin.

He seemed to be in a better mood than the last time when he'd dismissed her coldly. Briana's head was spinning. How could he change his emotions so quickly? Briana reminded herself that she would not have to worry about his moods for too much longer. After marrying Lord Edwards, he would become her priority and Cameron would soon return to treating her as the friend of the family that she is and nothing more. These moments of passion and the tumultuous peaks and valleys that seem to be part of their recent relationship will end.

"Thank you, as do you," Briana said quietly. She met his eyes briefly before pulling her hand away and returning it to her side. Cameron made a joke about their late arrival due to Jake getting himself stuck in a fight with his boots. Briana had laughed quietly and politely, still confused by his current mood. She was saved from further conversation when Wallace announced the arrival of Lord Edwards. With a sigh of relief and a contented smile, she met his gaze across the room. Wanting nothing more than to get away from Cameron, Briana nodded a goodbye before crossing the room and greeting Lord Edwards.

Cameron watched as Briana laughed at something Lord Edwards said. It wasn't the quiet and polite laugh she'd given him, but instead was the full, throaty laugh he'd always heard from her. She was being distant and polite with him, but seemed to have no such reservations with Lord Edwards who always wanted to control her passionate side. Something was going on to make her behave so openly with him. Even the way she stood arm in arm with him was different. They seemed to be pressed together a little more tightly than he'd seen them before, and Briana was so invested in what he was saying she barely heard Jake when he asked the two if they'd had a chance to read the review on the previous week's opera. Yes, something was different and for the life of him, he'd never felt as angry and jealous as he did in this moment.

Wallace came to announce that dinner was served, and as a group, everyone moved to the dining room. Lord Edwards escorted Briana and her mother, Cameron escorted his mother, and Jake escorted his sister, Emily. Everyone found their seats at the table and began enjoying the meal as the first course was brought out to them. The group enjoyed light conversation, although not everyone participated freely since Cameron did not seem to want to contribute to any of the topics being conversed. It was not until Jake leaned over to ask him if he was feeling all right that Cameron nodded and then turned his attention to the conversation. The last thing he wanted anyone to know was that his thoughts were fixed on the ravishing image of Briana and his pure hatred for Lord Edwards who was able to sit next to Briana.

Clearing his throat, Cameron was about to speak and divert Briana's attention from Lord Edwards. Unfortunately, Lord Edwards was faster and stood up and asked for everyone's attention. He held out his hand, and Cameron was surprised when Briana placed her hand in his and stood up beside him.

"We wanted to take this opportunity among family to announce our engagement. I asked Lady Valmont, I mean Lady Briana, for her hand this morning and she said yes." The shouts of joy that came from Briana's mother and the congratulatory words from everyone around the table were heard for the remainder of the dinner. While Emily and her mother asked for more details about the proposal, Jake poked fun at Briana by saying that she'd have to behave like a proper married lady now, which meant that climbing trees and playing tricks on others was not acceptable. The only one who did not say anything was Cameron. Instead, he simply stared in Briana's direction throughout the dinner and clutched his fork with a grip that tested the strength of the silver.

As soon as dessert was cleared, Cameron was the first to stand and leave the room without waiting for the hostess to invite everyone back into the parlor for further conversation. Instead, he turned down the hallway and found a moment to breathe in the Valmonts' study. He was soon joined by Briana, who had gone to retrieve a book from the study that she had borrowed earlier in the week from Emily. She paused as she saw Cameron meet her gaze with angry and troubled eyes. The warmth that was there at the beginning of the night was gone. She cleared her throat and looked away before stating, "I borrowed a novel from Emily and was just coming to fetch it for her. I didn't mean to intrude on you. I know we can all get a little loud for someone like you who likes his quiet and order. Don't worry, everything will return to normal now." She moved closer to the table near the window where the book lay, but was stopped in her path when Cameron stepped closer to her.

"If by *normal* you mean that you disappear again or that you interact more with my siblings than with me, then I'm not sure I can be happy about that," Cameron said in a gravelly voice. He grasped her arms and looked deep into her eyes as he asked, "Do you really think you'll be happy with him?"

Briana did not stop to think. She answered as quickly and directly as possible, hoping that the hurt she was feeling would be over the faster she said the words. "Yes. I think he and I suit well together and will be very happy. I thank you for your consideration."

"Consideration? Christ, Brie! You can't honestly intend to marry that dullard in there?" Cameron fumed. His grip on her arms tightened as he said angrily, "He'll bury the passion in you with all his social ideals. He won't be able to enjoy your passion, or know how to bring it out in you like I do. You know we're good together." As if to prove his point, Cameron's lips crushed down on Briana's hard. He was angry and hungry for her. He wanted to stake his claim on her and leave his mark as if to remind her that she belonged to him. As soon as he started to deepen the kiss even more, Briana pushed herself away with a look of pure disgust.

Touching her bruised lips with the back of her hand, Briana took in a few steadying breaths before saying, "I don't know what you are trying to prove or have me think, but I am marrying Lord Edwards, I mean Michael. He is my best choice and I'll be happy with a man who is kind, even-tempered, and honest with me and himself." Briana congratulated herself for remaining calm through her speech, although her legs were shaking under her gown.

"So, there's nothing else for me to say then, is there?" Cameron asked coldly.

"If they are not words of congratulations and best wishes, I believe not," Briana replied in the same cold tone.

The muscle in Cameron's jaw twitched and he gritted his teeth as he looked her over and replied, "Very well." He gave her a curt nod and strode toward the door. Briana followed after him and saw him collect his things. It took every ounce of willpower to not turn and look at her once more. He simply left the house altogether, without a word of goodbye to anyone. Social proprieties be damned.

Cameron loosened his cravat and removed his dinner jacket. He'd already paced around his library for the last hour since he arrived home. Cameron could not understand why he was so upset. Of course, he cared for her, but she'd been lying to him about her feelings and about her well-being. She'd told him that her family moved away after her father found success in a business venture in the countryside and that she was happy her family was no longer a burden to his. But, he'd never thought of her as a burden when they were younger. Yes, she'd been a spirited girl and was often getting into trouble with her brother, but he'd felt the same responsibility to care for her that he did for his siblings. Now, as an adult, he still felt responsible for her, but no longer thought of her as a sibling.

She'd looked ravishing, his little gem. No, she wasn't his anymore. She looked as beautiful, elegant, and happy as he always knew she would. The only problem was that she looked like that on the arm of another man tonight. And not just tonight, since she would be on the man's arm for the rest of her life. This would be the way he would see her from now on, with eyes that looked blissfully into the those of another man.

Cameron reached for the bottle of whiskey on the table and filled his glass. He wanted her desperately. He wanted to bury himself deep inside her and feel her convulsing around him, eyes glazed over in desire. He wanted to know her body and soul so that she wouldn't feel the need to lie to him anymore. He'd never before wanted to possess a woman like he did Briana. Just thinking about her made him hard and feel like he was on fire. Hoping to calm himself down, he filled his glass again and downed it in one swallow before filling it a third time. Why couldn't she trust him enough to share everything with him, including her worries and desires?

Cameron had worked his way through most of the bottle when Jake strode into the room. He shook his head as he took in the image of his brother. Cameron's leg was thrown over the arm of his chair, his right arm dangled by the side almost touching the floor, while his left arm was used to cover his eyes.

Jake nudged his brother's leg before saying in a loud voice, "Hey Cam! I thought I'd find you here after you left the Valmonts'." He plopped himself down in the seat across from his brother and decided to pour himself a glass of whiskey.

Cam didn't remove the arm across his eyes, but asked, "How was Briana after I left? Probably fine since she had Edwards there."

"Well, she was definitely as confused as the rest of us to see you leave without saying a formal goodbye. She smiled and talked a bit longer with all of us, but she was much quieter than she normally is. Did something happen between the two of you?" Jake asked with a lazy smile as he slowly sipped his whiskey. He knew something must have happened since he'd never seen his brother like this. Well, except the night their father died. Cam couldn't quite understand that the man he'd looked up to so much was no longer there and that he'd now have to fill his shoes.

Cam grunted in response. Dropping his arm and pulling himself into a sitting position with both feet touching the floor, Cameron added, "She's marrying that dullard. That boring excuse of a man who doesn't seem to understand our Brie."

"*Our* Brie? When did you begin thinking of her as 'ours?'" Jake asked with a grin.

Cameron downed yet another glass of whiskey before replying, "Hasn't she always been ours? I mean, she was always like another sister growing up, although now I can't quite look at her as my sister anymore. Not when I want her so damned badly." Cameron leaned forward and put his head in his hands.

"Oh man, you're in deep. *I* knew you had feelings for her long ago, but couldn't be sure if *you* realized it or not," Jake said.

"Yes, I realized it even though it doesn't seem to matter. She's lying. Why? Why does she lie?" Cameron was mumbling and his speech was slurred. "She never trusted me enough to help her, or our family for that matter."

"What are you talking about? Yes, she didn't tell us the true reason why they left or how that impacted them financially, but she told you she needed to get married fast to give her mother some security and protection. What does it matter if she didn't tell you all the reasons why?" Jake asked in an incredulous tone.

"Can't she understand that I would have helped? No, she had to go to Edwards. The man she thinks she suits well with," Cameron said with an eyeroll that was more of a full body wave due to his imbalance. "I tried to make her see she was wrong. I kissed her and she just pushed me away. Why can't women be simple like men?" Cameron said in a frustrated whine.

Jake laughed at his brother's frustration. He'd never seen his diligent, no fuss, workaholic, elitist, brother look like such a mess. If Briana could only see just how much his brother loved her, she wouldn't be making such a big mistake. Jake sighed and said, "Maybe you should get a woman's opinion on the matter. For as many women as we both have had, I'm not going to even pretend like I understand their minds. They remember everything and it is never the way we men remember."

"My Brie... my little gem... Ugh, women," Cameron mumbled with a huff before the empty glass in his hand fell to the carpet and he fell asleep. Jake sighed and, knowing he wasn't going to be able to move his brother on his own, simply picked up the glass and threw a blanket over Cameron's drunken form. He'd wake up sooner or later and stumble to bed. Jake let himself out with a smile and a shake of his head. He'd have to come over tomorrow and enjoy the hangover his brother was bound to feel in the morning. If only he could decide which loud noise he was going to use upon his arrival...

Cameron woke up with a stiff neck and an ache in his side. He'd fallen asleep in the chair hours ago, but his mind hadn't stopped thinking about Briana, even in his dreams. There must be something he was missing. He knew she had feelings for him. In fact, she had feelings for him when they were younger as well. There was no way she could just forget everything now and marry Edwards, a man who simply didn't understand her. Jake was right, he had to get a woman's opinion. Emily would probably know Briana's mind better than anyone, but he couldn't bring himself to discuss what her friend does to his mind and body. They were a close family, but that might be a little too close.

Running his hand through his hair, he thought of other women he could rely on to share his thoughts, fears, desires, and frustrations with. He needed a woman he could be honest with, who would not judge him, and who he was not afraid to discuss just how Briana drove him mad with need. He needed a woman who understood polite society, but also the passionate side of love that was not discussed in mixed company.

Cameron smiled as the only woman he'd felt comfortable enough to discuss all those things with came to mind: his previous mistress Serrafina. He'd write to her now that his hands were steady and the room was no longer spinning.

Standing up and walking to his desk on the right side of the room, Cameron took out paper and his quill and ink and began to write:

My Dear Serrafina,

It is with heavy heart and a confused mind that I write you. I'm in need of a woman's counsel and the only women I feel close to discuss my mind with are my sister and yourself. Although my sister would indeed have insight to share, I don't quite feel comfortable enough to discuss this matter with her.

I've lost her. Briana, that is. The emerald of my life. She's announced her engagement to another man and had the audacity to tell me I simply had to congratulate her. She's a vicious woman if she does not see what she has done to me.

No, she's not vicious. Much to the contrary. She is gentle and passionate, considerate and caring, responsible yet reckless. She cares so much for the well-being of others and forgets about herself.

I never felt the need to protect and be with a woman like I do with Briana. Even as children, she was the one who understood me best, yet she did not confess any of her troubles to me, and having returned to London, built a relationship with my family on lies. As much as I want to shake and throttle her for putting herself in such a situation where she would trade her happiness for money, I want to hold her and kiss her until she can't help but share everything with me.

I know during our time together, I never showed interest in marriage. You shared with me the joy and love you experienced with your husband, which is why you never married again. I want to know how does one make a woman understand that she is the only woman he wishes to marry even when he is angry enough to keep her locked in a room and teach her just how open and honest a man and a woman can be?

Serrafina, I'm sorry for my drunken rambles, but I had no one else to turn to. I find that I'm unable to leave my feelings for Briana behind. She is the only woman I am able to picture in my future and I feel that I am now being forced to go through the remainder of my life pretending not to feel as strongly as I do about her. I only wish she could understand the level of passion and affection I have for her and allow me to serve as her friend, lover, and protector instead of some dullard of a man who will slowly extinguish the flame inside her until she is simply another mild and docile wife of the ton.

I will leave you to your day since I am in desperate need of sleep in my bed and the sun's rays are slowly making their way in through my window. I thank you for your counsel and your friendship which allows me to speak so candidly.

Yours, as always,

Cameron Worthington

Cameron folded the letter and closed it with his seal before sending it out with a servant. He knew he would not get a response from Serrafina until much later, more realistically in a couple of days. But, if the letter was not sent now while he was in a relaxed state of mind, he knew he would lose his courage to do so. Without any input from Serrafina, he would have to confide his thoughts with Emily (and Jake, who would obviously be around to point out every way that Cameron had royally messed up his chances with Briana). Cameron was concerned whether or not Serrafina would be able to give him any peace of mind, but the need for sleep overwhelmed him, and with visions of Briana in his head as he ascended the stairs and entered his room, Cameron fell soundly asleep in his bed.

CHAPTER 23

Briana knew it would take time, if ever, to rid herself of the strong feelings she had for Cameron. He'd been the first boy she had ever loved, and now as a grown woman, her love for him had only grown. She knew that marrying Lord Edwards (she really ought to be calling him Michael now) and spending more time with him as they find their own routine would result in less time devoted to thinking about Cameron. Smiling to herself at the memory of how Michael proposed, Briana sat down to make a list of what needed to be done for the wedding.

With her ink and pen, she began with the items that needed to be taken care of the soonest. The announcement needed to be made with the date of the wedding, but Michael said he would take care of that. She needed to decide on a color for her dress, maybe a nice sage with her white bonnet and her mother's string of pearls. She also needed to decide on the flowers she would carry in her bouquet. Should she also tell Michael what to wear? His valet would take care of that, right? Also, where were they going to get married? In his church, most likely, since he has such a strong connection to it. She should probably sit down with him and her mother to determine who to invite to the wedding.

They were not getting married for another six months at the

earliest, but Briana couldn't help but feel overwhelmed. Setting aside her list, Briana rubbed the temples on either side of her head in the hopes that it would eradicate the anxiety and confusion. Making lists was always a calming mechanism for her, but now seemed to exacerbate her feeling of unease. Feeling trapped, Briana gathered her bonnet and gloves and decided a long walk would do her good. Calling for her maid, Lucy, Briana set out without a destination in mind. She was heading toward Grosvenor Square and Hyde Park as if by habit. It wasn't until Lucy asked which one they were going to that Briana decided on Grosvenor Square, with the hopes that she wouldn't run into too many people she knew and would have some quiet time alone.

Passing by the many shops and people walking about in the busy streets of London, Briana couldn't help but wish she was somewhere back on the outskirts of the city. She never liked being so far away, but didn't seem to truly enjoy being in the heart of the city either. The streets were always so crowded, and when paired with the foul smell and smoke looming overhead, it was enough to make one question how important a sense of fashion and social standing really were. It was nice that the Hereford had a family home in Surrey and how nicely situated it was in the country, but with its relative closeness to London. She knew that Michael had a small country home in Yorkshire, but it was so far removed from London that he only came to the city for the season. Would he even want to come now after they married?

Reaching the square, Briana found a bench to sit on while her maid sat next to her in silence. She could see her mistress' furrowed brow and knew it would be some time before they returned to the house. Lucy took out a small handkerchief she had been repairing and set her mind to her needlework. Briana, on the other hand, sat idly staring out into the distance. She vaguely remembered her manners to share some pleasantries with a few women she recognized as being friends with Emily or her mother, but once the women continued on their way, Briana returned to her mental list of everything she needed to do in order for the wedding to happen smoothly.

"Lucy, we are going to need to stop by the milliner while we are out. I want to buy some new silk stockings for the wedding day. Do you think Lord Edwards will be disappointed if I do not buy a dress specifically for the occasion?" Briana asked tentatively.

"I'm sure he will love anything you choose to wear. He will be so overcome with joy to have you as his bride that he may not even notice your clothing," Lucy replied reassuringly.

"I just want to make sure I'm presentable and that he is happy with me. I hope we can grow to love each other, but in all honesty, love isn't essential for a marriage. Look at how many members of the *ton* had a marriage of convenience and seem to be happy years later. I surely don't need a marriage of love, do I? I simply need respect, security, and stability to be happy," Briana finished mater-of-factly. She knew she was saying this for her benefit and not for Lucy's, but it didn't matter. She needed to keep reminding herself, so any notions she had of falling in love with her husband, as well as any notions of that husband being Cameron, would soon stop. She wiped a tear that fell down her cheek and blinked furiously before any others followed suit. Before she could adjust her bonnet to hide her face a bit better, she heard a soft chuckle coming from the bench next to her.

A woman in an elegant cerulean blue gown with black lace along the sleeves and bust sat with a gloved hand covering her mouth to stifle another chuckle at Briana's quizzical expression. The woman had exotic features with dark hair and eyes that were accentuated by her olive skin and voluptuous curves. She wore a pleasant smile that made her dark eyes warm up with flecks of gold.

"Forgive me dear, but you truly are wonderfully amusing to listen to."

"Excuse me, but I don't believe we are acquainted. I would ask that you not presume to know what my struggles are," Briana replied in a prickly manner. She turned away from the woman, hoping she would get the hint and leave. Instead, the woman sat back on the bench in a more comfortable fashion.

"Oh, but my dear, I do know some of your struggle. What would you say if I could share some information that would make you not have to convince yourself to want anything less than the life you deserve?"

"I'm sorry, but who are you and how do you know anything more about me than what you've overheard in the last few minutes? Have we met before?" Briana asked skeptically.

"No, my dear. We've never met, but we do have a friend in common. He has spoken of you to me before and I have seen the way he cares for you change and grow since you've come back to London. In fact, he has written those feeling down and sent them to me. I wished to share them with you and was hoping to find you either here or in Hyde Park on a partially sunny day like today." Pulling out a letter tied with a string, the woman passed it over to Briana.

Briana stared at the letter in her hands, afraid that after reading she would be more confused than she currently was. She didn't need the woman to say who their mutual friend was to know she was holding Cameron's letter. There was something in the confident strokes of ink on the envelope that echoed the strength of Cameron's character. Briana looked up at the woman smiling at her in an encouraging manner.

"I don't know if I should read this, especially since it was sent to you. Not to mention, he has made it clear that he cares for me, but that isn't enough." Briana continued to finger the string around the letter as she considered reading the letter or not.

"Please, read the letter. I will tell you now that I have been his mistress as well as his friend for some time now, and I think the words he wrote me in the letter are all words he wished to share with you." Serrafna continued to look at the expression on Briana's face as she was deciding what the next right thing to do would be. With a nod toward the woman, Briana sighed and began reading the envelope.

Briana couldn't believe her eyes. He really did love her. She could understand the anguish behind his words and the regret he felt for not speaking his emotions before Briana accepted Michael's proposal. Why had he never spoken of such feelings before? He'd shown her passion and desire with every caress, kiss, and heated moment they had where they came together. The need to consume and belong to each other in every way had always been there, and yet, Briana had pulled away from him since he never gave the words she wished to hear. Sure, they'd shared many conversations, both as kids and now as adults, but he never claimed to want anything more from her than her body. She'd thought he simply wanted another mistress, but now having read the letter he'd written, she knew he loved her. How could he write everything so openly with this other woman and yet never say these words to her? Was it because this woman was married before that she would understand his feelings, or because they had a relationship for such a long time? Could Briana really measure up to this woman with years more of experience and friendship?

Briana didn't even stop to fold the letter once she finished reading. Instead, she turned it over and read it again from the beginning. When she came to the line saying that he would have to live the rest of his life forced to pretend to feel something other than what he truly felt, she could not help but let the tears flow. He'd said the words that she thought when accepting her proposal to Lord Edwards. Could she really pretend not to love Cameron, especially after reading this letter?

Briana heard the bench moan under the added weight of another person. Taking the letter out of her hand and replacing it with a handkerchief, the exotic woman in the blue dress spoke softly, "Here. You can't let the other members of the *ton* see you crying like this in broad daylight, in a public square no less. Go on, dab your eyes and take a deep breath." She patted Briana on the shoulder as Briana quickly dabbed at her eyes.

"Thank you."

"Of course. I was the one who brought you the letter that made you cry in the first place."

"That's why I have to thank you. I would never have known how he truly feels if it weren't for this letter." Briana touched her forehead gently as she said, "If only he'd said any of this to me directly earlier."

"Well, if you don't mind me being so blunt as to say, you are aware of his feelings now and are still unmarried. So, what do you plan to do with this information?"

"What do you mean? I'm already set to marry Lord Edwards."

"You mean to tell me you are willing to sacrifice your happiness after knowing how deeply for you Cameron feels? Take some advice from me when I say that marriage is best when it is done out of love, not simply respect and compatibility. Love encompasses both those things and much more so that you can find joy and comfort in even the toughest moments. When you have a man who accepts every part of you and wishes to keep you from any sort of harm, even if that means changing oneself to fit another, you can't just ignore the depth of that man's love because it is not likely you will find it again. Trust me, I know," Serrafina said as she touched the corner of her eye delicately with a finger to catch a tear before it fell.

Briana sighed, "I don't want to lose Cameron. He's the only one I have ever loved, and no, I don't want to sacrifice my happiness, but I don't want to hurt Lord Edwards either. He is a nice man and I can't think of the words to say that despite accepting his proposal, I can't ignore the feelings I have in my heart."

"I don't see why you cannot simply say it in such a manner. I think as long as you are true to yourself and ask him to do the same, you will find that he too will understand that you will never be the delicate and pious wife he wishes you to be. Even if there is mutual respect and attraction, that is not enough for marriage, especially if one must change oneself completely to please the other," Serrafina responded sagely before standing up and bringing Briana up beside her. "Now, I insist you make your way home and read that letter again before speaking to either man again. Trust your heart. It will always lead you to the best choice."

Upon reaching her home, Briana sat on the settee in the parlor room and thought a bit more about the words in the letter, as well as the advice she'd received from Cameron's mistress. Well, more like his former mistress. She knew she would see Lord Edwards sometime today to decide on the wedding announcement as well as the length of their engagement. There was no need for a special license to marry sooner, so the wedding could be within the next six to eight months. Briana could feel her heart growing heavier as the thought of marrying Lord Edwards felt more like a cage trapping her inside.

There was a light cough at the door before her mother walked into the room and sat next to her daughter filling the empty space on the settee. She took her daughter's hand and smiled saying, "I am so happy for you, my dear. You have found a nice man in Lord Edwards who will treat you well. He should be here any minute for us to begin the preparations for the wedding announcement. I can hardly contain my joy that such preparations are beginning."

Briana smiled weakly at her mother. She wanted to be excited as well, but the truth was that after seeing those letters, she was unable to forget Cameron's words. She truly did not think she would be able to feel the same way about Lord Edwards as she did for Cameron. His smile would never warm her and send her heart racing like Cameron's. His voice would never hold the husky quality of Cameron's. His hands would never set her body on fire like Cameron's. She would have to live her life knowing that Cameron loved her and she willingly chose to walk away from him.

Briana's mother touched her hand and Briana refocused her eyes once again. Sighing, her mother asked, "Honey, are you happy?"

"Lord Edwards is a good man. He will take care of us," Briana replied robotically.

"Yes, he would, but you didn't answer my question. I feel saddened by the thought that you would never truly love him."

"Mother, love is a luxury that we do not have. I may not love him now, but maybe…" Briana trailed off knowing that she could not bring herself to lie. She shook her head and said, "No, I don't think I will ever love him."

Briana's mother gave her hand another squeeze not knowing quite what to say. She knew her daughter had feelings for Cameron that were not going to end anytime in the near future. She should be hoping for a marriage between them, but since it does not seem that Cameron is likely to propose, she had to find a way to encourage Briana to accept someone else who is proposing marriage and is able to care for them financially. Yes, she should urge Briana to look forward to her marriage with Lord Edwards and hope for their future happiness. She was spared from doing so when a knock came from the door and Wallace came to announce Lord Edwards visit. After she and her mother nodded, Wallace moved aside to allow Lord Edwards entry into the parlor where he greeted the ladies with a quick bow and sat himself in one of the vacant chairs opposite Briana.

Briana couldn't bring herself to be happy with their future. She knew it would be a comfortable one built on respect and companionship, but she wanted more than that. Knowing that Cameron felt the same way about her as she did him changed everything. She could only hope that Lord Edwards would understand and let her go and that Cameron would continue to love her as passionately and deeply as he had before.

Lord Edwards smiled at the woman that would soon be his wife. He could see on her face, past her smile, that she was very nervous to be with him. Michael couldn't help but be amused by the cuteness in her demeanor as she shyly looked away from him when he complimented her on her morning's beauty. To know that she was capable of such a shy expression further emphasized his belief that she could eventually become more docile. Taking a deep breath, he reached for Briana's hand and said, "I thought I would come and we could begin planning our wedding and our future together. Once you become the lady of the house, I know I shall not have to worry that we will, in time, be able to adapt well to one another."

"Is that all you want from me? Simply to be someone who you can adapt well with," Briana asked stiffly. She heard her mother sigh, but could not turn back now.

Lord Edwards cleared his throat in discomfort before replying, "I know you are nervous about our future together, but I am a man of my word and honor. We will have a respectable marriage built on friendship and understanding. Is that not what marriage should be?"

"I'm sorry, but I disagree. I know I said I would be happy with this kind of marriage because you are a kind man and would care for my mother and me, but I cannot lie to either of us anymore."

Dropping her hand, Lord Edwards stood up abruptly. He looked to Briana's mother who gave him a weak smile and slight shrug of the shoulders. Turning his attention back to Briana, he said in a stern voice, "I demand to know what you mean by all this?"

Squaring her shoulders, Briana replied, "I want a marriage that is full of passion, surprises, arguments, friendship, respect, and acceptance for every part of who I am. I don't think I will ever be the docile and demure wife you want me to be and that is not fair to either of us. I hope you can understand. "

Lord Edwards, who had moved to look out the window during her speech, did not say anything for some time. Although his pride was hurt, he couldn't but think about his time courting Briana and everything he knew about her person now. Yes, she is a kind and strong woman who would do anything for those she loves, but with that strength comes a fierce passion that he may not be able to control. Although he thought her to be just as much of a grand woman as his mother, she could never be the kind, demure, and selfless woman he hoped for. She'd spent most of their courtship lying to him and the *ton* and he had to commend her on finally being honest with him and herself. His mother always said that the measure of a true lady is her honesty, so it would only be fair for him to show his true gentlemanliness.

Pushing away from the window, Lord Edwards returned to where Briana stood wringing her hands together slightly. He reached down and took them in his own before saying, "My dear, I appreciate your honesty. Though it pains me to have to say, but I do believe you have more foresight than I. I had hoped that in time we would learn to how to forget about some of our desires and adapt to the desires of the other. I see now that my thinking would only lead us down a path of complacency and possible resentment, neither of which would lead to a happy marriage. I fear the respect, and possible friendship, we have for one another now would be ruined completely."

"So, you are not angry with me?"

"No, of course not."

"And you are in agreement with calling off our engagement?"

"I don't see how we could marry after such a confession," Lord Edwards chuckled softly. "No, we are not the ones who should be walking down the aisle together."

"Thank you for understanding. I know the perfect woman for you is simply waiting for your paths to cross. I pray that it happens sooner rather than later," Briana replied with a soft smile on her lips as she patted his hand in a show of friendly companionship.

"Yes, well, I believe your perfect match has been waiting for you as well. So, how long are you going to keep him waiting?" Lord Edwards asked with a slight nod toward the direction of Hereford House. Seeing Briana's eyes follow his gaze, he couldn't help but send up a silent prayer for their happiness after all the strife they have suffered through. When Briana's gaze returned once again to his, he bent and placed a kiss on her knuckles. "Well, I think I will take my leave. I have a wedding announcement that I must stop before its printing. Good luck to you both." Stepping back and grabbing his hat, Lord Edwards left the two women in the same spot he'd found them in earlier.

Briana's mother waited a full two minutes before standing up and, with arms on her hips and a mischievous twinkle in her eye, asking her daughter, "So, now that I no longer have a son-in-law to take care of us, just how long do you plan to sit here before finding me another one?"

Briana looked at her mother expecting to see the same worried expression she had seen ever since they left London years ago. Seeing the twinkle in her mother's eyes brought a smile to Briana's lips. She was happy her mother was not disappointed in her and understood her feelings. Briana wrapped her arms around her mother's neck and laughed.

"Hmph! I know you love me dear, but I really do think you need to go tell Cameron about your feelings. Truth of the matter is, I don't think he would like it if we had to move again with your feelings to each other being left unknown." Fixing a few of her daughter's errant curls, she placed a quick peck on her daughter's check before telling her to go find him once again. As Briana was leaving the room, she heard her mother call after her, "Don't forget your bonnet! It won't do for you to have freckles on your face when you reach him!" With a laugh and quick reply, Briana grabbed the bonnet she'd left by the door and made her way to Hereford House in the hopes that Emily or Jake would know where she'd find Cameron at this time of the day. She was fully prepared to make sure he took her confession seriously this time around.

CHAPTER 24

Briana found Emily and Jake in the library. One, it seemed, was engrossed in making some sort of list at the desk, while the other was quite comfortably sprawled out on the couch seemingly taking a nap. Upon entering the room, Emily quickly looked up from the desk and smiled softly.

"Oh, thank goodness you're here. It seems the preparations for mother's birthday next month are more than I remembered. It seemed to completely slip my mind this year," Emily said with a guilty look on her face.

Briana responded with a smile. "I'm sure you have everything in hand. Remember, you don't have to do everything alone. You have two brothers to help."

Emily simply pointed across the room at Jake and huffed. She rolled her eyes and said, "This is the help I get when I asked him to think about what colors mother would like for decorations. Apparently, 'thinking' is synonymous with 'sleeping' for Jake."

There was another huff from across the room and a reply of, "I did think of colors. It's not my fault you didn't tell me to share out my thoughts. So, I figured I'd take a nap until you asked or assigned me some other simple task. You really ought to be more specific in your instructions, dear sister. I am an officer in the Royal Navy who is accustomed to clear orders, after all," Jake responded with a wink at his sister.

"Ugh, when is it that you leave again? I feel like your leave has been for much too long. And, excuse me, but I was plenty specific. You don't see Cam in here claiming any differently, do you?" Emily asked haughtily.

Briana laughed at the exchange. This was the most lively she'd seen Emily since the kidnapping and she wanted to take it as a sign that her friend was beginning that horrible incident behind her. Briana truly loved this family and wanted nothing more than to truly be a part of it, but in order to do so, she had to find Cameron. Sitting down in the vacant chair across from Jake and to the right of Emily's desk, Briana asked, "Speaking of Cameron, where exactly is he today?"

"I sent him on an errand to pick out mother's birthday present. He always picks out the best gifts and I knew I could count on him to order everything with enough time for the party. He should still be in town, probably looking at jewelry or fabric," Emily responded.

"Yes, but didn't he say he was going to return to the exhibition again today if time permits? He claims he didn't get to see enough of the telescope and other inventions," Jake said with a roll of his eyes.

"So, if I wanted to find him now, I should head for town first?" Briana asked rising from her chair.

"Yeah... why? Is everything all right, Brie? You look very odd. Doesn't she, Jake?" Emily asked as she walked over to meet her best friend.

Jake also sat up straight in his chair and began to assess Briana with a scrutinizing eye before saying, "Yes, she does. She almost looks as if she might have some sort of secret she can no longer withhold. Do tell, minx!" Jake said with a lopsided grin.

"There's no secret, I just need to tell Cameron that I am no longer engaged to Lord Edwards. I think he needs to know... for propriety's sake," Briana stumbled.

"Right... for propriety's sake." Jake repeated.

"Wait, you're no longer engaged? What happened? I feel like you just announced your engagement to all of us. Poor Lord Edwards. Are you and Cameron now…"

Briana cut her off before she could finish. "Em, I promise I will tell you about it all later. I really need to speak with Cameron first. I'll find you both later. Wish me luck!" Briana called back as she raced out of the room, leaving behind a very stunned Emily and a laughing Jake.

"Well, it's about time. I'm telling you, there is only so much I can do for those two. I was wondering if I was going to be able to see these two get together before I ship out next week," Jake said shaking his head. "Honestly, I was thinking it'd be another ten years before either one of them confessed." Emily simply nodded, dumbfounded, in response.

Briana could not find Cameron to save her life! She visited the jewelers, the milliner, the silversmith, the bakery, the bookstore, and each time turned up empty-handed. Briana continued to walk in a daze due to the level of exhaustion and anxiety she was feeling. Trying to remain rational, Briana reminded herself that since her engagement to Lord Edwards was officially broken, there was no real rush to tell Cameron about her feelings. Despite having such a rational thought, her excitement of wanting to share her feelings with Cameron as soon as possible made it more of an emergency. She knew she would see him very soon at Hereford House or at any of the upcoming evening balls, but the excitement in her heart far outweighed all the rational thoughts she had earlier. As she continued to pass various establishments, Briana looked in through the windows in the hope of seeing Cameron. Not finding him, she turned away from the window and scratched her forehead where a stray lock of hair moved back and forth in the wind.

Suddenly, the easy breeze turned into a strong gust of air, blowing off her bonnet and sending it whirling off in the distance. Briana couldn't help but stomp her feet and bite her lip in a silent curse. She had half a mind to forget about her bonnet and continue her search for Cameron, but knowing that fashion would call for her to need the bonnet once again, she chased off in the direction of her elusive bonnet. Trying not to make a spectacle of herself, Briana walked with speed but did not run.

Coming to halt in front of an alley, Briana looked to her left and then to her right in search of the flying bonnet. Where was that blasted thing? Honestly, having to wear such a frivolous accessory was beyond her. Who really cared if she got a little tan or some freckles on her skin? Sighing aloud, Briana began walking down the alley looking along the street in the hopes that it blew in this direction and she'd be able to find it. Her thoughts of abandoning the annoying bonnet were forgotten when she made ran right into something hard and warm.

"Oh, excuse me! I was looking for something and wasn't looking at my surroundings. Forgive me."

"No, it was my fau… Brie? I didn't realize it was you. What are you doing down this alley?"

At the sound of his voice, Briana's head shot up to meet Cameron's eyes. Smiling, she answered, "I was looking for you, actually. I went to Hereford House and was told you were out buying a gift for your mother's upcoming birthday." Seeing his silent nod, Briana waited for more of a response. When none came she asked, "Did you find anything?"

"Uh, yes, I did. I found a beautiful brooch that I think she would like very much. Is this why you wanted to see me, to ask about my mother's present?" Cameron asked in a cold yet polite manner. He hated how he sounded, but they were both going to have to get accustomed to this tone of voice since she was soon marrying Lord Edwards and Cameron would be forced to be forever polite to her.

"Not quite. You see I came looking for you because I wanted to tell you something in regards to my engagement with Lord Edwards, but then my bonnet flew off and I went looking for it. Lucky for me, I found you," Briana said with a beaming smile.

Cameron's polite smile collapsed into what he knew was a scowl. He really was going to have to get better about masking his feelings when it comes to Brie. He really did want her to be happy; he just wanted it to be him that made her happy. Knowing he should say something, Cameron cleared his throat before saying, "Well, how can I be of assistance with your engagement? Does Lord Edwards need support in getting the license, or do you need support in finding where to be married?"

"No, it's nothing like that. We've...umm... decided that marrying for companion-sake is nice, but marrying for love is more important. Lucky are those who have a loving marriage, wouldn't you agree?" Briana asked with eyes that implored him to understand what she was trying to convey.

"Yes, they are very lucky."

"Right, well Lord Edwards is such a nice man and we get along well..."

"Yes, honestly, Brie I don't know why you are telling me all this in the middle of the streets of London. I've already told you my feelings about this marriage, but you insist on marrying him and if you really need my congratulations to do so then you have it. I'm happy for you and look forward to watching you walk down the aisle," Cameron said as he tipped his hat towards her and brushed past in a brusque manner hoping to end this torturous conversation.

"Thank you for that, but do you really mean to give me congratulations? You are happy to see me marry another man?" Briana asked pleadingly.

Dammit! Didn't she see that having this conversation was killing him. Did she really have to make him say those words to her? Why couldn't she just leave? Giving her another cold stare and putting his hands on her shoulders to move her aside, Cameron simply said, "Yes, I'm happy for you." Turning on his heel to leave, he remembered the bonnet in his hand. Offering it to her, he grumbled, "Why wear this damned thing when you can't even keep it on properly?" After she accepted it, he bowed quickly and said in a curt manner, "I wish you happiness."

As she was once more pushed off to the side by him, Briana

could not hide her feelings anymore. Blocking his path once again before he could exit the alley into the normal flow of people visiting all the stores and shops, with hands on her hips and hair flying wildly about as the wind picked up once again, Briana gave Cameron the angriest look she could muster.

"You are a liar, Cameron Douglass Worthington!" Briana yelled up at him. Poking him in the shoulder, she said, "You never say what you really feel and then blame everyone else for having the audacity to not know your true sentiments. Well, guess what? This time I do know your true sentiments and I can't believe you are lying to me!"

"What are you talking about? You're the one that has lied the entire time since you've returned to London!"

Briana pulled out the letter she'd received from Serrafina and read the lines aloud, "... how does one make a woman understand that she is the only woman he wishes to marry even when he is angry enough to keep her locked in a room and teach her just how open and honest a man and a woman can be?" Handing the letter over to Cameron for him to see, Briana returned her hands to her hips and eyed him with a look that dared him to feign ignorance.

"Where did you... how did you get this?" Cameron asked in confusion.

"Your friend, Serrafina, gave it to me. She thought I should have all the information before getting married. Why didn't you tell me how you felt?"

"I did! You were so set on marrying him that you wouldn't listen to me."

"You never told me you wanted to marry me! You told me you cared for me, that you desired me, but never that you wanted to marry me. You know my family's financial situation and that I needed to get married as soon as possible. What did you expect me to do?" Briana said accusingly. She knew her voice level was dangerously close to yelling, but she didn't care.

"How could you think otherwise?" Cameron reached out and grasped both her hands in his. Shaking his head slightly, he said, "I have never cared more deeply for a woman ever in my life. It is my love for you that is keeping me from killing Edwards for claiming you as his future wife."

"You're love for me? You love me?" Briana asked quietly.

"Brie, you've brought a balance to my life that I lacked. You helped me enjoy life outside of responsibility and made it so I stopped living as half a person. With you, I no longer question my ability to live as my father would have wanted. Of course, I love you, you enchantingly infuriating woman!" Cameron said loudly before grabbing her behind the neck and kissing her in a hard and demanding kiss.

Briana was breathless. She hadn't even had the chance to tell him that she'd called off her engagement hours earlier. Would he still want her now that the threat of another man was no longer? Looking into his eyes, she took a breath and set her doubts aside.

"Well, with a confession like that, what would you say if I told you that I called off my engagement to Lord Edwards?"

"I know confessing my love to you now is in vain, but must you make fun of me?"

"I promise that I am in no way making fun," Briana said in a serious tone. Reaching up to cup his face in her hands, Briana nodded and smiled. "I love you, Cameron. I only considered marrying him because I could not bear the thought that you could not love me in the same way I did you, but I couldn't do it. You've been my whole world since I was a young a girl, how could I think to marry anyone else? I'm only sorry that I couldn't bring myself to confide in you earlier."

Placing a light kiss on her lips before looking into Briana's teary eyes, Cameron responded by saying, "Well, I guess now that we both know how much we belong to and trust one another, we have our whole lives to make up for lost time." With a wide grin, accentuated by his enchanting dimples, Cameron tightened his embrace and said, "I'll say it every day. I love you. I love you. I love you."

EPILOGUE

Three Weeks Later

Briana took a small sip of her tea while Cameron rubbed his eyes and let out a sigh. They were in the formal sitting room at Hereford House looking over the various wedding invitations and decorations the Dowager Duchess had prepared for them. Cameron had barely waited a full week after confessing his love to Briana to propose marriage to her. He'd surprised everyone when he dropped to his knee at the dinner table during Lady Phillips' dinner party and asked Briana for her hand in marriage. Although everyone offered their congratulations and best wishes to the couple immediately after Briana had accepted, once the women and gentlemen separated for drinks and talk, it became obvious that their sudden engagement was shrouded in speculation.

Looking across the table at where her mother sat with Cameron's mother, Briana said softly, "People are speculating that I trapped you into a marriage by seducing you for your fortune. It is common knowledge that our families are close friends, but it seems the *ton's* opinion of me is not very favorable after ending my courtship and engagement with Lord Edwards. I am nervous that we will never be accepted."

Emily, who had been sitting quietly to Briana's right throughout the hour-long discussion of wedding invitations, sought to ease her friend's troubled mind by replying, "Brie, whatever do you mean? There were many at Lady Phillips' dinner party that were thrilled for you both. I'm sure many are not surprised at all by your engagement and rather are simply speculating as to how long this engagement will be."

Briana smiled at her friend's words of encouragement. She wanted to be as positive as Emily was, but her mother echoed her worries when she began speaking. Lardy Darby glanced over at Cameron first and then back at her daughter before saying, "I understand your concern, my dear. Lord Edwards was pretty open about his courtship and desire to propose marriage to you, Brie. He voiced his intention to many. To suddenly see that courtship end, and with little to no time to recover, Cameron offers a marriage proposal. Not to mention our financial troubles have been made public during the ordeal with Mr. Gutterson. I'm afraid the *ton* will see us as greedy social climbers."

Cameron moved in closer to Briana and, when she looked up at him, he kissed her cheek and said, "I'll just have to continue to show everyone how much I love you to set their minds at ease." Seeing a smile and blush spread across Briana's face, Cameron continued, "I am so happy we do not have much longer to wait since I was able to get us a special license. You've always been a part of this family and I can't wait for it to be official. In two weeks' time, Jake will be returned and you will be my wife."

Seeing the lovely pair, the mothers exchanged a secretive smile with each other. For so many years, the two always believed a marriage between the Valmonts and the Worthingtons would be wonderful, but they never thought Briana would be marrying Cameron. Elizabeth was thrilled to know that one of her children has now found someone they could be happy with, just like she was with her husband. That's all a mother wants for their children, to love and be loved.

"I believe the *ton* will see how this marriage was destined to happen. Even if the return of you all to London held a bit of deception at first, people will soon turn to the next big scandal.

Having said that, it's very important we don't have any other scandal among us for the *ton* to discuss," said Elizabeth.

Elizabeth moved her chair closer to where Cameron, Briana, and Emily were seated on the sofa. Grabbing Emily's hand in her own, she stated, "Emily, I am sorry to say that this applies to you as well. Now that Briana will be marrying, people will be watching how well you handle yourself in social situations to attract more suitors. You too must find a gentleman to help you carry on with your life and put the past ordeal and fears aside."

"Mother is right. It has already been mentioned how you seem rather different and reserved. It is leaving many in confusion, not knowing what to say when around you. We know you have been through an ordeal, but as your family, so did we. It's time we all pick ourselves up, and the best way to put something out of mind is to move on to other pressing matters."

"And of course, what could be more pressing than a lady finding a husband to build a life and family with?" Emily replied sarcastically. Looking to Briana for support, she wondered if the headstrong and fearless woman she'd known still remained now that she was engaged to marry. She was not disappointed when she saw her best friend nodding in support.

"Cam, you should know by now that a lady should also be allowed to discover and judge for herself what her most pressing matters are. Who better to make decisions for someone than the individual?" Briana asked while crossing her arms over her chest to send a message to Cameron. She could not understand the logic of the Worthingtons and, in keeping with her progressive views, she could not bring herself to agree with her future husband on this point.

"I'm not saying that a lady can't make decisions for herself, but sometimes it takes the family to help the lady, in this case Emily, see that finding a husband could be the best thing for her. She could find love, start a family, and be happy." Turning his attention to Emily, Cameron reached over Briana's lap and took his sister's hands in his. Waiting until Emily made eye contact with him, Cameron said, "Em, we just want you to be happy. Marrying one of the nice men Mother has in mind for you and looking forward to starting your family is not a bad thing."

Emily felt the tears stinging her eyes. She looked at the faces of all those gathered around her. They were supposed to be here for the happy occasion of wedding planning for Cameron and Briana, but now the mood in the room had soured. Her mother wore an expression that was a mixture of worry and exasperation, while Lady Darby wore an expression of kind discomfort. Emily's voice sounded as broken and frustrated as she felt when she said, "I understand that you are all concerned for me, but I truly do not think I am ready for marriage right now. Please, grant me some time to work through my thoughts."

"But, Emily…" Cameron began to protest, but the tug on his sleeve from his fiancée silenced him.

"Em, we know you've been through something horrendous and cannot imagine how it's affected you. We only hope it does not stop you from living your life. Anytime you need to talk, we're here." Briana gave her best friend a tight hug and smiled as she heard Emily whisper a thank you into her ear.

Once Briana and Emily broke apart from their hug, the air in the room felt a bit more at ease. Seeing the tired expression in her friend's eyes, Briana announced that it was best they head home since Cathy would be wanting to start on the dinner menu. Understanding that it was time to leave, Lady Darby stood and gave a hug to both Emily and her mother, thanking them both for all the help with wedding preparations the last couple weeks. Cameron followed suit saying he would excuse himself to walk the Valmont women home and then continue on to his bachelor lodgings.

Once Emily and her mother were left to themselves in the parlor, the air in the room that was previously full of joy and excitement was now one of awkward heaviness. Seeing her mother move to sit beside her on the sofa, Emily braced herself for the conversation of marriage once again. Her mother was nothing if not persistent, especially when the family name and image were involved.

"My dear, I know you do not wish to entertain the idea of marriage right now because you are suffering. I am not asking you or expecting you to be able to ever leave what happened to you behind. But this suffering cannot go on like it has. You have been sullen and quiet at every public outing we have been to. Even the ball you all put together for my birthday, with all the surprises you planned and tricked me with, was not enough for the smile on your lips to reach your eyes. When you are not sullen, you are jumpy and quick to suffer from a headache. Your suffering cannot be made known in the way it has been or you will never marry," Elizabeth said, stroking the side of her daughter's face.

"I don't know what you want me to say. I am trying my best, Mother," Emily said quietly.

"I know you are, my dear, but we women must suffer behind closed doors in silence. We cannot let the world and those who rely on us see us crumble. I learned this lesson when I lost your father, and then when you were kidnapped, even now I suffer to see you suffer. I am sorry that you must learn this lesson at such a young age, but it was always a lesson you were meant to learn one day."

Emily could feel her cheeks begin to flush with the evidence of the frustration and anger building within her. Standing and walking to the window across the room to put some distance in between her and her mother, Emily took five deep breaths before squaring her shoulders and saying, "Why must I suffer in silence behind closed doors and then present a false image of myself in public because it is what someone else has decided that is what women must do?" Emily had never questioned the importance of one's image and status in society, but now that she found herself struggling to meet the expectations of others, she could not help but question everything. Crossing her arms over her chest and lifting her head a touch higher than it was before, Emily continued, "Mother, until my thoughts and emotions can match those behind closed doors, I won't be able to trust or be happy with anyone else."

Losing patience with her daughter and feeling the exasperation of a parent watching their child struggling and not doing anything to change their situation, Elizabeth Worthington, Dowager Duchess of Hereford, replied in the tone she reserves for all formal occasions and decisions, "You shall see. I have a list of suitable marriage candidates and I'm sorry dear, but you will meet these gentlemen and marry one of them. I refuse to watch you live in fear and darkness any longer." Coming to stand before Emily, Elizabeth placed a kiss on her daughter's cheek before saying, "I'm doing this for the best, dear." Before Emily had a chance to respond, Elizabeth had gathered her skirts and walked out the parlor doors.

With her gaze fixed on the spot her mother just vacated, Emily couldn't help but stamp her foot in frustration. "Try your best, Mother, and so shall I. There will be no marriage until I so choose."

Acknowledgements

I have to start by giving thanks to my parents, Nancy Olivieri and Juan Colón-Santini, for their love and support throughout my life. From reading all my stories as a young girl (even with all the misspellings of a seven-year-old), to reading my short stories and poems written for open-mic nights in college, to cheering me on when I decided to begin pursuing writing as more than a hobby despite having a full-time teaching career. I would not have been able to do anything without you. ¡Los quiero mucho!

I also want to thank other members of my family who served as beta readers for me and gave me critiques and suggestions to help bring this story and the characters to life. To my sister, Ana Quinlan, thank you for reading multiple copies of my manuscript and for the many rambling phone calls where you helped me dig into the world of Briana and Cameron. To my mother-in-law, Paula McKinney, and grandmother-in-law, Merril Mountan, thank you both for taking the time to read my manuscript and give insight on my villain and his background. To my best friend, Laura Smothers-Chu, who took time away from setting up her new business (Befriended Heart) to read my manuscript, thank you for the edits and feedback! Truly, I can't express the amount of thanks to you all for your love, time, and support!

Another big thank you goes to my writing coach and developmental editor, Emily Tamayo Maher, whose words of inspiration, movtivation, and wisdom are invaluable. I am so lucky to be working with you and have loved all our meetings and conversations! Thank you for all your notes and guidance in plotting my story, talking me down from every ledge, setting deadlines for me, and encouraging me to push my writing beyond my comfort zone. You have such a way of keeping all who work with you positive and creative! Thank you for everything!

To my husband, Matthew McKinney, thank you for being my everything! Not only did you read a romance novel for me, but proofread it for all my mechanical errors much like you did for me in college. The amount of patience with which you listened to my ramblings, self-deprecation, and high-pitched excited squeals is second to none. Thank you for holding me to my passion for writing, giving me space to write instead of washing the pile of dishes in the sink, and for reminding me in my times of doubt just how proud you are of me. I love you!

Lastly, to my readers, whoever you are and whereever you may be. I hope this novel brings you joy and transports you to a different time where you are met with new experiences. May Briana and Cameron's story warm your hearts with the knowledge that depite any turmoil around us, we are all able to grow in strength, acceptance, and love. Thank you for reading and showing your support by purchasing this book!

Much Love,
Sela Colón